WENDY'S EVER AFTER

OTHER BOOKS BY JULIE WRIGHT

Contemporary Young Adult

The Art of Us

Swimming in a Sea of Stars

Regency Romance

A Captain for Caroline Gray

Windsong Manor

An Inconvenient Letter

Contemporary Romance

Lies Jane Austen Told Me

Lies, Love, and Breakfast at Tiffany's

Glass Slippers, Ever After, and Me

WENDY'S EVER AFTER

JULIE WRIGHT

SHADOW
MOUNTAIN
PUBLISHING

The epigraphs at the start of each chapter come from J. M. Barrie's 1911 novel, *Peter Pan* (originally published as *Peter and Wendy*).

Interior images: Unique Design Team/Shutterstock.com, Bakavets Sviatlana/Shutterstock .com, WiktoriaMatynia/Shutterstock.com

© 2025 Julie Wright

All rights reserved. No part of this book may be reproduced in any form or by any means without permission in writing from the publisher, Shadow Mountain Publishing®, at permissions@shadowmountain.com. The views expressed herein are the responsibility of the author and do not necessarily represent the position of Shadow Mountain Publishing.

This is a work of fiction. Characters and events in this book are products of the author's imagination or are represented fictitiously.

Visit us at shadowmountain.com

Library of Congress Cataloging-in-Publication Data
Names: Wright, Julie, 1972– author.
Title: Wendy's ever after / Julie Wright.
Description: Salt Lake City : Shadow Mountain Publishing, 2025. | Audience term: Teenagers | Audience: Grades 10–12. | Summary: "Wendy Darling embarks on a new journey where her past in Neverland collides with her future hopes for love, only to rediscover the adventure never truly ended"—Provided by publisher.
Identifiers: LCCN 2025000719 (print) | LCCN 2025000720 (ebook) | ISBN 9781639933877 (hardback) | ISBN 9781649333582 (ebook)
Subjects: CYAC: Romance stories. | Pirates—Fiction. | Magic—Fiction. | Characters in literature—Fiction. | Fantasy. | LCGFT: Fantasy fiction. | Romance fiction. | Novels.
Classification: LCC PZ7.1.W78 We 2025 (print) | LCC PZ7.1.W78 (ebook) | DDC [Fic]—dc23
LC record available at https://lccn.loc.gov/2025000719
LC ebook record available at https://lccn.loc.gov/2025000720

Printed in the United States of America
Publishers Printing

10 9 8 7 6 5 4 3 2 1

To McKenna, Merrik, and Chandler

You three are now adults with families of your own,
but I hope you are never too grown-up for fairy tales.

No matter where your adventures take you,
you will always be my greatest story.

I wish you all a lifetime of faith
and trust and pixie dust.

"All look your best," Peter warned them; "first impressions are awfully important."

CHAPTER ONE

1909 England

"I loathe them all." Wendy Darling stood in the parlor doorway, staring at the flowers that had overwhelmed every surface of the room. Roses on the side table. On the mantle, white violets sat on one side of the small Mora clock, and purple violets sat on the other. And a rather cheeky variety of tulips made the coffee table useless because it took up so much room. All from suitors, who hid their unimaginative personalities behind the bouquets they sent her.

"That's hardly a charitable attitude, Wendy." Her mother frowned and patted her brown hair as if somehow Wendy's declaration had caused her perfectly styled coif to frizz out of place.

Wendy wasn't trying to vex her mother, but could her mother not see how these suitors vexed her? Was her mother not also vexed that their London residence seemed more of a hothouse than a home as of late?

Granted, the fragrance was actually quite pleasant, but Wendy would not permit herself to admit any part of her approved of this garden-in-her-parlor nonsense.

"I'm not saying I loathe the *men* who sent the flowers," Wendy said. "Just the flowers themselves. I should respond to each of these young men with a sprig of hemlock to perhaps relay the message that I am not interested."

"Hemlock indeed!" If Mother had appeared vexed before, now she was positively ashen.

"I'm not saying I *would* send hemlock," Wendy explained. "Only that I wish I *could*." She often had to explain herself to her mother. Which was not to say she did not love her mother. Wendy loved her mother more than anything. It wasn't anyone's fault that they did not agree on the urgency for Wendy to marry.

In Mother's eyes, Wendy's refusal to accept Mr. Northbridge's proposal meant she was stubborn. Rejecting Mr. Tilney was Wendy being overly picky. Rejecting Mr. Barrit stopped short of scandal, only just.

Mother scowled, wrinkling her forehead in a way she preferred not to do because she said it made her appear haggard. Since Wendy's father died the year previous, Mother had changed, shifted like sand under the weight of a moving tide. Gone were the laughter and the pirouettes in the dining room. Gone was the hidden kiss in the corner of Mother's mouth. It frightened Wendy that Mother's kiss had disappeared. How could such a feature dissolve under her mother's grief? And if that part of her could go, what else could Wendy wake to find missing?

All because her father's heart had grown old and tired and stopped beating.

Her father's death had jarred loose memories of a faraway place with a boy who would never grow old, whose heart would never grow tired, who would never die. Nearly six years had passed since the grand adventure with her brothers.

She couldn't stop thinking of Neverland and the boy who would never grow old. It had never really occurred to her that getting old meant dying.

Which was ridiculous. Of course, she *knew* people *died*. She just hadn't known that when they left, they took pieces of those who loved them best with them.

"What was the point of your triumphant debut if you only intend on scorning every man to come into your vicinity?" Her mother's terse question snapped Wendy out of the dark thoughts that had invaded her mind yet again.

"I don't scorn *every* man." Wendy turned her back on the parlor and made her way to the staircase. "I'm quite fond of John and Michael. And Tootles is a dear. I daresay I like him better than the other two, sometimes."

"Liking your brothers does not count," Mother said as she followed.

Wendy gripped the richly polished handrail tighter when her mother added, "If only your father were here."

Her father.

It all came back to that. How could a heart just stop like a clock that someone had neglected to wind? The ache pinched Wendy's own heart so hard it felt like she couldn't breathe through the pain.

For as great as her own pain might be, she knew her mother's to be that much more horrible. Sometimes Wendy felt like a pirate, pillaging Mother's patience and hope with every saucy turn of conversation.

Her parents had wanted Wendy to marry respectably, to know what it was to love and be loved, but since Father's death, that one wish of her parents became her mother's obsession. The mourning period when Wendy had been sequestered away and isolated from the world had not agreed with Wendy at all. She'd felt confined like a ship in a bottle. Once the mourning period had been declared over, she should have been given a moment to reclaim herself, not thrust into marriage. If only her mother would let her breathe in her freedom for a little longer. If only her desire for another adventure didn't make her mother so sad.

Which decided everything. Wendy owed her mother some sort of compromise.

"I'll go to the ball tonight," Wendy said. She had previously argued that she would *not* be prevailed on to attend the Westridges' ball.

Wendy felt the rush of relieved air puff out from behind her. She could almost see her mother's heart being wound a few ticks.

Wanting to wind it a little more to ensure several more days of strong heartbeats, Wendy turned to gauge her mother's reaction as she said, "And I will send prettily penned thank-you cards for the flowers." She almost added that she thought wolfsbane might be a better option than the hemlock but decided her mother had experienced enough of her cheek that day.

Satisfaction swelled from her mother, who clasped her hands to her chest in genuine gratitude. "Thank you, Wendy."

"Of course, Mother."

Wendy left her mother to fuss over the flowers and went up to the writing desk in her room to make good on her promise.

The letter writing took the rest of the late afternoon, with sunlight sweeping across the curtains in its farewell performance for the day. Wendy turned on the electric lights her mother had installed in the house to finish her letter writing and didn't stir again from her seat until twilight.

She approached the window and opened the latch to let in the night air and to welcome any visitors who might choose to enter that way—though it had been a long time since Peter had left leaves on the floor just under the windows.

Outside, the gas lamps cast a warm, amber glow on the bustling London streets. Electric lights were replacing the gas, but the process was slow, something that came as a relief to Wendy. The gas lamps reminded her of fairy lights. A gentle spring breeze rustled through the tree branches, carrying with it the promise of a magical evening.

"It *will* be magical," Wendy whispered to the wind. She hoped that message carried over the housetops and oceans to the ears of one particular boy. Served him right to know she marched on with her life without him.

"Stubborn mule." Wendy hoped *that* message carried in the wind too. Didn't he know how much she needed him now that Father was gone?

Wendy turned away from the window when her maid, Wilson, entered to ready her for the night's festivities. Wilson smoothed her hands down the white apron over her dark wool dress while she waited for Wendy to be seated at the dressing table.

Wilson's service was a luxury to the family. The life Wendy now lived differed vastly from the one she'd known as a child.

Her father had finally managed to figure out those markets and stocks that he boasted to have known while courting her mother. And they were now quite well-off financially. They'd become respectable in the neighborhood, and her mother no longer needed to count the cost of every vitamin or pat of butter that crossed paths with her children.

Wendy's brothers were doing their part to make certain the family continued to enjoy their current financial ease. John was apprenticing and preparing to take over her father's business and grow it even further as soon as he reached his majority. Michael was still in school, but he was becoming such a proper little man that everyone had high hopes for him. Tootles had taken an interest in law and was focusing his studies in that direction. The boys no longer required her to mother them.

In the six years since their adventure, none of the Darling children ever spoke of that time with Peter in that other world, though sometimes they started conversations with "Do you recall . . ." or "Do you ever think about when . . ." And then they would trail off with a wistful, faraway look on their faces.

They didn't talk about it, however. To do so felt like it might spoil the memory somehow.

Sometimes, she wondered if she had dreamed it all, but she hadn't. She knew she hadn't.

The more society propelled Wendy into its spotlight, the more she thought she heard the melodic tones of a pan flute and the laughter of lost boys at swordplay.

The more she missed it.

Missed him.

She stared into the mirror as her maid worked to curl her hair into soft ringlets framing her face. She was no longer the silly girl in a blue nightdress and childish bow. Though some features persisted—her eyes remained the same pale blue, her lips were still naturally rosy, and her skin was still fair—everything else had changed. Her hair had darkened into golden amber. Her features had lengthened and softened and curved. She wore silk taffeta gowns in the latest styles from Paris.

Wendy was now a woman.

At least, society said so. Though at almost eighteen, she still felt like a little girl, no matter that she had been launched into society. No matter that she was to marry and put away childish things.

Wendy winced as Wilson twisted the back of her hair up and then let three loose coils tumble down from the twist. Wilson used a bit of the tulle fabric as a headwrap.

"Can you use this instead?" Wendy held out the comb that Peter had given her. It had belonged to one of the mermaids. The comb was made from opalescent seashells and was decorated with pearls and carvings of ocean waves. It was one of the tangible proofs that she had not dreamed up her experiences in Neverland. Wilson tucked the comb into her twist and handed Wendy the mirror to inspect her handiwork.

It was perfect.

Wendy stood so she could finish dressing and then stared at Wilson's completed efforts.

The woman who stared back at her from the mirror was a force of grandeur. The gown had been designed to capture attention everywhere Wendy went. The beauty of the deep blue silk taffeta with its meticulously embroidered sheer black overlay startled even Wendy when it shifted colors like liquid twilight as she moved. The hem was finished with a row of intricate beading that added to the gown's ability to both absorb and reflect light at its whim. The effect was as her mother predicted.

"Stunning," she murmured aloud at her reflection, then hoped

Wilson hadn't noticed whatever lapse in mind had sent Wendy prattling on to herself in such a conceited way. But how could it be conceited? Any woman would look stunning in a gown that was not simply a piece of clothing but a work of art.

What would Peter think if he could see me now?

Wendy turned away from the mirror and from that thought. Peter would not see her. And she would not see him. Not ever again. Wendy had endeavored to return to Neverland after the last "spring cleaning" he had picked her up to help him do. He'd said he'd come back, but then he hadn't.

She'd done everything she could think of to return. She'd followed manuals on how to capture fairies so they could bestow her with a wish. She had gone out on ships and lowered gifts of glittering jewelry into the oceans to entice a mermaid near enough to have a conversation. She'd wished on the evening star every night without fail for nearly two years.

Finally, she stopped wishing on stars. The years of hoping Peter would return for her were a dark smudge across her memory. She'd locked the latch on the nursery window to teach Peter a lesson in broken hearts so that he might know she would not wait forever for him. But she had been the one to curl up in bed and cry and cry and cry. Peter probably had no idea that anything was amiss because he had no intention of ever coming back for her.

The sound of a knock echoed through her room, bringing her back to herself. Her mother swept in, resplendent in a black gown not entirely unlike Wendy's, though much simpler in design. The little flourishes of embroidery and beadwork were missing in her mother's gown. She still wore the mourning black in honor of Wendy's father. Wendy imagined her mother would follow in the late queen's footsteps and never put off the mourning clothes.

"Oh, dearest!" Mother exclaimed. "You look . . . stunning." She echoed Wendy's own thoughts on her appearance. "And you'll dance tonight? You'll try to be agreeable to suitors, won't you? Really try?"

"Yes, Mother. I will really try tonight." Wendy only half-meant it. One-third meant it? One-quarter meant it?

Maybe she didn't mean it.

She longed for one more adventure before she had to take this step into true adulthood that was so much more severe than simply leaving the nursery. Could the universe not grant her heart one more opportunity to shake off the chains of being grown-up, to allow her to embrace her childhood once again?

Wendy's shoulders slumped. No. The universe would not make such an allowance. Society said it was time for her to marry and become a mother. And while she had spent a great deal of time *playing* at being a mother, she wasn't sure she wanted to be one in actuality just yet, no matter what society said on the subject. But what choice was there for her?

None.

Her mother frowned as if hearing her own overbearing tone and then placed a gentle hand on Wendy's shoulder. "I don't mean to push so hard, dearest. I only want you to have the same sort of love I've had in my life. I want you to know what it means to be cherished by someone so wholly. To know what it means to give your heart in such a way you never want to take it back."

How could Wendy explain that she had already given her heart? It was locked somewhere in the bowl of a thimble. And even if she wanted to, she didn't know how to get it back. "I'm ready to go," she said instead of responding to the uncomfortable conversation her mother had initiated.

"Right. Of course. But you almost forgot your mask."

Wendy *had* forgotten. The whole idea of donning a mask to hide her identity at a dance full of her neighbors seemed ludicrous. How would covering the bit of her face around her eyes cloak her appearance? Were her neighbors and friends really so unobservant as to not be able to guess who she was even though they had known her for the greater part of her life?

But Wendy sighed, fixed the blue, feathered mask in place, and followed her mother out to the waiting car, a Buick Runabout that her mother had purchased on a whim of pure frivolity. In truth, Wendy hated it and missed their carriage. But her mother was intrigued by all things new and modern. The stable master had learned to drive it and do repairs on it, and Wendy had once caught him talking lovingly to it as if it were one of the horses, leading her to believe he enjoyed the vehicle as much as her mother did.

As the footman helped Wendy into the back of the car, she caught a glimpse of her father's overcoat folded neatly on the front seat. Her mother kept it there because she said it made her feel like he was with them on their outings. Wendy then caught a glimpse of the starry sky. Again, memories of adventures within those starlit skies flickered into her mind. She shut those memories out with a deep, cleansing breath. No more. Tonight, she would try. She'd promised. She would put off the dual mourning of her heart and try to find happiness in the world in which she now lived. But even as she thought it, her hand went to the acorn button on the chain under her gown, nestled close to her heart.

No, the acorn button whispered to her. *You will not forget me so easily.*

The car rumbled to life, and Wendy dropped her hand. *You just wait and see*, she thought.

Once they arrived at the ball, Wendy took another deep breath to summon the courage to carry out her mother's wishes. She faced the house all lit up with electric lights.

Mr. and Mrs. Westridge were much like her mother. They were in love with discovery and all things new. So it was that they were among the first in the neighborhood to install electric lights in their home. The Darling household had been quick to follow. Wendy's grandmother hated those lights. Called them the devil's work and insisted they were much too bright and gave her a headache. This was not so bad because it meant she did not visit Wendy's home nearly so often, which meant she wasn't lecturing on all the ways Wendy was failing her mother by not being married already even though

Wendy was far from what anyone would consider an old maid. Her grandmother was steeped in the traditions of her own generation and didn't think a woman should ever reach twenty without having aligned herself with a man for protection.

Mr. and Mrs. Westridge greeted their guests as they entered, and Mrs. Westridge handed Wendy a fan with a gold cord to attach to her wrist. A dance card, Wendy realized, though the metal and silk lady's fan was the most elaborate dance card she'd ever seen. It was destined to become the most cherished keepsake of the evening— probably of the entire season. Wendy made her way to the ballroom and glanced at the press of people as she tried to count how many young ladies were present, wondering how much it had cost Mrs. Westridge to create such an elegant little party favor.

Wendy shouldn't have bothered with the worry. The society her family could now afford to keep didn't think twice about such extravagances. Her mother and John often reminded Wendy that they no longer needed to count their coins and pen down every expense while checking and rechecking the budget. They were quite comfortable. More than comfortable, really.

But as a child, Wendy had spent enough time at her mother's side counting those coins and double-checking those numbers. It was a hard habit to dispose of. Wendy looped the gold tie around her wrist after glancing quickly at the variety of dances offered. The polka, a quadrille, several more waltzes, and even the minuet, which her mother would be pleased by since she dearly loved that archaic form of dance. Wendy snapped her fan closed and entered the ballroom.

The waltz, already in progress, flowed like a silken river under the lights. The swirl of glittering gowns was mesmerizing. And Wendy had to admit, she did not recognize one in four of those masked faces. Wendy, poised at the edge of the dance floor, felt adrift in the current of dancers. Her smile, practiced over years of etiquette lessons and tea, never felt more forced. Tonight, she had to be serious about finding someone. Tonight, she had to stop straining against phantom echoes of windswept skies and laughter against a Neverland moon.

"Is it Miss Darling I see?"

Miss Cynthia Meyer's strawberry blonde wavy hair was pulled up into a loose bun that was really quite fetching. Her rust-red fox mask accented her hair color perfectly.

"Cynthia!" It was a relief to see the face of her friend, even if part of it was covered. "You look positively charming."

"You don't think it's silly?" Cynthia touched her mask self-consciously.

"Absolutely not. You look perfect."

"Miss Darling," a man's voice said from behind her, interrupting her conversation.

She cringed, recognizing the voice that had addressed her, wishing her mask had hidden her better from its owner. What good was a mask that didn't keep her safe from men who were objectively not very nice? The big midnight unveiling promised to be an abysmal disappointment if people were so easily identified. Mr. Hurst wore a mask designed to look like a tiger's head. This man was the sender of the tulips. She smiled to thank him for the flowers. The tulips, it could be argued, were certainly a unique choice. Perhaps there was more to him than she had first thought? She needed to give him a chance. She had promised her mother that she would try tonight. "Mr. Hurst." She inclined her head in acknowledgment.

"Dance with me, Miss Darling." He held out his hand, indicating he wasn't asking but rather expecting.

She had no excuse to refuse. There was no reason to insist he scrawl his name on the dance card since the dance had already begun, and she had clearly not been claimed or she would be swirling with the rest of them. She wanted to say "no," but she had promised her mother, and Mr. Hurst had been tolerable enough at dancing, even if his breath smelled like freshly chewed garlic cloves, even if he was a wantwit when it came to conversation, and even if he had spent their every interaction together acting as if she were a possession in his grip and not another human person. But maybe if she allowed herself to get to know him, she might find he was not so brutish. She might decide to like him.

"Of course." She tossed an apologetic glance to her friend and settled her hand lightly over his so he could lead her away from the sidelines and into the eddying couples.

He curved one hand over her shoulder blade as his other held her hand tightly. "You arrived very late."

She almost laughed out loud at his censure of her timing as a conversation starter. It was ill-conceived for a man to lecture a woman on such a subject when he was trying to win her favor, especially when her arrival had nothing to do with him. "I was sending thank-you cards for the many flowers I received. The endeavor took much longer than anticipated."

She watched his reaction and felt satisfied when his features tightened in response. Good. He should know his was not the only bouquet she'd received—that he was not the only one to take an interest in her. That he did not own her.

After a moment of silence in which his arms felt stiff around her, and her neck felt tight from holding her head away from his garlic breath, he finally said, "You received many bouquets then?"

That others could find any value in her clearly surprised him.

Her cheeks flamed hot at the implied insult. "Mm." She murmured her assent, letting him make what he would of the noise.

"Who sent them?" He asked as if merely curious, but the way his fingers curled over hers tighter than necessary actually caused her pain.

No. She was not wrong about this one. He was the sort of man who would always insist she fell into line with his wishes and never allow her to have opinions of her own. This was not the one. Her mother would understand when she explained it. "At a masquerade such as this, you surely would not wish me to unmask my personal business, sir. It is not even midnight yet." She kept her tone playful and light but hoped he was astute enough to feel the bite in her words.

Beneath the silk ribbon holding his tiger mask in place, his ear tips flamed to an alarming shade of red.

Wonderful. He understood. He wasn't nearly as dim as she'd feared.

Another round of silence made her wish they were dancing the quadrille, where one needn't be in such close proximity to one's partner. And where the exertion of the dance left little room for talking. She'd been looking over Mr. Hurst's shoulder, trying to escape the barrage of garlic—really, did the man have access to no other form of produce?

That was when she saw him.

Someone new entered the ballroom.

Wendy couldn't say why she thought of him as "new" exactly. She'd already determined she couldn't recognize a quarter of those present under their masks. Only that he swept in like a wave from a distant shore with a presence that shook her to her core. He was cloaked in velvet the shade of midnight—an anomaly in the sea of pastel gowns and starched shirts. The domino mask would not have been enough to hide his identity if she'd known him, which was why she was certain she did *not* know him.

She opened her mouth to ask Mr. Hurst if he knew the man when she realized it was hardly polite to inquire after another gentleman while dancing, even if Mr. Hurst had a grip on her that was cramping her fingers. Sending hemlock to the man would have been kinder.

She closed her mouth again and let her gaze follow the stranger as he moved across the polished floor. He was tall compared to many of the other guests, which made it easier for her to see him even when he entered the press of skirts and waistcoats. His dark hair was longer than most men wore theirs and tied back with . . . Wendy squinted to see better . . . a black leather cord. His clean-shaven jaw was all angles, highlighting his perfect cheekbones. Handsome, she decided immediately. This stranger was brilliantly handsome. But it wasn't just that he was handsome. He was so much more than that. His presence held a new note—a dissonance in the perfectly orchestrated manners of society—a dissonance she had not realized she'd needed until he swept into the ballroom.

"It is nice to feel you relaxing in my arms. We are becoming more comfortable with one another, are we not?" Mr. Hurst's grip around her had become a cage.

She realized that she had indeed relaxed and had drawn inappropriately closer to her dancing partner. "Excuse me," she said, making her voice reflect her own revulsion with herself for being so careless. "I'm afraid I am quite unwell and might be sick." She sagged like a limp flower.

"Oh dear." Mr. Hurst hurriedly cast his eyes around the room in a desperate attempt to find a chair in which he could safely dispose of her before she erupted her sickness all over his expensive clothing.

Good. Now he could take her "relaxation" for illness and get those inappropriate ideas out of his head, because Wendy had no intention of allowing Mr. Hurst to keep her caged like some pretty bird. She breathed deeply as Mr. Hurst settled her in a chair by the window and scurried away to fetch her a drink, or her mother, whichever he came across first. Wendy frowned, tilting her head to the side so as not to lose sight of the man in the domino mask and felt a tingle of memory. Pretend games of hunting in Neverland. She knew what it was to hunt, and she now drew on that experience. Her prey never left her sight.

She had every intention of catching him.

The many gentlemen who had been boys when she was a girl discovered simultaneously that they loved her.

CHAPTER TWO

Wendy vacated her chair as soon as Mr. Hurst was out of sight. No matter what her mother said or what Wendy had promised, she did not have it in her to entertain the idea of such a man. Her father had cherished her mother. Wendy would not settle for a man who would treat her like property.

Mr. Hurst seemed like a man who had a temper simmering beneath his smiles, the type that expected his wife to always be under his complete control. He would likely expect an heir right away, and while she had played at motherhood to her brothers and to the lost boys, and she'd even mothered Peter on occasion, she felt certain she wasn't ready for the real thing. Avoiding Mr. Hurst was definitely her best option.

Searching for the stranger in the domino mask, Wendy diligently skirted around pockets of people talking. She couldn't have explained her reasons for searching the man out. She couldn't understand why he, out of everyone present, interested her. But there was something—a promise of adventure, a hint of intrigue. It was silly to think so, and yet . . . she strained to hear the stranger's name whispered on the lips of several as she passed. The murmurs carried the weight of a secret as they discussed him.

"His name is Mr. Liam Blackwell," one said.

"In His Majesty's Navy. Lieutenant, I believe."

"Poor soul," said another.

"Dreadful business," said yet another.

"Mother just died." This came from a woman on Wendy's right. Wendy absorbed the information with the intent to continue hunting her quarry. But then the woman said, "His mother was a great friend of mine. He's spent a lot of time with me while getting his mother's affairs in order."

Wendy stopped and looked at the woman, mentally unmasking her. Mrs. Alison Connolly.

Mrs. Connolly dearly loved to play matchmaker and had tried, without success, to match Wendy on two separate occasions. Wendy decided it only fair to allow Mrs. Connolly the possibility of success with a third attempt.

"Mrs. Connolly," Wendy said with warmth. She was not faking the emotion. She truly cared about the woman who had lost her son and then become a widow early in life and, instead of retreating into herself, had become the mother, aunt, and friend that every other person in society never knew they needed until they spent time with her. There was a special place in Wendy's heart for a soul as gentle and kind as Mrs. Connolly.

"Wendy Darling, may I just say you *are* a darling." Mrs. Connolly loved that particular joke. "How are you, dear?"

"Quite well. And how are you? I hear you've redesigned your music room. I would love to see it sometime."

Mrs. Connolly flapped her hands excitedly. "Yes! I have! And you must come see it. I insist. Oh! And you must meet my young friend." She raised up slightly on her tiptoes to scan the room. "Where has he gone off to? I really must introduce you. Young people require other young people, I always say. And you both seem suited to one another." Mrs. Connolly looked Wendy up and down in a way that Wendy knew to be a full assessment and approval. The introduction Mrs. Connolly made would be full of insistence and hints at a lifelong connection. She would be intent on making a match.

Wendy was glad to have run into Mrs. Connolly since she didn't want the woman making that same assessment and conclusion for some other young lady. Far better to work *with* Mrs. Connolly than against her.

Wendy's determination regarding this young man whom she had never met surprised her. After all, she knew nothing of him aside from the few whispers and Mrs. Connolly's assurance that they were well-suited. Why then did she feel this need to meet him? Especially since she was not actually wanting to be matched up with anyone.

"Oh, here he comes now." Mrs. Connolly was looking past Wendy's shoulder, but Wendy resisted the urge to turn and look for herself. She did not want to appear too eager. Also, she needed a moment to try to understand herself and her own wishes.

"Liam," Mrs. Connolly said. "I've been looking for you. There is someone I wish for you to meet."

"Of course, Mrs. Connolly. If they are a friend to you, then they are a friend to me."

Wendy turned to face him and nearly buckled to the ground. Thinking him handsome from a distance was like admiring a star in the sky. She imagined that a star up close would have the same blinding flawlessness as Mrs. Connolly's friend. He was taller than Wendy by several inches, so she tilted her head to see him clearly. Fringed by dark lashes, his eyes were the most brilliant blue she'd ever seen. His dark hair was tied back with a leather cord like it had been done hastily and without much thought, and yet, he looked incredibly well put together and composed. She had to fight against the unexpected impulse to run her fingers against the angles of his clean-shaven jaw.

Mrs. Connolly kept speaking as if the light from this one perfect man had not rendered her speechless and breathless, though Wendy could scarcely understand how anyone could utter a syllable when met with such an open, direct gaze from those forget-me-not blue eyes.

But more than that . . . his gaze stirred something familiar in Wendy.

"Liam," Mrs. Connolly said. "May I present Miss Wendy Darling, a dear friend of mine. And Wendy, this is my closest friend's son, Liam Blackwell."

Wendy curtsied deeper than she would have done if she'd ever been presented at court. Mr. Blackwell bowed and then looked up from his bent position with a smile. "It is a lucky person who can call Mrs. Connolly a friend. I know she was my mother's dearest and closest confidante. I don't know how my mother would have managed without her while I was away."

"Away, sir?" Wendy was glad she'd found her voice. She'd begun to fear it might never work again.

Mrs. Connolly jumped in before Mr. Blackwell could reply. "He is serving in the Navy. Go on, Liam, tell her where you were."

"I've been serving on the HMS *Indefatigable*. We were stationed in New Zealand. I was allowed to return home as soon as I discovered my mother had taken ill."

She opened her mouth to offer her condolences on the loss of his mother but stopped herself since she wasn't entirely certain that the whispered rumor she'd heard in passing was true. *Ill* and *gone* were not the same thing. Though the pitying look Mrs. Connolly bestowed on him confirmed the truth of it.

"And your mother is . . . ?"

"Was," he replied. "She was too ill. She did not recover." His whole body tightened as he spoke, and never had Wendy felt more of a kinship. Losing her father had left the same sort of hole in her. She had more questions, like did he make it home in time to say goodbye, and did he have siblings or other family to rally around him? Wendy, for once, held her tongue. In this first meeting, she did not need to demand he flay open his heart and reveal its contents to her. His pain belonged to him, and he did not owe it to anyone to share.

"I am so sorry," she said.

He must have seen how the words had been burrowed into her soul because he said, "You've also lost someone?"

"Yes. My father." Wendy normally didn't like talking about her father, but as she stared into the depths of his eyes, she found they reflected her same insecurities and worries. And grief. It startled her to see such an equal depth of mourning mirrored in his gaze.

"I am sorry for your loss as well."

So many people had shared that sentiment with her. Dozens, if not hundreds. Never before that moment had she believed it. "Thank you, Mr. Blackwell. It means more, somehow, coming from someone who understands."

"My, but aren't you two a solemn pair!" Mrs. Connolly declared after having leaned over to whisper something in Mr. Blackwell's ear. "You're too young to be carrying such heavy burdens. Especially at a party. Now is not the time for morose musings. Now is the time to dance. If you were a smart man, Mr. Blackwell, you would scratch your name on her dance card before it's filled. I assure you that Miss Darling is a treasure not to be ignored. She'll be in much demand once the vultures are aware she's arrived."

Wendy felt her face grow warm with the less-than-subtle review Mrs. Connolly had bestowed on her. But she did not look away from his gaze. She'd meant to meet this man, and now that she had, she wanted to dance with him, to talk more with him, to know all there was to know about him.

If he didn't want to spend time with her, she would not make it easy for him to extract himself from her presence.

"Miss Darling, I would love to dance with you if you have room on your dance card."

Happiness swelled in her. "As it so happens, I've not been here long enough to put a single name on my card yet." She brandished her wrist with the dangling fan. He took it up and began to write.

And write.

Goodness! Had he decided to put his middle name and perhaps list his pedigree as well? How long could it take to write a name?

When he finished, he took her hand before she could see what he'd written. "I believe this next dance belongs to us."

It was the quadrille, she realized as the music shifted. Why couldn't it have been a waltz? Why could it not have been an excuse to step into his embrace and converse privately for a short time?

But Wendy lamented only a moment for the lack of intimacy. Any dance with this man should prove to be enjoyable. They joined another couple on the floor and bowed and curtsied to the partners in the set. Each time she joined hands with Mr. Blackwell as the dancers formed the intricate patterns and figures, she couldn't help but smile. He was easy on his feet and graceful as he performed the dance. Across the room, other couples mirrored their steps, but after a moment, Wendy stopped noticing the other couples. Every time she and Mr. Blackwell moved together and then apart again, they exchanged fleeting glances. Did his heart stammer and stutter like hers?

When the music ended, Mr. Blackwell led her back to the edge of the room. "I am so glad you agreed to dance with me. I was quite nervous."

"Were you?" Wendy could hardly imagine him being nervous about anything.

"Quite nervous," he repeated. "Do you know what Mrs. Connolly said to me on that subject?"

Wendy shook her head.

His lips quirked up in a wry grin. "She said, 'Stop fidgeting, dear. Women of society can smell fear.' How was that for not exactly comforting?"

They both laughed. Wendy could readily imagine Mrs. Connolly saying such a thing.

"Would you like a drink, Miss Darling?" he asked.

"Yes, please." She went with him to a table decorated like a fairy woodland, with the punch bowl made to look like a pale pink pond in the center. Wendy began to calculate the cost again before stopping herself.

While she stood to the side and waited for Mr. Blackwell to get her a glass, she was approached by Mr. Tilney. His straw-colored hair slightly stuck up in the back in a way that always reminded Wendy of a baby bird.

"Miss Darling." He squinted at her from behind his silver mask. He wiped at his perspiring brow with a handkerchief and then wrenched the poor handkerchief in his hands as if it had done something wrong and needed to be punished. "It *is* Miss Darling, isn't it?" He spoke timidly as if worried she might laugh at him or turn him away.

A thing she would never do. The man was just the sort she felt protective of. She would never make him feel small. "You guessed accurately, Mr. Tilney. Bravo."

"Ah, and you guessed me as well." He wiped the handkerchief once more over his brow.

She smiled in response.

"I hoped I might request your next waltz."

"Of course." But she opened her fan to find that her dance card was full. How?

She peered closely at the names. *Mrs. Connolly's friend. Your new acquaintance. Liam Blackwell. Man in the black mask. Mr. Blackwell. Lieutenant in His Majesty's Navy. My mother's son.*

Mr. Blackwell hadn't put his name down once—he had used various methods to fill her card entirely. When he turned her direction with their drinks, he met her incredulous stare and shrugged with an impish sort of grin that looked apologetic without being at all repentant.

"I am sorry, Mr. Tilney, but it appears my dance card is full."

Mr. Tilney drooped but nodded. "I expected as much. It took me a long while to find you. Perhaps next time."

"Yes, of course. Thank you so much for asking. In the meantime, there is a young lady who has been unattended all evening and might truly love to dance with a kind young man." Wendy pointed him to the lady in question, whom she'd mentally unmasked as Mary Sadler. Mary was quiet and kind and reminded her of Mr. Tilney's gentle nature.

Though Wendy had outright rejected a marriage proposal from the man, she saw no reason not to be his friend and wanted to guide him to someone with a disposition that matched his.

"Thank you, Miss Darling." Mr. Tilney twisted his handkerchief again and squared his shoulders before approaching Mary.

"Nicely done." Mr. Blackwell handed her a cup of the pink liquid.

"Are you complimenting me or yourself?"

"Why would I compliment myself?"

Wendy narrowed her eyes at him. "Because you seem altogether too pleased with the mischief you've unleashed on my dance card."

"What's wrong with your dance card?"

She flipped the fan open and showed it to him. "It's full."

"Ah, that. Well . . . if Mrs. Connolly declared you a treasure, you shouldn't be surprised by a full dance card."

She raised her right eyebrow high enough to be sure it was visible above her mask. "The man in the black mask?"

"Him. Oh, I've heard he is very handsome. You're lucky to have caught his eye."

"Mr. Blackwell! Truly, what were you thinking?" She tried to sound exasperated but failed, she was sure. She could not hide that she thought him to be amusingly clever, and the compliment of him wanting to spend his time with her was not lost on her.

"I was thinking that the thing about a masquerade is that it is hard to keep track of the various identities of your dance partners. How is anyone to fault a couple for accidentally connecting again and again?"

Wendy shook her head and laughed. "Did it not occur to you that I might want to dance with others?"

"Did you?" His eyes were earnest then, finally looking truly repentant.

"Not especially. But you could not have known that."

His features loosened at the confirmation that he'd been right.

"It was presumptuous." She continued scolding him because to let him off easy would be to give him permission to do such a thing again. When her younger brothers did something wrong but amusing, she always told them the first time was funny. The second was mildly humorous. The third time was a switching.

Not that she ever switched her brothers and not that she'd threaten Mr. Blackwell with such a punishment, though she was determined to let him know the truth of it if he persisted in such naughty behavior.

"It *was* presumptuous," he agreed. "If you'd like, I'll procure a new dance card at once."

"How will you convince Mrs. Westridge you need a dance card?"

"I'll tell her I spilled punch on yours."

"You'd lie?" Wendy couldn't say why that thought disappointed her so greatly.

"Of course not. I would take the trouble of actually spilling punch on your card before taking it to her. What kind of amateur do you take me for?"

Wendy laughed and took a sip of her effervescent punch.

"And actually . . ." He scratched the back of his neck—a sheepish little mannerism that was fairly adorable. He was every bit a grown man and held himself erect like she would expect from a military man, but try as he might to hide it, the boyish gesture made him a curiosity to her.

"Actually?" she prompted.

"I *did* promise Mrs. Connolly one dance. She loves the minuet, and I would not want to deprive her of the pleasure of dancing."

With one simple statement, he'd inserted himself firmly into Wendy's good graces. She truly cared about Mrs. Connolly and worried for the widow, all alone in her big house. That he was taking care of her, watching out for her needs? Well . . . not one of the other gentlemen who had previously proposed had ever done anything half so perfect.

She looked at her dance card. "Well, *friend of Mrs. Connolly.* The minuet is a way off, and it seems this dance is yours."

"I believe you're right." Mr. Blackwell settled their drinks back on the table and led her out to dance to the lively polka music that had just begun. They moved in rhythm to the music, gliding and hopping—movements that seemed to mirror their previous playful conversation. They circled the floor several times over before the final strains of the song hung in the air.

The fast-paced dance left them both smiling as they faced one another. She imagined her face must be as flushed as his from the exertion, and she didn't mind at all. Amid the laughter and applause, Wendy had the thought that her mother would be so pleased to learn she'd finally met someone worth mentioning.

"So tell me, Miss Darling," he said. "Are you fond of long walks in the park?"

"I am fond of many things," she replied as they walked together back to the punch table. She'd enjoyed the punch and, after the exertion of the polka, needed some refreshment.

He made a noise low in his throat that might have been a chuckle. "All right. I'll bite. What are those many things?"

"All of them? You want me to list every single activity that gives me pleasure? I'm not sure I would even know where to begin."

"Begin with the first thing that comes to your mind."

"Fencing." She felt herself grow hot with the admission, and the rise in her temperature had nothing to do with the exertion of a dance. Divulging that she enjoyed fencing would alarm any respectable man. She hadn't meant to blurt out such a truth. That was the trouble with speaking before thinking. Wasn't that what her mother always said?

"Do you mean you enjoy watching or that you enjoy participating?"

Wendy could have lied. It would be easy enough to do. She could pretend that she meant that she enjoyed fencing as a spectator might. She could flip open her fan and flutter it gently in front of her face to hide the truth.

But what would be the point? If she liked Mr. Blackwell as much as she suspected she did, then she needed to know if he was the sort of man who could like her back—the genuine Wendy, not the Miss Darling she had to be in society.

"I like to participate. I'm quite good if I do say so myself. I can best my brother John nearly half the time when we practice, and I best my other brothers, Michael and Tootles, and their friend, Slightly, every time we practice together." She glanced at him to gauge his response as he swept his gaze up the full measure of her body and then smirked in disbelief.

His thoughts were written all over his face.

"You don't believe me," she said.

"I'm trying to believe you. Very hard, in fact." They'd arrived back at the punch table, but if he thought she would let the matter drop and return to their expected roles as man and woman in society, he was sorely mistaken.

"You doubt me based on my size? I'll have you know that fencing is not just about physical strength. It's also about strategy, timing, and mental agility."

He handed her a fresh cup of punch and took a sip from his own before saying, "Indeed it is. And I've no doubt you can best your brother with a foil."

"Not just the foil, but the épée and the sabre as well, naturally."

"Naturally." Mr. Blackwell took another drink, but his glass was insufficient to hide his smile.

She'd wipe that smile off with a blade tip. "Would you care to place a wager on the fact that I can best you at least once when we practice tomorrow?" It was a bold move to assume he would meet her, that he wanted to ever speak to her again after she'd been so decidedly opposite of the demure housewife most of the men who courted her were looking for. But she felt bold. And if he did not want to meet her to fence, then was he really the man she wanted for herself?

Not at all.

"No wagers, Miss Darling. I would feel terrible taking your

money, and I have no intention of going easy on you simply because you're a woman."

"Are you saying you actually agree to such a scheme?"

"Honestly, Miss Darling, if it meant that I would get to see you again, I'd go as far as agree to a duel with pistols." He settled his gaze on her in a way that seemed he was charmed, not alarmed.

"I . . ." She faltered, suddenly unsure of what she'd been saying. Had she been making a point? She didn't know. But she was certain that she was also charmed.

She was about to say something that surely would have been brilliant, but he said, "Alas, I cannot meet you tomorrow for fencing. Unfortunately, I need to leave town for a short while to help my uncle with a project."

He must have seen her disappointment because he hurried to say, "But I am very unhappy about it now that I know I could have been with you instead. I shall dip my arrow in devil's snare so that my uncle feels even a small portion of the torture I feel at having to miss a chance to spend time with you."

Wendy blinked. "Devil's snare?"

He grinned. "The saying goes that devil's snare makes people hot as a hare, blind as a bat, dry as a bone, red as a beet, and mad as a hatter."

"Yes," she replied slowly. "I know that saying."

"Do you? That's funny. I hardly know anybody who knows it."

"So how is it a saying then? If not very many people know it?" The twisting in her stomach tightened its grip.

"It's a common saying among my uncle and his friends."

Wendy could barely breathe. Edges of her vision felt like they were narrowing and going dark. Captain Hook had been the only person she'd ever heard use that phrase. Hearing it from Mr. Blackwell meant . . .

She was almost sure that it meant . . .

But she was being ridiculous. Mr. Blackwell was a man of the sea, that was all. Why would hearing this phrase make her think this man, who was friends with Mrs. Connolly, was in league with Captain Hook? She could not really, *really* be sure of any such thing. How could she? Mr. Blackwell hadn't actually said anything too nefarious. Perhaps that particular phrase was something commonly said among all seafaring folk. Regardless of where they dropped their anchor.

She emptied her punch glass as if it were filled with liquid courage and then said, "It's a shame you're leaving town. I should like to have trounced you at fencing."

"Do not count me out of that plan so quickly. I am determined to prove myself as fierce as Blackbeard's bosun. Otherwise, Uncle James might be ashamed of me."

Wendy felt her smile freeze on her lips. Uncle James? Blackbeard's bosun? Her fingers went of their own accord to the chain of the acorn button, but she didn't pull it out. She was being ridiculous. Uncle James was how half the English referred to one of their uncles. It didn't have to mean James Hook. Just because Hook had been reputed to have been Blackbeard's bosun didn't mean Mr. Blackwell was talking about Hook. It was probably some seafaring saying.

Still, the words "James" and "Blackbeard's bosun" elicited a shudder from her. But the words had to mean nothing more than what they seemed. Why was she jumping at nonexistent shadows?

He took her hand. "I believe it's time for us to dance again."

So it was.

Wendy shoved aside her strange misgivings and turned her focus to the man in front of her.

She found that she didn't need the adventure of crossing swords with Mr. Blackwell. Dancing with him and talking to him were their own adventure. The rest of the evening, they danced and laughed their way through conversations full of verbal lunging and parrying. The entire exercise of banter was mentally delicious. Every syllable, an exquisite burst of flavor. She told him all about her family. He told her all about his mother and how much he missed her, which prompted her to share her own pain over losing her father and how she was still reeling from that loss.

When he gazed at her, she felt her metaphorical mask slipping long before midnight. He saw past all the things she had to *be* according to society, to her grandmother, and even to her mother. He saw her as she was and didn't shrink back in contempt at what he found.

She had never before delighted in a waltz the way she did when he took her hand in his and stepped forward as she swept back. The world around them melted like candle wax. He held her closer than anyone had ever done before. Or maybe it was that she held him closer?

The warmth of him so close would have been stifling if it had been anyone else, but the feel of him so close to her made her feel safe, *comforted*.

It made her feel not alone anymore.

That thought startled her. Mr. Blackwell must have noticed the shift in her thoughts because he said, "What's wrong?"

"Nothing," she said, and meant it.

When Mr. Blackwell danced the minuet with Mrs. Connolly, Wendy was claimed for the dance by Mr. Amesbury, a tall mountain of a man with fair hair and a perpetually serious look on his face, especially with the black, silver, and gold mask designed to mimic the face of an old Roman gladiator.

Mr. Amesbury was startled when she greeted him by his name. "You know who I am?"

Well, that was unexpected. She had assumed he recognized her since he had asked her to dance.

"Do you *not* know who I am?" she asked carefully.

He shook his head. Wendy was certain he wasn't pretending, and she found herself looking for the one man who would be amused by this man who knew her well not recognizing her.

But Mr. Blackwell was not visible in the crowd, and a pang of . . . *something* twinged her heart.

She missed him. After such a short time, she missed him.

Mr. Amesbury looked at her expectantly as if she would at any moment reveal her name to him, but she smiled and said, "It is not yet midnight, Mr. Amesbury. Until then, let us be content to dance." The minuet took an age, and she spent most of that time trying to catch glimpses of Mr. Blackwell and Mrs. Connolly. When she finally spotted them down the line, Mrs. Connolly wore such a serene smile that Wendy could only feel gratitude that Mr. Blackwell took the time to give her friend this one pleasure. Would anyone else have thought to ask the lady to dance? Wendy thought it unlikely.

Watching him take Mrs. Connolly by the hand and lead her through the forms before they parted again, all while maintaining eye contact with his dance partner, softened every instinct in Wendy. Here was a good man—a man she could trust, a man who did not flinch when met with a young lady with peculiar pastimes such as fencing, a man who saw to the needs of an aging widow.

Wendy had never thought herself to be so silly as to love someone at first sight, though her mother had often told her that she had loved her father from the first moment. But now . . .

Now, Wendy believed she had met the man who could possibly be destined to have her heart.

"That crocodile would have had me before this, but by a lucky chance it swallowed a clock which goes tick tick inside it, and so before it can reach me I hear the tick and bolt." He laughed, but in a hollow way.

"Some day," said Smee, "the clock will run down, and then he'll get you."

Hook wetted his dry lips. "Ay," he said, "that's the fear that haunts me."

CHAPTER THREE

While Wendy watched Mr. Blackwell and Mrs. Connolly dance, she considered all the ways she admired him. It was so much more than simply him being handsome. It was his quiet understanding of her heart that attracted her to him. As soon as they locked eyes, she knew he knew. He knew what it was to lose and to grieve that loss.

Her own grief was a tangible creature, lurking in her shadow and trailing her every step. But in Mr. Blackwell's presence, that phantom seemed to evaporate like morning mist on a hot day.

Then there were all the things he had said to her over the course of the night. He'd told her that he often wrote little mental notes to his mother as if, somehow, she might be able to look down from heaven and read the words he etched into his heart for her benefit.

"What would you tell her about tonight?" she'd asked.

"Oh, I've already started one for tonight."

"Really?"

"Truly. I began it by describing a certain young lady introduced to me by her dearest friend."

"How would she respond, do you think?" Wendy asked.

His eyes had taken a faraway look as if mentally conjuring the words his mother might pen to him. "She would want to know all the particulars of what everyone was wearing and what food was served at the Westridge ball. She'd always liked the Westridges. And of course, she would ask whether or not this mysterious Miss Darling was fond of riding horses."

He gave her a meaningful look.

"I do like riding. A great deal."

He'd asked her several questions after that under the guise of asking for his mother. She'd responded by informing him that his method of writing to his mother was brilliant, inspiring her to write a similar letter to her father. This allowed her to ask him the sorts of questions she imagined her father would want to know, were he alive to ask them himself.

Wendy smiled, thinking of the conversation now. He was funny and charming and quick to match her wit for wit.

Several other young men tried to engage her in conversation, and she tried to be polite. She had to force herself to pay attention to them and not turn her head to scan the room for Mr. Blackwell to see if he had escorted Mrs. Connolly off the dance floor yet. She shivered when his low voice whispered from behind her, "Did you miss me while I was away?"

She did not turn to face him, but hoped he felt the smile in her words as she answered, "Not at all. I've been much too busy to be missing people."

"So I noticed." He moved around to face her directly. One gentleman who had seemed determined to stay at her side for the rest of the night flinched and scampered away when Mr. Blackwell fixed him with a stare. "Are you always in such demand by other men?" he asked.

A proper lady trained in the etiquette of society should have been humble and demure and cast her eyes down while assuring him she was not *always* in such demand.

Wendy did not do any of that.

She shrugged, making him laugh—a sound she felt she could never grow tired of hearing.

Mrs. Westridge stood atop the small stage where the musicians played. She clapped her hands lightly to call attention to herself. Conversations died down to give the proper respect to the hostess.

"It's almost midnight. As the clock strikes twelve, you may all remove your masks and reveal your identities. The dancing will resume at that time."

There was a space of scarcely a moment after this announcement before the tall clock struck its first mournful peal to mark the changing hour. People all seemed to be holding their breath, waiting for the full twelve chimes.

"Are you ready?" Liam whispered in her ear at the sixth chime. He'd leaned in close to be heard over the crowd.

Seven chimes.

"I'm ready."

"Promise you won't be disappointed in what might be under the mask?"

Eight chimes.

"Your face is barely covered under that scrap of fabric," she scoffed.

Nine chimes.

"True. But I could be horribly disfigured around my eyes."

Ten chimes.

"And you think it would sway my opinion if you are?"

Eleven chimes.

"I suppose we're about to find out."

Twelve chimes.

The room erupted in noise as masks were flung from faces, and people cheered and laughed.

"Come now, Miss Darling. It's time." Mr. Blackwell reached his hand to the back of her head. His fingertips brushed her cheek and then grazed across the top of her braids and curls. What was he doing? He couldn't plan on kissing her here now in front of everyone. Of course he wasn't planning any such absurdity. Why would she even think such a thing?

Of course he wouldn't.

Which was altogether too bad.

He did not draw her near to him the way her brain seemed to think he should. Instead, he tugged on one of the silk ribbons tying her mask to her head. The knot loosened, and the mask slipped just a little.

Her breath caught at his nearness at the same time that her fingers caught the mask. Her eyes never left his as she pulled the mask away from her face.

Once, Wendy had seen her father at the unveiling of *The Lady of Shalott*, painted by John William Waterhouse, when it had been donated to the museum. Her father's eyes had softened, and he'd looked at that painting as if it had been bestowed by heaven itself.

Mr. Blackwell's eyes softened in that same way. He seemed startled to be staring into her unmasked face. "I knew you were beautiful," he said. "But truly I had no idea how heart-stammeringly stunning you are."

She blushed. Many suitors had said words to that effect to her, but never before had the compliment felt so sincere. She swallowed hard and smiled to thank him. Unsure of what else to do, she simply said, "Now it's your turn. Take off your mask and reveal yourself at last."

He laughed. "There is very little that my mask actually conceals. But as you desire, my lady."

He wasn't teasing regarding his lack of concealment. The domino mask did little to hide his features. And yet, removing the mask and allowing her to see the whole picture made him twitch his shoulders as if he had made himself vulnerable in a way he had not anticipated.

Her eyes trailed over the jagged scar that went from his left temple and down over his cheekbone. "So you were telling the truth," she said, "about being disfigured under your mask." She smiled to let him know she was teasing.

"Is it terrible to look upon?"

"Quite the opposite. It enhances your handsome features."

Wendy felt certain that had her mother heard her, she could have expected a severe scolding for her brazen assessment.

He burst out laughing. "Oh, Miss Darling. I am so glad Mrs. Connolly introduced us." He sighed as he pulled out his pocket watch. She wondered at the action since social events such as this ball could go long into the morning.

When he met her eyes again, he hesitated, then said, "Miss Darling, do you perhaps recall—"

"Wendy, I have someone I'd like you to meet." Her mother had managed to sneak up on them and slide between Wendy and Mr. Blackwell, though Wendy wasn't certain if she'd done it on purpose or if she truly hadn't noticed him there.

"Hello, Mother. May I introduce Mrs. Connolly's particular friend? Mr. Liam Blackwell."

Her mother turned toward him but still didn't really look at him. "Mrs. Connolly's friend?"

"Yes," Wendy confirmed.

Her mother finally said, "It's so nice to meet you, Mr. Blackwell."

"A pleasure, Mrs. Darling."

Her mother stayed and talked for a moment before deciding that Mr. Blackwell was mostly harmless. Then she left them alone again so that they might join the next dance.

"You'll have to forgive my mother," Wendy said as she took his hand and followed his lead through the steps. "She desperately wants me to form an attachment but is immediately distrustful as soon as a man shows sincere interest. The woman is a quandary sometimes."

He shook his head to indicate no apology was necessary. "She simply sounds like a mother," he said. "My own was much the same way. For as much as she wished me settled, she never seemed to fancy any of the young ladies I fancied."

"So you've fancied many young ladies then?"

The question startled him enough to make him stumble on his steps of the waltz.

Wendy smirked at that. "Watch your step, Mr. Blackwell. You'd hate for your future fencing partner to think you were clumsy."

"Fencing again. Might I ask where you learned such a skill?"

"I have younger brothers. And they have a half-dozen friends who were always underfoot. Who else is supposed to protect them from the pirates?"

His lip twitched as if amused. "Pirates? And how often did you and your younger brothers encounter sorts such as that? I would imagine one doesn't see many of those wandering around Hyde Park."

They glided with ease across the floor. "You'd be surprised how many pirates walk the streets of London."

"How do you know if someone is a pirate? I hear they look just like everyone else."

"That's the reason one must keep her skill sharp and her blade sharper." Wendy shouldn't have begun such a conversation. Why did she keep mentioning fencing? Was she trying to frighten him away? But she couldn't seem to stop herself, and she tilted her head slightly. "Do you enjoy fencing, Mr. Blackwell?"

"Very much."

"Are you any good?"

Wendy was certain he couldn't have stopped the smug grin crawling over his face if he'd tried. "I have not been bested in a very long time."

She couldn't tell if he was teasing her or not. "Really. And how did *you* get to be so accomplished?"

"Pirates," he said simply.

"But of course." She laughed.

"How do you know I'm not a pirate?" he asked.

"You don't smell of salt and gunpowder." She glided under the arch of his arm and then back into place within his arms.

His expression became unreadable as he said, "It seems we are very much the same sort of person, Miss Darling. So it is that I must ask, is it your opinion that all pirates are evil?"

"I've not met one who isn't. As a man in the service of His Majesty's Navy, have you met a good pirate?" Wendy nodded with the confidence of one who knew she was right. She'd met enough pirates to know.

"Would you believe me if I told you that some pirates are heroes?"

She laughed. "Not even for a moment."

He maneuvered her into the Viennese cross and a natural spin. He retreated away from that conversation and began a new one. "What do your brothers think of a sister who fences and has such strong opinions regarding pirates?"

"They're grateful, I think. My peculiarities have given them a great deal of entertainment. When we were young, I told them stories of great battles. We often acted them out. Once the boys began official fencing lessons, where they were learning from the masters, they came home and taught me everything they knew. I think they didn't want the story to end."

She felt the twisting of nostalgia in her heart as she glanced across the room to the double doors leading to the balcony. She could just make out the shine of stars through the windowpanes.

"Are you all right?" he asked when she went several long moments without saying anything. He followed her gaze to the doors.

Wendy shook her head and fixed her eyes on him, almost surprised to find him there. She felt like a fool for letting herself get caught thinking about Peter. "I'm sorry. I apparently wandered off. Memory Lane is such a funny place. If I'm not careful, I might get lost there sometime and not be able to find my way back."

"Were they at least good memories?"

"Yes. Of a sort." She gave a tiny laugh and a slight shrug of her shoulders. Her fingers tightened over his. "Who can really tell if a memory is good or not? Often, either way, memories make us sad, don't they?"

"Quite right, Miss Darling," he said. "I would call any memory with my mother a good memory. Yet all of them make me sad, at least a little."

She took a deep breath and forced herself to mentally shove away the rain cloud she'd invited to settle over the top of them both. "But we should not dwell on the sad. Let us instead think of happier things, like how much fun it will be for you to try to beat me at fencing when you come back into town."

He laughed outright but sobered quickly as he said, "Sadly, I could be gone for quite some time. I'm afraid I don't know when I'll be able to meet you for such an activity." He glanced toward the double doors, which were much closer since he and Wendy had moved that direction as they'd danced.

"Where will you be going for such a long time?"

"I will follow the second star to the right. Straight on 'til—"

"Morning," she said at the same time he did. Her heart quickened as she stared at him with wonder, suspicion, fear, and excitement. What was this game they were playing? "What is your business that takes you so very far away?" she asked.

They were now at the doors. "It's a secret. I'm afraid I can't tell you. But . . ." He stopped dancing and pulled out his pocket watch. "I must go now, or I won't be able to get there. Some doorways do not stay open for very long."

"You're leaving now? In the middle of a ball?" What doorways was he talking about? The doors next to them were closed.

"I have to. If I don't, I won't be able to get there."

Did he know he was being cryptic? His behavior had gone from charming to downright suspicious. What could he possibly be talking about? "I wish we had more time," she murmured, trying to stall him.

"I wish we did as well." He looked like he meant it. "Time is the enemy sometimes. I suppose it's like the ticking crocodile, isn't it? Time is chasing after all of us, snapping its jaws at our heels."

She was sure her eyes widened to the size of moons.

"Farewell, Miss Wendy Darling. I don't know how long I will be gone, but I will think of you every moment." Mr. Blackwell pressed a kiss to her fingers that he let linger for far longer than was strictly necessary, and he seemed to feel a real pang of regret that he had to leave her side.

Mr. Blackwell left her standing by the double doors as he exited out of them.

As soon as the door closed, Wendy wrestled with herself as to what to do next. Who was Liam Blackwell? A pirate? A criminal? An excessively tall lost boy with a five o'clock shadow?

The last option was just her being ridiculous, but still . . . He said a great many suspicious things. And who left in the middle of a ball out the back entrance rather than the front door?

No one.

At least no one who wasn't up to no good.

Which was why Wendy couldn't let Mr. Blackwell get away.

His presence had been like the moon to the ocean. She was compelled to follow his pull.

There was nothing to be done except to follow him.

"Second to the right, and straight on till morning." That, Peter had told Wendy, was the way to the Neverland; but even birds, carrying maps and consulting them at windy corners, could not have sighted it with these instructions.

CHAPTER FOUR

As soon as the door closed, Wendy cast her eyes around her, trying to take inventory of her options. There was nothing in her immediate vicinity that could aid her with anything. She touched her fingers to the handle on the double doors Mr. Blackwell had exited through and made her choice as she tossed a quick glance over her shoulder and opened the door to follow.

"I'm sorry, Mother," Wendy murmured. But following a suspicious character into the night was spades better than flirting with men who wanted her to get married and have babies for them and invite their neighbors to tea. She rushed to catch up to Mr. Blackwell but then worried he would see her following. She hung back a little to avoid detection.

Mr. Blackwell slowed as he passed by where the carriages and motors waited for their owners inside the ballroom. At first, she thought perhaps he was trying to steal a motor and was glad he'd already passed her mother's so it wasn't a temptation for him. Her driver was nowhere to be seen, likely down in the kitchen with the Westridges' household staff getting a light supper. That was when she realized Mr. Blackwell was with a young stable hand who had apparently wandered close to one of the new motorized vehicles from Ford in America. The vehicle's driver was yelling at the boy, and he raised his fists to strike the child.

Wendy was about to step out from where she'd concealed herself behind her own motor so that she might protect the boy when Mr. Blackwell caught the man's fist before it could land a blow. He shoved the man back. "Only a monster strikes a child," Mr. Blackwell growled, appearing as though he barely suppressed his anger enough to keep him from throwing a punch of his own.

The driver's mouth hung slack, revealing teeth that sat crooked in his mouth like old gravestones in a long-neglected cemetery. "He was scratching it up."

"With his *eyes?*" Mr. Blackwell asked.

"Well, he would have if I hadn't stepped up just now. And then I'd be the one in trouble. Just see if I wouldn't."

Mr. Blackwell released the man's hand once it seemed there was no further threat. "If you're worried for the welfare of this conveyance, perhaps you should spend more time looking after it and less time preening for the young ladies." Mr. Blackwell jabbed a thumb in the direction of several housemaids who were watching the altercation from the safety of the stairwell.

The driver finally slinked away, and Mr. Blackwell sent the stable boy back to the safety of the stables.

No pirate would ever do anything to protect a child. It was against their very nature.

So . . . not a pirate.

Then what?

She supposed that was what she was following him to discover.

At the last moment, Wendy opened the door to her own motor. Inside the glove box was a small bag. She'd placed it there when she'd gone on a little adventure that may or may not have involved her sneaking into an old monastery. The bag held a lockpicking set Michael had given her for her last birthday. He'd done it as a joke, saying she would need it when Mother became fed up with her and decided to lock her in her room, but Wendy had taken the gift as a challenge and learned how to use it. John did not love that Wendy could use it to get into his rooms. And, apparently, Michael didn't love that she used it to sneak into a monastery and dragged him along with her. He'd felt guilty and told on them both, which was irritating. He then felt guilty for getting her lockpicking set confiscated and so liberated it from where her mother had put it and given it back to her.

She should have felt guilty for including Michael in the escapade and probably should have felt guilty for doing it at all, but she'd had to. There had been a rumor that someone had hidden a scroll in the monastery library that gave a detailed account of the method of catching fairies. She'd needed a fairy at the time to help her get to Neverland. Michael, of all people, should have understood her dilemma.

On the front seat, her father's overcoat, top hat, and umbrella were all laid out as if waiting for him. Mother said it made her feel like he was with her when she traveled. Wendy impulsively grabbed all of it and wrestled herself into the coat. She pulled on the top hat and used the umbrella as though it were a walking stick. It made for a grand disguise should Mr. Blackwell turn around and see her following.

As she quietly closed the door to her mother's motor, she worried for a moment that she'd taken too long and lost Mr. Blackwell, but she saw him again making his way around the hedgerow.

Wendy wasn't certain whether to be impressed or annoyed with his ability to be such a sneak. He would have been a better companion than Michael had been for the monastery escapade.

She followed at what she hoped was a safe distance.

Wendy felt like a shadow trailing Mr. Blackwell's steps through the London streets. He was quite a fast walker; his long legs carried him much more quickly than her shorter legs carried her. Not that she was short. For a woman, she was actually quite tall. It was just that in comparison to him, she had to take one and a half steps for his every single one.

That meant she had to work hard to keep her breathing quiet. She also had to walk on her tiptoes in order to keep her slippers from clapping against the cobblestones. Her feet were going to feel like torture if she had to keep up this particular pace.

But she did keep it up, matching his stride as best and as quietly as she could. Three times, Wendy had to duck into the alcove of a doorway or behind a tree in order to avoid detection as Mr. Blackwell glanced around him to be certain he was alone on the streets.

They walked for such a long time that Wendy couldn't understand why he hadn't brought a carriage. Though, in truth, it was better that he wasn't in any kind of conveyance, otherwise she might not have been able to follow. Wendy was agile enough that it was easy to grab hold of the back of a carriage or motor should the need arise. Regardless, she was glad she didn't have to.

The man and his shadow wove through the London streets until they came to the high gates of the Kensal Green Cemetery.

What on earth could he possibly have to do in a cemetery? Perhaps he was a grave robber.

The thought shouldn't have been exciting for Wendy, but she sometimes couldn't help herself.

She followed Mr. Blackwell inside, removing her top hat and leaving both it and the umbrella by a grave with another silent apology to her mother. Wendy used gravestones and mausoleums to hide her presence until she and Mr. Blackwell came to a large mausoleum topped by an opulent dome with an entrance flanked by tall stone pillars.

Mr. Blackwell entered the mausoleum, and Wendy waited a moment before approaching. She peeked around the thick, iron-reinforced door. Mr. Blackwell was barely visible in the thin sliver of light shining in through a small glass window at the back.

He shoved his hand into an alcove and twisted it as if turning some sort of mechanism behind the statuette. A rumbling, like the earth itself was moving and groaning, quaked underneath her feet. Stone grated against stone until a hole opened up in the wall. Mr.

Blackwell pulled a lantern out of a pack that had been lying on the floor, apparently left there by him, and lit it. The light meant that Wendy could no longer depend on the shadows to hide her, and she had to scramble behind a pillar in case he looked in her direction. He turned his head and glanced around, holding his lantern aloft, probably because he heard the scuffling noises she made as she ducked.

After a moment, the light faded, and the ground began to rumble again. Only then did she dare to peek out to see that Mr. Blackwell had entered the dark space in the ground and it was now closing up again. Panicked, Wendy leaped into action and hurried to the opening that was narrowing by the second. She snatched up the hem of her gown and overcoat around her so that they didn't get closed up in the stones after she made it through the door, and it closed behind her.

"Breathe, Wendy," she whispered and then mentally admonished herself for allowing even that much sound to escape her. With a glance around, she found that she stood on a small landing. The light from Mr. Blackwell's lantern somewhere below her helped her to see that there were stairs in front of her. She took another deep breath for courage and began her descent into the ground.

Wendy started counting the stairs after a short time, but she stopped when she reached number four hundred and twenty-seven. She felt like she had been creeping down the stone steps for an eternity while trying to stay above the sphere of lantern light. Surely, she had to have reached the center of the earth by now. Where were they going? Her imagination got the better of her as she followed. Perhaps he was a necromancer intent on raising the dead. Maybe he was releasing an evil spirit into the world—though Wendy wasn't certain why she assumed the spirit had to be malevolent. Couldn't there be friendly spirits? Maybe he was Hades and was on his way back to the underworld. Whatever he was doing, now she was trapped under a crypt, and her calves ached from the careful tiptoeing she'd had to do to keep her slippers from making noise against the stone.

Staying quiet was tedious business. A few times, she almost began humming to herself out of boredom and had to bite down on her lips to stop.

The cold air was thick with the scent of damp earth and ancient secrets, and Mr. Blackwell's lantern cast eerie shadows of his form as he moved ahead of her, making her feel dizzy and frightened and determined all at once. Wendy had time to contemplate her feelings as she crept behind him, yet she had no idea what it was she actually felt. She had felt a genuine attraction to this man, and now she felt a curiosity as well. What secrets could he have that would lead him down this path into the dark?

Twice, she almost turned around and went back the way she'd come because, really, did she want to know what he was doing in the belly of the earth? But she didn't go back because she didn't have a lantern to light her way, she wasn't entirely certain she could get the stone door to open from this side of the wall, and more, she felt a desperate need to know the truth.

The truth of him.

And in a way that made no sense, the truth of herself.

After a while longer, the cold, damp air finally gave way to something warm and tropical. Her overcoat was entirely too warm, but there was no way she could take it off without wasting time and losing her footing. If Mr. Blackwell got too far ahead of her, she'd no longer have a portion of the light he swung in front of him. The faint sounds of water dripping grew louder with every step she took. And then, just when she was sure she would have to stop and rest or otherwise break her neck stumbling down the stairs because she was so tired, there were no more stairs. Suddenly finding herself on a landing she hadn't been expecting, she stumbled and fell with an "Oof!" and a few choice words her mother would scold her for using. She was glad she hadn't removed the overcoat since it helped pad her fall so she didn't get too scratched up.

"Who's there?" Mr. Blackwell said from somewhere in front of her.

Did she answer? Did she stay silent and hope he thought it was an animal of some sort? Not that Wendy thought animals could curse aloud, but she could hope he thought they did. But then she heard footsteps that rang against the rock. Mr. Blackwell must have forgotten all about the noise from behind because his now-familiar footfalls were moving away from her.

His light faded away entirely, but she didn't dare move just in case he doubled back. When several minutes passed without any noise or activity, Wendy carefully pulled herself to her feet and crept forward in the dark, feeling her hands along the wall. A faint glimmer of light ahead pulsed softly. She'd followed Mr. Blackwell's lantern long enough to know that this light wasn't from that source. Yet it must have been the way Mr. Blackwell had gone because the corridor from the stairs led in no other direction. Mesmerized, Wendy approached the light to discover that it wasn't just one but many lights. It was a midnight blue door with glowing constellations etched into its surface. The brightest of the stars being the second one to the right.

"I'm here," Wendy whispered. "I've found you at last, Neverland." She reached her hand out and touched the ornate handle to open the door. As she pulled down on the handle, the door didn't swing open as she had expected; it dissolved in a shimmering fall of stardust. Wendy now stood in an arched entrance to a vast sea cave. Stalactites hung from the ceiling like the teeth of a giant crocodile and the stone landing gave way to uneven ground, slick with moisture. And the smell of damp earth yielded to the smell of the sea.

She took a shaky, relieved breath and crossed the threshold into the grotto.

Instantly, Wendy doubled over with a feeling of sickness. Her stomach roiled and bucked in rebellion against something twisted and wrong.

No, she thought. *This cannot be my Neverland.* It felt nothing like the happy, bright place of her memories. Where had Mr. Blackwell led her?

Then she heard another voice, a deep, rumbling tone with an accent that sounded as if it were from the aristocracy. Wendy crept closer, keeping low and crouching behind stalagmites to stay hidden.

"I trust your mission went well?" the voice asked. Wendy gasped then covered her mouth to try to call back the noise she'd made. She knew that voice, that haughty, condescending tone. It had cropped up in her nightmares on many occasions—even now.

She peered out from where she hid.

There, in the center of the cavern at the shore where the ocean lapped up at the cave floor, Mr. Blackwell stood with his back to her. A tall, imposing figure dressed in a crocodile-skin coat and wide-brimmed hat stood in front of Mr. Blackwell. The man was shaking his head, making the black candle coils of his hair bounce over his shoulders. The pirate's hook gleamed menacingly in Mr. Blackwell's lamplight.

Wendy's blood froze in her veins.

"Hello, Uncle," Mr. Blackwell said.

No. How was it possible?

She had *liked* Mr. Blackwell—enough that she'd intended on telling her mother all about how much she liked him when she arrived home from the ball, enough that she'd hoped he would call on her. Wendy had gone so far as to believe she had met the man who was destined to have her heart.

But Mr. Blackwell's uncle was none other than her greatest enemy, Captain Hook.

"Proud and insolent youth," said Hook, "prepare to meet thy doom."
"Dark and sinister man," Peter answered, "have at thee."

CHAPTER FIVE

Mr. Blackwell stood taller as Hook approached him. "Everything went as planned."

"Then where is the prize?"

"It's a delicate situation. I'll handle it," Mr. Blackwell said. Wendy had the feeling he was talking about her. "How did you know I was here already?"

Hook waved his hook hand like he was explaining something everyone should have already known. "Oh, that? I placed a blood tracker on you, of course."

"You've been tracking me?" Mr. Blackwell clearly felt affronted by this information.

"Of course I'm tracking you, but not like you think. I'm sent an alert through the bluebells whenever you cross the border into Neverland."

So they were in Neverland. Certainly, she had hoped, but to have it confirmed nearly undid her. Wendy felt a burning in her eyes with the relieved tears. She'd truly made it back. She was in Neverland. She glanced around, expecting to see Peter crouching behind another one of the stalagmites and raising his finger in front of his lips to tell her to stay quiet as he ambushed the pirate. But Peter wasn't there. There was no chime from Tinker Bell. She peeked out from her hiding place to see better. The grotto opened into a larger cavern carved out by the ocean tides. The rugged walls curved toward the dome at the top, their sides shimmering with the dampness left by the tide. Streaks of minerals stained the walls and glinted in the faint light coming from the cavern's opening that framed the vivid expanse of blue water and bluer sky.

The ocean rippled gently into the sea cave's bay, the sound echoing against the walls. Anchored there in that bay was a little jolly boat bobbing on the water's surface. A man sat knitting what might have been a scarf in the boat and seemed to be ignoring the conversation between Hook and Mr. Blackwell. The dark outline of the *Jolly Roger* could be seen on the horizon.

Yet, she couldn't understand how this was truly Neverland. The oil-slick feeling in her stomach when she'd crossed the threshold into the grotto was nothing like the elation experienced when she'd come before. Something felt off about the island. A muted keening hung heavy in the air.

The sinister feeling settled over her bones. Neverland had never felt like this. Sure, Neverland had its darkness, but this was different. Regardless. If she was in Neverland, then she could find Peter. Hadn't she spent years trying to get back? She was here. Really here.

Hook waved his arm, making the crocodile-skin coat flap in the air. Wendy had never seen the coat before. She had wrongfully assumed the crocodile had killed Hook, but apparently, Hook had been the one to win that battle. He continued his explanation. "I did it when you were still an infant. It was to keep you safe. To make certain that that cocky boy never took you and turned you against me by making you into one of his monstrous lost boys. I could never live with myself if your mother had to live with the pain of losing her only child at the hands of my greatest enemy."

Mr. Blackwell nodded.

The entire exchange confused Wendy. How could Mr. Blackwell be talking with Hook with such cordiality?

"Was it terribly difficult?" Hook asked Mr. Blackwell.

"No. Well, not the mission part. But seeing the old house without my mother in it . . ." Mr. Blackwell cleared his throat and tried to look away.

Hook placed the tip of his hook under Liam's chin and gently lifted it so Liam was forced to look into his uncle's eyes, now shining with unshed tears. "I'm sorry, lad. Your mother was a good soul. You can take comfort in her goodness. She leaves for a far better world than I can expect when I am gone."

"Don't say such things, Uncle. You've only done your duty. No heavenly place could hold that against you."

"Couldn't it?" Hook gave him a knowing look and lowered his arm. "At least your mother is with her sister now. They've missed each other a great deal since your aunt passed. I now get to miss them both. Your mother's presence in the world was a solace to me as she reminded me of my own dear wife. Her absence leaves a hole in me that I do not know how to grieve."

"Going home . . ." Mr. Blackwell said. "Well, my emotions are a little raw at the moment, as you can imagine."

Hook clapped his hand on Mr. Blackwell's shoulder. "I *can* imagine. My grief is a drop of water compared to your ocean in this. I know that. So how do we proceed with our *delicate* situation?"

"Please trust me to fulfill my duties," Mr. Blackwell said. "I'll handle things and meet you at the ship."

Hook made a scoffing sound. "You're implying that I cannot be delicate. Did you hear that, Smee?" he called to the bosun in the jolly boat as he waited to row his captain back to the *Jolly Roger*. "My nephew thinks me a bull in a porcelain shop! What do you think?"

Smee muttered something that sounded suspiciously like an accusation that Hook had broken one of Smee's mother's teacups but then loudly said, "I think you have the grace of a dancer, Captain."

Hook held out his hands—well, his hook and his hand—and said, "You see, lad? I'm a dancer."

"Can we discuss this later, back at the ship? As I said, it's a delicate situation." Mr. Blackwell sounded impatient.

"Is that how you treat me?" Hook asked. "After all I've done for you? I could have left your mother destitute, but I cared for you, fed you, sheltered you, made you a gentleman in a society that shuns all other stations. And you tell me to go sit in a corner and wait for the only prize I crave?"

The information fascinated Wendy. Hook had done all that for Mr. Blackwell? To see unshed tears in Hook's eyes . . . to see him speak with any degree of compassion and to hear of any kind deeds was nothing short of mystifying.

Hook inspected his nephew. "I cannot leave until I know you've accomplished your mission." The feather in his wide-brimmed hat swished in the breeze.

"It's done." Mr. Blackwell kept his posture stiff, but his head turned slightly in Wendy's direction.

Hook stepped forward, his blue eyes targeted on Mr. Blackwell's. "It's not done until I have assurances. Say the words, lad. Say what it is you mean for everyone in hearing distance to hear. You must spell it out if you want me to believe you sincere."

Wendy held her breath behind him, waiting to hear what it was he was being forced to say, certain he was being forced to say it precisely so *she* could hear.

Mr. Blackwell gritted his teeth as he said, "I'm here to help you kill Pan once and for all."

The chortle of manic joy would have been disconcerting if Wendy hadn't been expecting it in some part at least. This war with Peter had been all Hook cared about in the past. Why would that be any different now? What she hadn't expected was that Hook expected Mr. Blackwell to join forces with him. She hadn't expected Mr. Blackwell to be heir apparent to the pirate king of Neverland. She hadn't expected the man she had spent a night dancing and talking and flirting with to be able to say such horrible words.

She hadn't expected Hook's dramatic mood swings from doting compassion on his nephew to a surety that he planned to gut his nephew right then and there. Hook seemed to be so much more malevolent than he had been before. While she had no doubt that he'd kill Peter if given the chance, he wasn't so far gone that he'd slice through Mr. Blackwell, was he? Could her memory be so distorted that she had not adequately recalled the evil seeping from Hook?

The pirate's hook was back under Mr. Blackwell's chin. "Well then. That's a different mix of pixie dust altogether. When can I expect you?"

"Can you send a boat for me in an hour?"

"What's an hour in Neverland? It is not even the single beat of a pixie's wings. I can wait that much longer. One hour and then we plan for the downfall of that cocky boy!" Hook swept his arm away from Mr. Blackwell, accidentally, or maybe on purpose—Wendy couldn't tell from her vantage point—nicking Mr. Blackwell's throat with the sharp point of his hook. "Don't be late!" Hook called over his shoulder as he sauntered back to his boat.

Mr. Blackwell nodded but didn't turn away from the boat, the captain, and the bosun, Smee. He waited until they were almost back to the *Jolly Roger* before he said softly, "I know you're there."

Wendy gasped but hurried to clap her hand over her mouth.

Mr. Blackwell wasn't fooled. "Come out, Miss Darling. Or I suppose you are just Wendy on this island so far from society's rules of conduct. I'm sure you have questions."

Wendy *did* have questions. She did *not* come out.

Mr. Blackwell walked back into the smaller cavern. He obviously couldn't see her, or he wouldn't have veered the wrong way. "It's all right," he assured her. "I can explain everything."

"Explain everything?" Wendy was sure her voice sounded strangled and wounded. She hoped it bounced off the stalagmites and stalactites in a way that made it hard to discern where it came from. "How can you hope to explain anything?"

"Wendy, come out. You're worrying me."

"You *should* be worried. Wait until I tell Peter your plan."

He made a scoffing sound. "Wendy, come out now. We need to talk."

"No!" With no other choice before her, she ran.

"Wendy!" He gave chase.

How had this happened? How was Liam Blackwell, friend of Mrs. Connolly, charming man in the domino mask, this same man chasing her through Neverland caverns? Wendy had *liked* him. How was such a man the nephew of the great specter of her life?

Mr. Blackwell gave a growl of exasperation as he went deeper into the little cavern to get her. "Wendy, please. I'm begging you."

She pressed herself against a boulder, waiting for him to go a different direction before she made another run for it. A scuffling noise to the right of the boulder gave her the motivation to creep around the left. She squinted off to the right, trying to see where he'd gone, when a hand clamped onto hers.

Wendy cocked back the fist of her free hand and socked him in the jaw. He almost let go of her in his surprise and pain but managed to keep his grip even as she tried tugging away. She felt gratified knowing she'd landed a hard hit. It made the throb in her fingers absolutely worth it.

"Wendy," he said, trying to reason with her. "Please, let's talk."

She had no intention of being reasoned with. "Are you taking me prisoner? Will you take me to your captain? Am I to walk the plank?"

"Of course I'm not taking you prisoner. Not like you think," he amended, which meant she *would* be his prisoner if she didn't come willingly—which she wouldn't. He continued. "But I do require your help, Wendy. Please. Stop. A great evil is in Neverland, and I'm asking for a service only you can give. Let's discuss this like adults."

Indignation flared inside her chest. "Adults? The kind of adults who kill children?"

"Curses, but you're being ridiculous."

She threw another punch in his direction, but he pulled back, so she missed. Then without warning, the fire seemed to extinguish itself in a wash of sorrow. Any potential they might have had in a future together was gone. "How can you . . . How is it . . . How can you be a pirate, Mr. Blackwell?"

"Does it matter to you if I am? You said earlier this evening that we were the same type of person."

Her chin went up. "That was before I knew you were the enemy."

"You could never be my enemy, Wendy."

She narrowed her eyes and gave a meaningful look at where he held her captive.

He let go of her hand and raised both of his own in surrender. "You, who once escaped Neverland with your brothers, must understand why my uncle requires my help."

She shook her head. "I don't understand. You were so perfect. How are you this . . . this . . . pirate."

"I'm not exactly a pirate."

"You're an adult in Neverland. You can't be anything else."

Mr. Blackwell took a step toward her, but she took a step back and coiled, intending to flee if he reached for her again. He raised his hands once more to show he had no intention of doing so. "Wendy Darling, you are *also* an adult in Neverland. What does that make you?"

She took another step back and glared at him. "I'm not an ad—" She broke off.

She'd been about to say she wasn't an adult, but she couldn't deny such a thing, could she? She was launched into society, preparing to start her life. Wasn't that why she'd been at that ball?

"And what do you mean by escape?" she demanded to know, determined not to think about what it meant that she'd been at that ball. "Peter took us back. The only person we'd had to escape from was Hook!" The fire was back in her soul. If she'd had a cutlass, she'd be holding it to his throat for making such implications.

"If my uncle took you, it was to return you to London. To return you to your families."

Was the man addled? Did he not know his uncle? "You're wrong. He tied us up and said I was a curse. He made me walk the plank!"

"He would never have harmed you," Mr. Blackwell said.

"He certainly would have. He told me he meant to kill us all."

Mr. Blackwell took another step forward. Wendy took another step back. "He's a lot of talk. He always has been. Come with me. It will only be for a short while. And then I'll get you back to London, Wendy. It will all seem like a dream if we can get you back soon."

She crossed her arms and stared Mr. Blackwell down. "I'm not going anywhere, and I will *never, ever* let you kill Peter Pan."

As if all of Neverland wanted to put an exclamation mark on her declaration, the ground under their feet began to rumble, a deep guttural sound that seemed to come from the very bowels of the earth. Wendy and Mr. Blackwell shared a terrified glance as the cave shuddered and groaned, the once-solid walls quivering like sails in a vicious wind. Mr. Blackwell stumbled, and his lantern dropped and went out. Wendy faltered and instinctively grabbed Mr. Blackwell for support. "Watch out!" he cried.

A deafening crack echoed through the cavern. Wendy and Mr. Blackwell dove to the side, narrowly avoiding the deadly spike as the stalactite broke free from the ceiling and plummeted to the ground, shattering into jagged shards.

"We need to get out of here!" Wendy shouted, her voice sounding as shaken as the walls and ground around them.

But before they could make it back to where the little cavern opened into the larger grotto, stalactites cracked and splintered and began to fall all around them. "Wendy!" Mr. Blackwell leaped to her and tugged her out of the way as one viciously sharp stalactite pierced the sand where she'd been standing. Pieces of the stone and sand splayed everywhere, pelting her skin like arrows. He had just opened his mouth—most likely to ask if she was all right—when she yanked them both to the side as another stalactite shattered where they'd just been.

The shaking grew more severe, and they clung to each other for stability. A deafening crash came from where the little cavern had opened up into the larger one, and rocks tumbled into the space.

And then it stopped.

Nothing shook or quaked. All was silent.

And everything was pitch black.

"Can anything harm us, Mother,
after the night-lights are lit?"

"Nothing, precious," she said; "they
are the eyes a mother leaves behind
her to guard her children."

CHAPTER SIX

Wendy's breath hitched in her throat. And it had nothing to do with the cloud of dust that had swept over them with the cave-in.

The darkness. She was surrounded by darkness. She could feel the panic rising up. Trying to explode in a scream that had also somehow become caught in her throat. No air. No sound. Nothing but the panic in her heart. Her belly. Her head. Desperation clawed at her chest.

"Trapped," she managed to rasp out around the clog in her throat. They were trapped.

"Wendy, are you all right?" Only when he spoke did Wendy realize Mr. Blackwell's arms were wrapped around her shoulders, holding her tightly from behind. He'd used his own body to shield her from the cave-in.

"Wendy," he said again. "Please tell me you're all right."

The concern in his voice was enough to make her want to melt into him and let him protect her forever, but she pulled away, annoyed that he persisted in using her first name just because they were in Neverland. She would not let herself forget what she'd overheard. Mr. Blackwell was the enemy now. She had to escape him and find Peter. Peter would know what to do.

Peter.

The thought of him was almost enough to make her forget she was trapped in a cave in the dark with the enemy. Peter was here in Neverland, somewhere close. She would see him again after all these years. She'd feared he had forgotten her. Neverland had a way of erasing memories, like a wave washing away sandcastles on a beach.

"We can't stay here," Wendy said. "There's no way of knowing whether or not another shake will happen."

"There are never earthquakes in Neverland," Liam said.

"Our current situation would indicate that you're wrong. If it can happen once, it can happen again. Dodging stalactites that you can see is hard enough, but it would be impossible in the dark." She was proud of the fact that her voice had steadied. Proud at how rational she sounded. Her mind tumbled over Liam's words, however. There never had been an earthquake in Neverland. How could such a thing have happened?

Wendy also considered the fact that Liam had saved her from one of those falling stalactites. True, she had saved him as well. She would never have been able to forgive herself if she had not pushed him out of the way, even if he was a pirate.

"We'll need light if we have to travel through the caverns in the dark." With that comment, Liam whistled a tune.

Wendy had never heard this tune before. And could not account as to how he was able to make such a sound with his mouth. The trilling song was light and lovely and unlike any whistle from any human she'd ever heard. Was Liam not human? For all she knew, he was a kraken or a merman or minotaur. With everything else she'd discovered that day, him being some kind of mythical creature would be the least remarkable.

As he continued whistling, a small light floated into the cavern. It moved slowly, and when it grew near, Wendy could see that it was a pixie, a trail of dust shimmering in her wake. Her face was slack, and her eyes stared into nothing. Her iridescent wings, which were sometimes orange and sometimes blue, beat barely steady enough to keep her aloft. A pixie's wings normally beat so rapidly that they were almost a blur, making the pixie flit here and there erratically and with no concern for whether or not someone else could keep up.

The pixie had hair the color of sunset orange and wide eyes the color of evergreen. Her burnt orange silken clothing looked patched together from leaves and flower petals. Perched on her head was a crown that looked to have been woven from twigs and dewdrops.

Her mouth was slightly agape, elongating her face, making her high cheekbones and pointed chin look sharper somehow.

As she drew closer, her light illuminated Liam. Wendy saw the tiny pan flute in his hand that he had pressed to his lips as he played the lilting tune.

"What are you doing?" Wendy asked, horrified by what she saw. "Did you put a pixie in a trance?"

The pixie hovered in front of Liam now. Wendy reached up to yank away the flute at the same time he dropped it, seized the pixie, snatched up his lantern, and closed the pixie inside. She shook off whatever trance he had placed her under, looked around the lantern cage, clearly startled to find herself locked up, and began to pound her tiny fists against the glass as her face turned fiery red, making her glow that much brighter.

"Did you just kidnap a pixie?" Wendy was as enraged as the little pixie caught within the lantern's glass.

"We need light. What else would you have me do? Can you magic light from your fingertips?"

"You could have just asked her. But to take her against her will like this. She's a person."

"It's a pixie. Not a person. Have you never caught a butterfly? Besides, pixies are the worst sort of vermin. Mischief-making meddlers. But don't worry. I'll let it go as soon as we're back into the light. It's not like I'm keeping it forever. I do not kidnap anyone."

Wendy lunged for the lantern, determined to let the pixie go, but Liam danced back and held it out of her reach. Earlier that evening, when she'd thought he was handsome and charming, she had liked that he was so much taller than her, but now she wanted to cut him off at the knees, take the pixie, and run. But run where? She glanced around the cavern. There was a darker shadow in the far-left corner that looked like it could be a tunnel. Liam was right about needing the light.

"Let me at least talk to her," Wendy said.

"You understand pixie?" Liam said with a scoff.

"Anyone who takes the time to listen can understand a pixie."

His jaw tightened, but he relented and lowered the lantern to Wendy's level. "No tricks," he said.

Wendy muttered that the only one playing tricks had been him when he'd pretended to be an honorable man. Liam either hadn't heard her or was purposely ignoring her. Her heart ached at the sight of the delicate creature. Wendy looked sadly into the lantern at the pixie, who was filled with too much fury to be sad about anything. Pixies were so tiny that they were incapable of holding more than one emotion at a time. Or so Peter had once explained to her. "I'm sorry," Wendy said. "I would get you out if I could, right this instant, but I promise I won't let you be in there very long. And I won't let you get hurt."

The pixie's wings slowed their frantic beating, and the little creature tilted her head to look at Wendy.

"My name is Wendy," Wendy said. "What's yours?"

It took all of Wendy's energy to not try to wrench the lantern from his grasp and to free the little pixie right then and there. Maybe she could find a happy thought. Maybe this pixie would shower her in dust and help her fly.

But Liam had the build of a formidable foe. Even if she had a sword, he was just as likely to win as he was to lose. She couldn't take a fifty-fifty chance while she was stuck in a cave. She didn't take gambles of that sort. She turned back to the captive in the jar and listened to the chiming language of the pixie. "Your name is Starna? That's lovely."

"Insipid, you mean to say," Liam muttered.

Wendy ignored him. "That's right. Tinker Bell and the lost boys did call me Wendybird . . . a long time ago." Could Wendy's heart twist any tighter than it already had? From Liam and his actions to her missing Peter to the fact that Peter was so close and yet still so out of her reach, she could barely stand it. It all wrenched her heart tighter and tighter until she felt it would burst.

"Wendybird?" Liam asked. His tone didn't have the derision she would have expected. Instead, he sounded mystified.

The pixie's response to Liam's interruption was the sort of thing that Wendy's mother would have locked her in her room for saying out loud to anyone.

"No. Don't say that. Mr. Blackwell isn't going to hurt you," Wendy answered, her heart now wrenching and shattering at the same time because she didn't believe herself at all. Reassuring Starna had to be the right thing to do. There was no reason for both of them to be afraid and angry and sad. "He's simply making some bad choices right now. I'll make sure he lets you go as soon as we're through the tunnels. What? What's that you say?" Starna chimed and gestured dramatically. Wendy tossed a glance at Liam and then back to the pixie. "You say you know the way out and you'll show us?"

"No," Liam said firmly.

"No what?"

"No, I am not letting the pixie go with the hope that it will lead us out of here. We'll be fine without that help. You can get to any place you'd care to go in Neverland if you know the way through these caves."

"And I suppose you know the way?" Wendy stood to her full height and put her hands on her hips.

He opened his mouth to tell what was likely the largest lie in all of history, but then he snapped it closed again before shaking his head and muttering, "Well . . . no."

"So let her out and be nice to her so she can help us."

Liam's cheek twitched as if he was clenching and unclenching his jaw. Finally, he flicked the latch on the lantern and freed Starna.

The little creature shot out of the lantern and around the cavern, intermittently diving at Liam's head.

Liam threw his arms up to protect himself from having his eyes poked out. "I told you it wouldn't help us. Pixies are known for troublemaking, not giving service."

As if to prove him wrong, which, honestly, she probably *was* trying to prove him wrong, Starna stopped and hovered close to Wendy's face, chiming her little bells with energy. "I quite agree," Wendy said. "He should apologize if he wants your help."

Both the pixie and Wendy faced Liam with their arms crossed and their faces waiting. "Well?" Wendy said.

"Well what?"

"Use your words. An apology is not hard."

"The only words I have are not appropriate for a lady's ears."

"Apologize now." Wendy gave him the same look she'd given her brothers on many occasions.

Liam blustered and flustered. "You want me to apologize for being the means of getting us light? Even though if I hadn't, we'd still be stumbling around, tripping over the rocks and running into walls? No. I will not apologize. You're being unreasonable."

Wendy and Starna gave each other a look and then turned their backs on the pirate.

"Curses, but this is ridiculous," he said.

Wendy wasn't quite sure if Liam would resort to violence or not. He was, after all, a pirate. And his uncle had resorted to violence. How could she trust that he wouldn't stick a sword in her back while she had it turned to him? But she didn't give in to her fear. She didn't turn to face her enemy head-on as was her instinct. She couldn't because part of her wanted to trust him. The man who had spent hours talking with her and dancing with her and listening to her and dancing with Mrs. Connolly and saving little stable boys couldn't be all bad, could he? Were her instincts about people so run aground that she couldn't tell the difference any longer?

While at the ball, she'd had the feeling that she could fall in love with the man who danced with her. She was sure the stirrings of that emotion had swirled in her.

Now?

She wasn't sure. She still thought well of him, though it made no sense.

She hadn't known before that moment that such feelings of love were something that could not be turned on and off. It was not a light switch. Not some modern invention. Love followed its own rules, and once you had fallen into it, you would be falling forever.

She considered herself fortunate that she'd not stepped off the abyss into that fall with this man. She had been dangerously close.

This man was Hook's family. She was afraid of him. She was furious with him. And Wendy wanted nothing more at that moment than for her mother to give her guidance through all of these contrary emotions. How could all of those things be true while Wendy still thought well of him?

"Fine. I'm sorry," Liam said gruffly, not sounding sorry at all but rather impatient.

Wendy finally turned back to him. "Say it like you mean it." She knew she was treating him like a child, but if he was going to act like one, he had to expect to be treated accordingly.

His mouth flattened into a thin line before he blew out a long breath. "I'm sorry."

"Not to me. Say it to Starna."

Liam shot Wendy a withering look that told her she might be pushing him way too far, but he then faced the pixie and repeated the apology.

"But don't you think an apology is so much better when you use the offended person's name? One more time with Starna's name."

He opened his mouth to begin again when Wendy interrupted him.

"And remember to say it like you mean it."

He took another deep breath. "Miss Starna, please accept my humble apology. I hope my behavior hasn't been too painful for you and that you can find it in your tiny heart to forgive me for my many apparent faults, errors, and missteps. I am deeply, painfully, truly in agony over how sorry I am." To his credit, he said all of this with a straight face, which was more than Wendy could say for Starna, who was holding her sides and chiming with a delighted laugh. Pixies had a very odd sense of humor.

"It appears that will do as Starna looks as if she has forgiven you, though she's laughing so hard, I can't make out what she's actually saying." Wendy shook out her skirts, poofing up a cloud of dust. "Well, Starna, please lead the way."

Starna flitted off in a pattern that made her seem somewhere between reckless and intoxicated. She led them toward the shadow in the corner, which was where Wendy would have gone on her own without the guidance. Liam gave Wendy a look that said he was thinking the same thing. Without a word to Liam, Wendy marched forward to follow their guide.

They walked in silence for a long time, every now and again having to scramble over rocks or crawl through tunnels to keep up with the pixie. Wendy refused all offers of help from Liam, even when she genuinely needed help. Her heeled slippers were meant to look elegant and charming. The shoemaker did not have scrambling over boulders in mind when designing them.

"You're just being stubborn," Liam said more than once when she turned her nose up at his hand of service.

He wasn't wrong. But he didn't need to know that.

"Your little pixie guide called you Wendybird earlier," Liam said after they'd been traveling for what felt like hours in silence. "I heard stories of the Wendybird from a friend of mine."

"You could have no friends who would know me by that name," she said hotly. The lost boys, Peter, Tinker Bell . . . *they* would know her as the Wendybird. The pirates didn't know her as such.

"He said you told the most marvelous stories."

She turned sharply in his direction.

He was looking at her. His expression curious.

"Who told you such a thing?"

"His name is Slightly, one of Pan's lost boys. He joined His Majesty's Navy a few years back. We all called him Sly. Nice kid."

"I knew he was in the military." She was maddened that she was unable to do anything about her frown. "I sent him a few letters." And then she remembered something from one of the replies she'd received. Slightly had told her that an older boy was taking care of him and keeping him from trouble. Slightly had given the older boy a nickname as well. "He called you Inkpot."

Mr. Blackwell laughed. "Yes. He did. Told me Blackwell was a stuffy name and renamed me on the spot. When he mentioned the Wendybird, I didn't realize that he meant you or that such a name had any connection to this place. It seems we have yet another way that we are thrown into one another's path. I knew I'd be meeting the bluebird at the ball. But I didn't realize that the Wendybird and the bluebird were one and the same."

Wendy wasn't sure if he was talking because he really wanted to get to know her or if he was bored and trying to entertain himself. "Bluebird was Hook's name for me," she said with disgust at the memory.

"You say my uncle's name like it's a slur," Mr. Blackwell countered.

Wendy glared at him. "So would any decent, law-abiding person. Your uncle is a *pirate*."

"So is yours."

Wendy sputtered and fumed before being able to say, "He absolutely is not!"

"You're a hypocrite because he absolutely is too."

Wendy wished the pixie glowed brighter so that Liam could catch the full measure of her glare. "My uncle is not a pirate!"

"How can you say such a thing? Of course, he's a pirate."

"Are you trying to tell me that my uncle has been to Neverland?" She was sure she had him on that one.

"No. Don't be silly. He's a pirate in London, which is so much worse in my opinion. He's destroying real families. Futures. In London. Every day."

Wendy stilled and stared at him. "You know nothing of my family."

He smirked, an expression that seemed to be his favorite and one she was growing to loathe. "Don't I? At the ball, you gave me quite a lot of information regarding your family. You said your uncle buys farms that are failing, even though their owners are only in such financial desperation because of bankers like him, bad weather, or pestilence. He sees their distress, and he sails in to offer to buy them out for a couple of quid when he should be paying hundreds—if not thousands—for the land he's purchasing. He leaves them with no choices and no futures. He destroys legacies. Your uncle is the worst sort of pirate I've ever heard of, and I've met enough to know that I'm a good judge of such things."

Wendy hated the logic in his words. Her legs wobbled, and she had to sit, or she would have collapsed altogether. "I need to rest. Starna? Can you wait a moment?" The pixie fluttered to a rock up high, likely keeping her distance from Mr. Blackwell, and who could blame her?

Mr. Blackwell sank to the ground as well and looked relieved to do so. He must have suffered some sort of sprain during the rockfall because he had a slight limp as he walked. "It hadn't occurred to me that you might be exhausted as well," she said. "I always assumed pirates had boundless energy, fueled by their cruelty and evil deeds."

"Don't be mad at me for saying your uncle's a pirate, Wendy," Mr. Blackwell said after a moment.

Wendy looked up sharply. "Yes, well, at least my uncle doesn't make dark pacts to kill little boys."

"Pan is hardly a little boy. He's been around longer than you and I or our parents or even our grandparents. He's ancient like the mountains. He's the age of the sky itself."

Wendy wanted to argue that fact but found she had no argument. Peter had given flippant responses to Wendy every time she'd asked him how old he was. Technically he was much, much older than her, but his childlike demeanor made it hard for her to remember that such things were true.

"But he has the mentality of a child," she persisted. "It isn't right to consider killing one such as that. What justification could you possibly have for your uncle and for yourself, for that matter? I heard you say it. You are going to help your pirate uncle kill Peter Pan. But how can you? How can you possibly when it's *Peter*, rescuer of lost boys, friend to Tiger Lily's tribe, hero of the mermaids? And your Captain Hook is what? The scourge of the land? *That* is who you're siding with in this war?"

Mr. Blackwell's face darkened with her every word. She tensed, worried his anger would make him lash out. He scrubbed his hand over his hair, which had fallen loose from the leather cord at the back. "Is this really what you think of me? That I am siding with the scourge of the land? You should not pass judgment when you do not have all the facts. The truth is—"

"I have all the facts I need." Wendy turned from him, tightened her father's coat around her primly, and tried to look like she wasn't bothered at all by the things Mr. Blackwell said.

"No," Mr. Blackwell insisted, picking up a handful of rocks and slowly sifting them out of his hand before starting over again. "You have all the facts as given to you by Pan. Which means you have nothing but a series of fiction, stories like the kind he makes the kidnapped young girls tell his lost boys."

"Peter Pan did not kidnap me!"

Mr. Blackwell hadn't called her out specifically as being kidnapped, but she felt that he was talking about her. "You don't think so?" He shook his head and picked up another handful of rocks. "I feel sorry for you. That you connected so deeply to that demon that you do not understand you were his prey all along."

Wendy jumped to her feet and pointed a shaking finger at Mr. Blackwell. "Take that back!"

"No."

"Take that back, or I'll—"

"You'll what?"

She stuttered for a response. Really, what could she do? Decide to loathe him forever? She'd already decided that, hadn't she? Decide to tell Peter his plans? She'd already decided that too. "You're wrong about him. You don't know a thing about him."

"Or is it *you* who do not know a thing about him?" Mr. Blackwell countered. "He's a demon, kidnapping children because he's alone and bored and living an empty life, so much so that he has to steal the lives of others to fill his own existence. Chances are he sucks away their youth, and that's how he stays so young. No one knows why he takes them, only that he does."

"You're lying."

"I'm not. He kidnaps children. He would have kept your brothers if you hadn't been there to protect them."

"That's not true." Wendy shook her head as if she could drown out the echo of his words in her own skull. She then realized the opportunity in front of her. She was standing. He was sitting— reclining really—against a rock. He had that limp, which meant he would be at a disadvantage. Before she could change her mind, or think too hard about it, she turned and ran. Starna must have noted her leaving because she immediately followed, offering Wendy a bit of light and likely leaving Mr. Blackwell in the dark, which would make it harder for him to follow her. She might be able to escape.

She could make it to Peter, and then they could plan.

Wendy stumbled several times as she scrambled over rocks, but she didn't stop. She heard Mr. Blackwell cursing his way through the corridor behind her. He was stumbling too, which was good. Starna passed her and led the way, and when the corridor split into several choices, Starna went through the center corridor off the right and waved frantically as if Wendy wasn't doing enough to keep up. They twisted through an unpredictable path, Wendy's feet sloshing through several puddles that they encountered. She slipped in one of those puddles and slammed against the side of the cave wall, her face warm with the blood that trickled out of the scrape, but still she didn't stop. Mr. Blackwell's voice calling out for her to see reason quieted as the distance between them grew.

Wendy passed through a cavern that opened up into dizzying heights. The walls glowed with pinks, blues, and greens, and a clear pool shimmered with those same colors from underneath the water's surface.

Wendy would have stopped and gawked, in awe of the splendor of the natural marvel, but the primal fear of knowing she was chased and not knowing how far behind her pursuer might be propelled her forward.

She heard crashing from the corridor where she entered and realized that Mr. Blackwell had nearly caught up, though how he'd done so in the dark and with his limp, she couldn't fathom.

Starna guided them to the narrow opening, and Wendy tried to quietly follow, though it was difficult between the impracticality of her shoes and the way the pebbles and rocks crunched under her steps. She slid over the two boulders at the end of the passage and pressed forward, turning a corner into another corridor and then another, before she saw it: light. Light that was not from Starna's pixie shine.

"We did it. We did it, Starna," Wendy whispered, feeling like she might cry with relief to almost be out of the dark.

Her relief was mingled with something else. She felt sad to be leaving Mr. Blackwell behind in the cave—sad because she had thought him to be so amiable. She was disappointed in herself for falling for his charms and disappointed in him—whether that was because he was so charming to begin with or because he had turned out not to be very charming at all.

She could not think of such sadness or charm. She could not let herself feel guilty for leaving him to stumble in the dark. Not now, not when she was so close to freedom. She skirted around another set of boulders and broke out into the light, feeling the tightness in her shoulders ease slightly under the bright light of a Neverland sun.

A waterfall near where she'd come out of the cave system crashed down to the left of her, a rainbow of light dancing over the droplets. The verdant, leathery jungle leaves could have been used as large umbrellas. Songs from a dozen different birds filled the air, and frogs chirped from underneath the leaves.

"Hello, Neverland," she whispered.

The waterfall followed the river's path to the ocean, where Wendy saw the *Jolly Roger* anchored in Pirate Cove.

And that was when her shoulders tightened again because she was not in friendly territory. The jolly boats on the water were rowing in her direction. Starna's eyes went wide as she flitted into the sky. A couple of the pirates took shots at the little pixie—her pixie shine making her a vibrant target—but she got away. At least, Wendy hoped she got away.

Though Wendy was too far to make out the details on the pirates, one thing was certain: They had seen her.

Wendy didn't wait for them to take aim. She dove headlong into the foliage to make her escape from the pirates on the water and the pirate in the form of Mr. Blackwell in the cave.

She wasn't sure which threat frightened her more. The pirates on the water were certain to want to do her physical harm. They had done so in the past. She'd been tied up and made to walk the plank and had been threatened with swords.

But Mr. Blackwell threatened her belief in Peter, in Neverland, in herself.

Which was why she couldn't allow any of them to catch her. She was certain she'd evaded capture when a voice came from behind her. "Well, well, well," said the silky-smooth voice. "This is most unexpected that you should come out alone. You haven't happened to see my nephew, have you?"

Captain Hook.

"No, lads, no, it's the girl.
Never was luck on a pirate ship
wi' a woman on board."

CHAPTER SEVEN

Four pirates besides Captain Hook surrounded her. Wendy had no intention of being so easily overtaken, not after she'd already escaped Mr. Blackwell twice, not when she could see the Neverland sky. When the pirate on her left moved in her direction, she leaped forward. A well-placed kick to his knee with the heel of her dancing shoe buckled him. A sharp elbow to his jaw sent him sprawling.

The pirate on her right swung his sword at her, but she ducked his blade, and, in a move taught to her by her brothers, grabbed hold of the pirate's wrist and wrenched it hard, forcing him to drop his weapon. From behind him, she used his forward momentum and slammed him into a tree. She hurried to pick up the two swords and pointed them at the others.

Two left. Well, two and Hook. But now she was armed. She'd take those chances.

At that moment, Mr. Blackwell emerged from the foliage.

Hook stood watching the entire scene with interest and obvious amusement.

"Is there a problem here, Uncle?" Mr. Blackwell asked.

"Friend of yours?" Hook waved a hand in Wendy's direction, obviously recognizing her and obviously tossing the taunt at Mr. Blackwell for some cruel reason Wendy couldn't understand.

Mr. Blackwell seemed to be considering the question. "We're becoming friends, yes."

"No!" Wendy said at the same time he said yes.

"She'll make a lovely addition to our crew," Hook drawled. "She's quite a vicious little pirate."

Wendy turned both of the swords she held on Hook. "Did you just call me a pirate? You blackhearted monster of a villain!"

Mr. Blackwell stepped between them. "Uncle, Wendy, please. This is clearly a misunderstanding."

"I understand everything perfectly," Wendy spat, not sure who she wanted to run through more: Hook or Mr. Blackwell.

In a quick move she hadn't been anticipating, Mr. Blackwell removed one of the swords from her possession. He'd done it in much the same way she'd done it to the pirate on the ground. He had twisted her wrist, though he hadn't done it hard enough to cause the damage she had done to the pirate on the ground. He stabbed the sword into the soil near the pirate, who was only now getting to his feet. "Uncle, may I introduce you to Miss Wendy Darling of London." He said this evenly, as if they were still in the ballroom and not in a standoff at Pirate Cove.

Hook leaned forward, peering at Wendy as if seeing her clearly for the first time. The blue of his irises heated to something frightening—the fiery red of her nightmares. "Wendy Moira Angela Darling. Isn't that how you so cheekily introduced yourself to me all those years ago? And now, you've come back to us." Hook walked around her. She sliced the sword she still held in the air as if to warn him away, but he merely tsked at her.

"I've waited a long time to see you again, little bluebird." Hook used his silky, patronizing voice. "You were one of Pan's favorite toys there for a while, so I thought you would be back. He would not forget a favorite so easily. But then you never returned. We had to go and fetch you because he *did* forget you, didn't he?"

Wendy sucked in a sharp breath.

"Of course he forgot you," Hook continued. "How could he

help it when you're now a grown woman? He would see you as the enemy now. He would see *you* as a pirate."

"Stop!" Wendy shouted. "You will not twist me into knots, Hook. You forget that I know you. I see you for the monster you really are."

Hook spared a brief glance to Mr. Blackwell as his lips twisted into a wry grin. "Well, this is a fine cannon full of powder, Nephew. Tell me you didn't bring her here to insult me. I thought you told me she would help us. That she would be the reason Pan finally came out of hiding so we could finish his reign of terror on this island once and for all."

Wendy slashed her sword out again, slicing the air with a swish. "I'm not helping you!"

Hook tsked again. "That changes everything then, doesn't it?" He snapped his fingers at his crew. "Take Miss Darling, men, and make sure she's comfortable."

The pirates began to leer and laugh as several others that Wendy hadn't noticed before rose up from the jungle foliage. They took hold of Wendy, wrenching the sword from her grasp and dragging her away as she yelled and tried to kick and punch her way free. They dragged her to where the jolly boats had been pulled up on the shore. Then they lashed her hands together and dropped her rather unceremoniously into one of the boats.

"Was it necessary to tie her up, Mullens?" Mr. Blackwell asked the pirate who was keeping watch over her.

"She's a spy for Pan's side," the pirate, who was apparently named Mullens, said. "We can't be letting her get the chance to escape to tell Pan about Cap'n's secret plan." Mullens scratched under the eye patch covering his right eye.

Wendy didn't know if the man had a damaged eye or not, but the idea of scratching under the patch made her swallow in distaste.

"What is the captain's secret plan, Mullens?" Mr. Blackwell asked.

Mullens seemed surprised that Mr. Blackwell didn't know the answer already. "Well, *she is*, o' course."

"So she doesn't really have to say anything to Pan if she were to go to him. Her presence would be enough, wouldn't it?"

Wendy smirked at that logic since it proved Mullens was not the sharpest of the pirates. But then she felt the disappointment at understanding Mr. Blackwell's part in all this and said, "You told me you were in the navy."

"I am," Mr. Blackwell said at the same time Mullens said, "'e is."

Her disdainful sniff was her only response.

"It's true," Mr. Blackwell insisted.

Wendy was unconvinced. "Oh, yes? Then tell me, how are you here now?"

Mr. Blackwell didn't seem to like the implication that he was lying to her, but he answered her questions regardless. "My uncle came to visit me several times once I joined the navy. He told me stories of Neverland, of his life's work here, of his crew, and of the evil he fought. I didn't believe the stories at first, but one day, on my birthday, a fog rolled over the sea that put every man aboard my ship to sleep. Every man but me. My uncle sailed the *Jolly Roger* through the sky and dropped a rope down next to me. I had to believe after that, didn't I? And I met the whole crew that day as we celebrated my birthday."

"That was a great party," Mullens interjected.

"Indeed it was," Mr. Blackwell said. "Are you satisfied, Wendy?"

"Not even a little." She went back to looking out at the ocean instead of at him.

"Wendy . . ." Mr. Blackwell stopped himself. She peeked at him to see what had stopped him. He was looking at Mullens. "Why don't you go in Murphy's boat?" he said to Mullens. "I can take the oars here. You deserve a rest."

"Cap'n would be angry," Mullens said thoughtfully, clearly considering the idea of not having to row if he could get out of it.

WENDY'S EVER AFTER

"I'll take full responsibility," Mr. Blackwell promised. "If he gets angry at anyone, it will be me."

"But the prisoner . . ."

"I'll see to it that she doesn't escape."

That was all the convincing Mullens needed as he moved to Murphy's boat.

"I'm surprised that worked," Mr. Blackwell said out loud.

She watched the man slosh through the shallow surf to the other boat. "Hook's biggest fault, aside from being an evil pirate, is that he surrounds himself with idiots."

"I am sure you mean except present company."

"No. I do not mean any such thing."

"Curses. This is ridiculous. You have no right to be angry with me." The signal was finally given to shove off, and Mr. Blackwell pushed the boat out into the water before jumping in and beginning to row.

"I absolutely do. You're here to help a wicked creature kill a young boy and probably several other young boys at the same time. Nothing else in the world could give me greater reason to be angry with you." She squinted, hoping that the gull in the distance would come closer and reveal itself to actually be a flying boy. She was looking for her deliverance.

But Peter would have no idea she was here.

"If you could just trust me and let me explain—"

She jerked her gaze to him fast enough that she rocked the boat, sloshing water up over the sides. Mr. Blackwell had to struggle to steady it. "You want me to trust you?" she demanded, the fury rising up in her chest. She thrust out her hands. "Then untie me."

He stared at the rope digging into her skin and looked like he might actually want to untie her. But his gaze went ahead to where Hook's jolly boat was hoisted into the air by pirates on the deck of the *Jolly Roger*. She watched as he stepped off to greet them.

Wendy followed his gaze back to the ship. "Of course. Tell me again all the ways I should trust you when you're nothing more than a dog to that foul creature." She turned away from him again and considered her options. She could just jump out of the boat and allow her body to sink down into the water. She couldn't swim with her arms bound, so the hope of swimming to safety without help if she did jump was out of the question. Perhaps the mermaids would find her there and get her to safety before she drowned. But she didn't know if the mermaids would actually help her.

What she did know was that she would figure out how to escape her bonds. She would not let that codfish harm Peter Pan. She would make sure that Liam Blackwell felt as terrible as she did over his betrayal. She felt his eyes on her but refused to give him the satisfaction of meeting his gaze.

The farther away from shore they rowed, the choppier the waters became. Liam handled the little boat expertly, which irritated her to admit to herself. Wendy instead focused on the horizon and the silhouette of the imposing ship looming ever closer with its skull and crossbones flag flapping in the wind.

"Are you all right?" Liam asked her.

She didn't look at him but held up her wrists as evidence that, no, she was *not* all right, and he was an idiot for asking. He fell silent for a while, which was good because she needed to plan. Wendy glanced at the churning waters below and once again dismissed the idea of jumping. The mermaids hadn't exactly been friendly to her before because they'd been too busy flirting with Peter. Depending on them to save her was like depending on Hook to hand over the *Jolly Roger* to her and to wish her good luck with it. It just wasn't going to happen.

She looked around the boat. Perhaps there was something she could use to cut the rope from her wrists, but the only thing inside the boat besides herself was Mr. Blackwell. That meant she had to look at him to see if he had anything readily available to help her escape. Looking at him did not mean she was going to admire the way his arms bent and flexed as they rowed the boat, or the way his hair had come undone from the leather cord that had been holding it off his face so that a few strands stuck to the sweat on his cheek. She would not think how handsome his jawline looked now that it had a bit of scruff from missing his morning shave. She would not allow her previous attraction to him to impede her good sense now.

Her eyes landed on the dagger tucked into his belt. A half dozen scenarios entered her mind and were dismissed just as rapidly. She couldn't get it just yet, not without a struggle and both of them landing in the water. And though she suspected Liam might try to save her from drowning, she wasn't sure he would. It wasn't like she could best him with her hands tied.

Liam pulled the rowboat alongside the *Jolly Roger*, and tied off the boat to several ropes that hung down. Pirates above hoisted them into the air where Captain Hook waited for them on deck, looking every bit the tidy, well-kept gentleman. Hook eyed her with glee. "Fame, fame. That glittering bauble is mine," he said with a manic laugh.

Wendy decided to put her vow of silence to an end. "Surely you are not referring to me. It is terribly impolite to call a lady a bauble. Have you no manners at all? And capturing a lady? It was hardly a fair fight, Hook. Your *eight* men to capture me? Some might even call eight against one bad form. I know *I* certainly would."

Hook glowered at her comment.

"What are you doing?" Mr. Blackwell whispered in her ear with a tone that carried a definite scolding as if he'd been imitating her mother.

He thought he knew what was best for her in this little prisoner situation. Well, she would *not* be a good little prisoner. Little did he know that she *would* escape. She was certain of it. She'd done it before.

Even as she faced Hook directly, she was taking inventory of everything within her visual range that might tip the scales in her favor. A few of the pirates lounged against the bulwark, not paying attention to the new captive, intent on whatever daydream they were dreaming. One was playing with dice—scooping them up in a cup, shaking them about, and dropping them to the deck before starting the process over again. Several more were scrubbing the decks like their lives depended on it, which their lives probably did. Chances were good they had gotten in trouble for something and were trying to win their way back to their captain's good graces before he decided to throw them overboard.

"What bad form do you speak of?" Hook asked, circling her like the vulture he was. "If I remember correctly, you'd disarmed two of my men. The number of men against you was necessary to compensate for your uncanny skill."

"A compliment?" She wanted to track him as he circled her but became far too dizzy. "How generous."

He finally stopped circling and stood directly in front of her, his gaze calculating and a sinister smile curving his lips. "My dear bluebird. I'd forgotten your sharp tongue. How lovely to have you as a guest once again."

Several of the crew laughed at that.

Wendy could not account for why they laughed. Hook hadn't said anything funny. "What do you want from me? Do you need me to teach your crew how to tie a decent knot? These bonds are dreadfully sloppy."

He didn't rise to the insult. She had thought he would since he was particular about every detail regarding how his ship was run. "What I want," he said, "is a solution to my problem. And here you are. Solution given. That cocky boy has a soft spot for damsels in distress. He'll come for you." He stroked one of her curls that had escaped the twist at the back of her head with his hook, causing her to shudder in revulsion.

She squared her shoulders. "You're wrong." It hurt to admit the next part, a hollow thud in her gut. "He's off doing whatever he pleases and not thinking about me at all. He will not come for me. As you said, Peter doesn't even remember me."

Hook's eyes went wild. "Do not use that devil's name in my presence!" He shouted directly in her face. "Do you hear me?"

She considered doing it again just to spite him, but his crew surrounded her, and she wasn't keen on receiving a swipe from that hook.

Hook composed himself, then said with a sneer, "Take her to the brig. We need to get word to that cocky boy that we have something he will want." Hook turned with a swish of his cloak and sauntered away as if Wendy was not of any concern to him at all. If only that arrogant man knew what kind of concern she could cause when she set her mind to it. She had every intention of making his life as difficult as possible.

The men who had captured her in the first place took hold of her again and began to drag her off. Mr. Blackwell stopped them and said, "It'll all be over soon, Wendy. And when it is, I'll get you safe to London in no time. You won't come to any harm."

She allowed herself to meet his eyes, and his earnest gaze was nearly her undoing. But she kept her chin held high. "Do not trouble yourself, Mr. Blackwell. For you see, I do not require your assistance."

The pirate with the goatee and the missing front tooth pulled her toward the hatch that led to the brig. The last time Wendy had been dragged this particular direction, she'd been accompanied by her brothers. She'd had to be brave for them, as a good big sister should be. But now, there was no one to put on a brave face for. Once they were down the stairs, not even Mr. Blackwell was there to watch her pretend that she was not at all concerned. When the missing-tooth pirate brandished a knife, she swallowed hard.

"This place used to mean freedom to us," he said as he thumbed the edge of his blade. "Now it feels like a prison. Cap'n won't let us leave 'til we catch Pan. Makes you wonder who the real captives are, don't it?"

He lifted his knife higher. So, they were going to kill her here and now after all. But he sliced through her bonds and shoved her hard into the brig, where she landed in an undignified heap on the wooden floor. He hurried to slam the door before she could get her feet underneath her, and she heard the rusty iron lock click. Then the pair of pirates walked away, talking about what Cook might be making for supper. Her own supper felt like years ago. Would they feed her too? Probably not. She was alone down here. And she was very much afraid. Afraid and furious. Fury was the emotion she would focus on. That was the emotion that would help her to escape.

Wendy sat breathing deeply in the dim, oppressive confines and tried to find some semblance of calm to help her think her way through her situation. Her heart pounded with equal parts fear and determination as she listened to hear if a guard had been placed anywhere near her. All she heard was the creaks and groans of the ship. She surveyed the barred door and tried to lift it up off its hinges, but the weight of the door would have required a kraken to remove it.

She pushed and prodded at the bars at the top of the door to see if there were any weak spots that she might be able to shove aside enough to let her squeeze through. But there were none. Not that it would matter if she could get out the door. If she did, she would still have to contend with the pirates.

Wendy glanced around her cell. There was a small metal cot and a bucket in the corner. She didn't want to think about the uses for that bucket. The only other exit was the porthole window, but it was also barred. She moved closer and examined it from all angles. It was sturdy, but the rudimentary frame gave her a glimmer of hope. Wendy flipped the small cot on its side and wrenched one of the metal legs free. She gripped the leg in her hand and returned to the porthole, where she pried up the slats of the frame at the top. When the wood groaned in protest until the frame finally popped free of the nails holding it in place, Wendy saw what she had hoped to see. The bars had been set into the spaces for each one, but it was only the wood frame holding those bars in place.

She made quick work of removing the rest of the frame and then prying out each of the bars until the porthole was clear. Wendy assessed her new exit. It was small, but she clung to her determination like a talisman.

The rough wood scraped against her skin as she wriggled through the narrow space, but she ignored the fiery pain as she forced herself through the opening. Getting through the porthole while also hanging onto it proved to be an acrobatic effort, but finally, she was outside the ship, though she had to refrain from looking down so she didn't fall from such a height into the water.

"Take that, Captain Hook," she whispered. "You cannot keep me in your prison."

She was free again.

"Wendy, one girl is more use than twenty boys."

CHAPTER EIGHT

Being free wasn't all that Wendy had hoped. She clung to the porthole and surveyed what her options might be now that she was out. She'd managed to find rather tenuous footing on one of the ornamental carvings on the ship's hull and was glad for that since she didn't have the arm strength to stay hanging from the porthole for much longer. The mistake of not tying up her skirts nearly made her fall as they swished around her ankles, but there was nothing she could do about it now.

The deck above her thumped with the reverberations of the crew's activities, and their voices floated down to her in persistent, but faint, nattering. One was talking about the romantic entanglements of the ship's cook and a mermaid. Another was talking about how several of the midshipmen were always shirking their duties, and how he had to be the one to pick up the slack. Pirates were such gossips.

Should I drop into the water now that my hands are unbound? she wondered. No. She was too tired to make the swim. She'd never make it.

There. Out of the corner of her eye, she spied a rope dangling from the bulwark. Above it was one of the rowboats they'd used to bring her over. Wendy stealthily eased herself up along the outside of the ship, finding footholds and handholds along the garish carvings that ornamented the ship. As she passed by another porthole, she quickly peeked in to make sure no one was inside to see her. She saw a glass tank in the center of the room filled with water and something coral-colored. A big fish? She squinted and dared to take a longer look. Not a fish at all.

It was a mermaid.

She was entirely coral-colored, from the ends of her silky hair to the tips of her fins. She was achingly beautiful. Why was she in there? That was when Wendy noticed the lock on the lid. And the tiny holes at the top so that there was oxygen going to the water. Hook had captured a mermaid and kept her prisoner. Wendy wondered whose room this was, but a glance around proved what she'd already instinctively guessed. The lavish furnishings could only mean that she'd discovered the captain's quarters.

Wendy considered going inside and setting the creature free, but the door to the room suddenly swung open. She ducked to the side and bit her lips to stifle any noise. The pirate inside sang a jaunty little sea shanty to the mermaid. From the voice, Wendy could tell it was Smee.

No. She couldn't hope to rescue the mermaid *and* save herself. She would have to come back once she was armed and had Peter and the lost boys to help her. There was no choice but to continue to where the rope hung, grab hold, and begin climbing until she reached the top. Wendy paused, listening for any sound of alarm, but no one had noticed her escape.

She slid over the bulwark and crouched behind the crates and barrels that littered the deck as she crept toward the rowboats swinging gently with the rocking of the ship. With her heart in her throat and her stomach in her shoes, Wendy kept low and sneaked toward the freedom of that rowboat. Each step was agonizingly slow, but to risk everything by rushing an escape would have certainly put a sour spin on her cleverness.

Wendy reached the rowboat without incident. She lowered it,

cringing at the creaking sound of the ropes. The boat's bottom hit the water with a soft splash. Wendy hurried and looked up to see who had heard, but no shouts or cries of alarm went up. No faces appeared from above to look down at her. The cannon doors remained closed.

Wendy grabbed the oars, her muscles burning with the energy she'd already exerted, and she pulled hard. The water lapped against the side of the boat, and relief filled her entire being as the *Jolly Roger* moved farther and farther into the distance.

Wendy rounded a bend in Pirate Cove that took her out of the open water of the ocean and deeper into the cove. It was the same route they'd taken to get her to the *Jolly Roger* and, therefore, was the worst possible choice since they would search it first, but it was also out of their immediate line of sight.

Her arms trembled from exhaustion. There was simply no way she could keep rowing. Each stroke had less force than the one before it. Soon, she would be dead in the water and floating back to the *Jolly Roger*. She spied an inlet up ahead and fixed her gaze on that. Only twenty-seven more strokes. Only twenty-six. Only twenty-three. Only fourteen. Only thirteen. Only ten. Only five. Only four. Only two.

The rowboat hit sand, the waves pushing it up higher onto the beach. Wendy stumbled to get out of the boat, plopping down with a splash and then using reserves of energy she hadn't known existed to pull it higher up out of the water. Her legs wobbled underneath her. The forest edge seemed to be taunting her. It was so near. She glanced at the boat. Yet so far.

She had to hide it. There was nothing else to be done. Her arms ached as she pulled the boat into the cover of the dense foliage. "More branches," she murmured to herself and then went to find branches and leaves to make certain no one knew which way she'd gone. Not Hook. Not Mr. Blackwell.

She used one of the branches to sweep away the imprints of her feet and boat and then took a deep breath of satisfaction.

"I've done it! I escaped. Take that, Liam Blackwell. Mr. I'll-get-you-safe-to-London-in-no-time. I'll jolly well get myself safe to London if I choose to go back." She snapped her fingers in the general direction of Pirate Cove.

Wendy fled through the jungle. Well, fled might be the wrong word because her dress seemed to catch on every single twig, branch, thorn, and bramble. Even with her father's overcoat covering it, the beautiful gown had been shredded into tatters and splattered with sand, mud, and debris. Her mother would be displeased to see it. Wendy certainly was.

Her hair didn't fare much better. The elaborate updo of the previous evening that her maid had painstakingly pinned and curled likely resembled one of the bushes she passed.

The greater concern, however, was not her gown or her hair. It was her safety. Wendy was certain her mother would agree. Pirates were bound to come after her. Tearing up a dress and scuffing up brand-new dancing slippers were nothing compared to that.

For a moment, she considered removing her slippers since she was sure she had blisters, but a sharp stick or rock would likely hurt far worse than an ache due to inadequate, frilly footwear.

She was on a steady march up away from the shore. Sharp branches reached out and clawed at her as she passed, leaving long scratches and gashes in her hands and wrists as she tried to shield her face. She would look like she'd been through a war when she got back.

If she got back.

How would she get back?

She slowed her step, taking ragged gulps of air, and finally stopped. The pirates might not know she was gone yet. They might not be in pursuit.

That thought gave her the briefest idea that she should stop and rest, but the panic of her racing heart after seeing Captain Hook again and then the cave-in and then Mr. Blackwell drove her forward.

"No," she whispered to herself in gasps of breath. "I will not stop."

The path before her had different ideas.

As she broke through the last line of trees, her heart sank into the bottom of her half-destroyed slippers. The jungle abruptly ended at the bottom of a jagged cliff. Wendy tilted her head back to try to see the top of it to no avail. Hadn't she done enough climbing in a dress for the day?

The late afternoon sun shone hot on her, especially with her overcoat. She hadn't removed it because the protection of her father's coat made her feel safer somehow. She wiped at the sweat on her forehead to keep it from running into her eyes but gasped in dismay when she pulled her hand away and saw blood— probably from one of the many gouges she'd experienced in the jungle, but maybe from her time in the caverns.

She allowed herself only a moment to rest. A glance down at her gown hem and then back up to the cliff face should have been enough to stop her. But the Wendy Moira Angela Darling of Neverland did not retreat.

She pulled off the overcoat and set it to the side. Then she took a deep breath and grabbed the hem of her skirt at one of the places where the jungle had already torn it. Wendy ripped the dress up to past her knees. The tearing noise gave some odd sense of satisfaction. She then took the two portions of loose skirt and tied them up together so the entire hem, train, and all were up past her knees. Not willing to lose her father's overcoat, she tied it around her waist so that it hung behind her and then reached for the cliff.

The cool stone was rough on her fingertips. "This is madness," she said to the rock protrusion. But the sun lowering in the late afternoon sky meant there was no time for her to hem and haw over her decision. She had to act quickly. Otherwise, she would be climbing in the dark. Wendy gripped the rock and hoisted herself up. Her feet slipped on the mossy surface, but she managed to climb above the moss and find better footholds in the rock. Even tied up, her skirts seemed to be tangling her legs and making the entire process that much more treacherous. "Just breathe," she said to herself. Higher and higher she climbed, wishing she had pixie dust and a happy thought. Reaching above her head, she gripped a part of the stone face, but when she tried to lift herself up on it, the stone crumbled under her fingertips and she skidded down several inches before she could catch herself on the stones.

She felt like she was hugging the wall as she stood on legs that trembled. Her muscles weren't used to this kind of activity.

Lungs were supposed to work better, weren't they? Wendy's lungs were incapable of anything but rapid, shallow breaths. "I should have taken off my shoes," she said. The dancing slippers were made to glide on a dance floor, not provide traction on a cliff face.

"Do not continue until you are sure your handhold and foothold are secure." This was the mantra she now repeated in her mind over and over. Looking down was simply out of the question, at least until she was at the top. She agonized over each inch when, finally, she came to a small ledge that led to a narrow path that was still steep, but not climbing steep—walking steep. She pulled herself up over the ledge and collapsed against the cold stone. The palms of her hands and her fingertips were raw and sore. And the muscles in her arms, legs, and back trembled in a way that made her wonder if they would ever be still again.

"I'm alive!" she shouted to anyone who cared to know, not even worrying that someone might hear her shout. Only then did Wendy dare peek over the edge to see how far she'd climbed. Her stomach twisted at the dizzying height. The jungle below looked like a swirl of green tapestry in the early evening light. All seemed quiet below her. Perhaps the pirates had not followed. Unlikely, but possible. More likely, they were combing the jungle for her. But they would not look up. They would not guess that she had climbed a rock face and conquered a mountain in an evening gown and dancing slippers.

Now that she was on relatively safe ground, she rolled to her back and stared up at the sky ablaze with the setting sun.

Liam Blackwell—that blackhearted pirate—had tricked her into following him to Neverland. But in that moment, as she stared up and watched fiery clouds drift lazily above her in a purple Neverland sky and listened to the neverbirds trill as they rode a wind funnel before they retired to their nests for the night, she couldn't be sorry.

Her heart swelled with joy as the weight of her responsibilities back in London slipped away from her shoulders. She felt the wild freedom in this land that was alive, breathing, welcoming her back to its shores and jungles. A bubble of laughter escaped her lips. "I'm back."

She'd wanted to be here. And now she was.

"Did you miss me?" she whispered to the sky.

Then she frowned. It felt like the earth beneath and the tree branches waving above all seemed to groan in response. Was something wrong? How could anything be wrong in Neverland? Especially now, when Wendy had the advantage over her would-be captors—when she was out of their reach, giving her a chance to rest and breathe. Once her heart rate had slowed to something that could be called normal, Wendy got up, straightened out her tied-up skirts as best she could so they didn't get in her way and slow her down, and began taking the steep winding path upward.

Satisfaction swelled in her when she reached a plateau that led into a tree line of more jungle. Wendy turned to take in the view from the cliff and gasped. "There you are, Neverland," she said to the wind. "I'd almost forgotten how painfully beautiful you are." She stood on a peak that allowed her to look over both Pirate Cove and Mermaid Lagoon. From her vantage point, she could even see Skull Rock, surrounded by mist and swirling, cawing seagulls. The verdant green jungle met the golden sands of the various beaches, which then stretched into a blue that reminded her of Mr. Blackwell's eyes. She swatted that thought away.

The air was thick with the sweet scent of wildflowers and the salt of the sea mingling together in a perfect dance. The sun hung low in the sky, reflecting its molten rays across the ocean. She'd never been to the peak on which she now stood, and the experience left her breathless and giddy over her sense of self-accomplishment. Her mother had assured her again and again that she needed to wed in order to have someone take care of her. Absurdity and nonsense. Wendy could jolly well take care of herself.

To think she had considered Liam Blackwell as one who might be up for the job of being her husband. "Figures I'd choose a pirate," she muttered. How had he fooled her so completely? He'd seemed so marvelous.

Wendy sighed. What did it matter how he had seemed? She was only glad her heart hadn't had time to get too attached. It was only bruised at his betrayal, but not broken. Wendy caught herself staring out to Pirate Cove and wondering if Hook would punish Mr. Blackwell for her escape.

She turned away, feeling the frown drag at her face as if it had its own gravity. "It's not because you care what happens to him. It's only that you are a nice person who doesn't want misfortune falling on others—even if they are pirates." She said this all quite sternly as if scolding a small child, but she wasn't sure she believed herself, which bothered her a great deal.

Better for her to worry about herself at the moment. She had no idea how to find Peter. Wild animals could make a quick meal of her if she wasn't careful. Wendy yawned. "I need to sleep," she told herself. She hadn't slept for nearly two days, and she was exhausted. She needed food, too, and water, but sleep felt like the most pressing matter at hand.

Wendy untied the overcoat from her waist and laid it over the grasses under the shade of a tall pine before settling herself on top of it and closing her eyes. At first, she feared that sleep would never come no matter how tired her body felt, but the thrum of the ocean rolling into the sand on the shores below her and the chirring of insects in the trees soothed her soul with memories.

Tiger Lily teaching John to shoot a bow and arrow. Nibs showing Michael how to weave a basket to gather berries in the forest.

Peter flying overhead, crowing and laughing and saying, "One girl is worth more than twenty boys."

"You're right about that, Peter," she murmured, half asleep, to the trees. "I challenge any twenty boys to escape Hook as neatly as I just did."

She needed to find Peter, or Tiger Lily, or even Tinker Bell, though that vexing little pixie was not often helpful. "But I need to sleep." Her mind hummed as it descended into slumber. She was almost certain she heard Peter whisper on the wind, "Wendy, Wendy, when you are sleeping in your silly bed, you might be flying about with me saying funny things to the stars."

"But I'm not funny, Peter," she murmured. "No one laughed when I made the joke that stars stay positive because they have a lighthearted attitude."

"I laughed," her phantom Peter said.

"No, you didn't," Wendy responded before her body sank deeper into sleep. Her breathing slowed and steadied. Her heart rate became a rhythmic drumbeat in the quiet of the Neverland evening. She surrendered to dreamland at last, even as she felt a shiver of something dark slither her direction.

Then she turned up the light, and Peter saw. He gave a cry of pain; and when the tall beautiful creature stooped to lift him in her arms, he drew back sharply.

"What is it?" he cried again.

She had to tell him.

"I am old, Peter. I am ever so much more than twenty. I grew up long ago."

"You promised not to!"

"I couldn't help it."

CHAPTER NINE

Wendy awoke to the feeling of tiny thumps on her chest. She opened her eyes to find a pixie standing on her and staring at her.

"Starna," Wendy said with a yawn. "How did you find me?"

Starna made a chiming noise as she moved her fingers to pinch her nostrils.

"I do not smell bad!" Wendy insisted, though she considered it was probably true. A lot had happened since her last bath.

Wendy sat up and stretched out her cramped muscles, then halted. The hairs on the back of her neck pricked up. Someone was watching her. She jumped to her feet and whirled in the direction she felt certain someone lurked, hope rising in her chest that it was Mr. Blackwell, which made no sense that she should hope for such a thing. It was just that her sleep had been filled with terrible nightmares of him hurt and calling to her and feeling the guilt as she turned her back on him and fled. Why he should be hurt and why she should feel guilty about it was completely lost on her, but dreams had a habit of making no sense. "Mr. Blackwell?"

The cawing seagulls in the distance were her only answer. She frowned, noticing that parts of the plant life around where she'd slept had shriveled and turned to a gray, ash-like color. She reached out to touch one of the shriveled leaves when a slight rustle of leaves on a quivering branch forced her to look up, and there he was.

Not Liam Blackwell.

Peter Pan.

He perched on the branch and was framed in the tree's foliage, his green clothing nearly blending in with his surroundings. He tilted his head to the side as if he were a curious little bird up there on that branch. When their eyes met, Wendy was pulled in entirely. She had waited for this moment for years. Her heart forgot to beat. Her lungs forgot to draw in air. He was here. She was here. They were together. Peter jumped down from the tree and landed softly next to her. Starna flew away immediately.

Peter peered hard into Wendy's face. "Wendy?" he finally asked. "*My* Wendy."

She wanted to weep with relief. He remembered her. She was not entirely forgettable. But then she stiffened. She was not *his* Wendy. She belonged to no one but herself. Didn't she? Yet, she loved that he claimed her still.

Wendy and Peter stared at one another for what seemed like eternity before Wendy threw her arms around him and hugged him tightly. He went stiff in her arms, clearly not expecting that kind of response from her, but she didn't care. She was here, in Neverland, with the boy who could fly her to the stars.

"Wendy?" Peter's confused voice sounded muffled against her shoulder.

"Sorry." She pulled away, feeling her cheeks burn hot with embarrassment. Ladies did not throw themselves at men. It was then that she looked at Peter, *really* looked at him. A terrible realization struck her. He was *not* a man. She was taller than he was now—not that such things mattered. But it wasn't so much that she was taller. It was that she was older.

The elation fled her soul as quickly as it had filled it upon seeing him.

"You've changed," he said with a frown, as if the thought had just occurred to him as well. His hand reached toward her face, but he stopped himself just short of her cheek. He drew his fingers back and folded them into his palm. She couldn't say why that action hurt her so much, but it did.

Peter shook off whatever melancholy had come over him and reached for Wendy's hand. He took hold, which hurt her just a little since her hands hadn't exactly healed overnight, but she didn't pull away, glad to have him with her again. "I'm so glad you're back. Just wait until you see what I've done with the place!"

He took a little jump into the air, but because he was holding her hand, she tethered him to the ground. "Well? Come on. It's time to fly."

Wendy *wanted* to fly. She wanted to feel the kiss of the clouds against her cheeks and the liquid light of the stars dripping through her fingertips. "I don't think I can. Gravity weighs heavy in my soul."

This concept of gravity made no sense to Peter. He tugged her hand again and again as if he could will her into the sky. "It's easy," he insisted. "Just think of a happy thought. Remember the mermaid lagoon? You love it there."

"I didn't love it when the mermaids were trying to drown me."

"Aw, they were just playing."

"That's the problem with your sorts of games. Peter. They don't feel like games to some of us." She shook her head. The realization that she had changed so much while he hadn't felt like an anchor. "I can't fly, Peter." The admission tasted like failure.

"Why can't you fly?" Peter poked her shoulder as if she were something strange and dangerous.

"I forgot. Sometimes people just forget things," she snapped. "Why don't you know how to speak French?"

Peter shrugged and laughed. "I don't even know what that is." He clearly missed the point she was trying to make—that he didn't know everything just because he knew how to fly.

Before she could explain that it was a language from people in her world, he shook his head and said, "You just need some pixie dust."

He cupped his hand around his mouth and yelled, "Tinker Bell!" He waited only a moment before calling again. "You gotta do it a few times. Sometimes that pixie has dandelion fluff in her ears."

Wendy thought about Starna and wondered where the little pixie had gone. Not that she was surprised that Starna was wary. Tinker Bell was the pixie who had claimed Peter's friendship. The others steered clear for the most part. Then Wendy heard it. She recognized Tinker Bell's chiming sound. Tinker Bell flew around Peter in a crazed pattern, leaving a small trail of dust as she went.

She landed on his shoulder and chimed something to him. Peter laughed but then waved his hand. "No. We're not putting mud in Jinx's goggles. But maybe later we can." Peter's ear tips turned red at her next suggestion. "No, I didn't rip my trousers again. And anyway, if I did, Wendy could fix them." He gestured to Wendy.

Tinker Bell turned and noticed Wendy for the first time. Wendy felt certain that the little pixie was less than thrilled to see her, though she hoped that this time, Tinker Bell wouldn't be encouraging the lost boys to shoot her out of the sky. Tinker Bell tilted her head to the side and chimed again. Then she did something wholly unexpected. She smiled.

Wendy smiled too. "Of course I rescued Starna. It was my pleasure. She helped me too, you know."

Peter flapped his hands, not wanting to be bothered with the conversation between the pixie and Wendy. "Wendy needs to fly. We need some dust."

"If you please," Wendy said, shooting a meaningful glance at Peter, who had not asked nicely at all.

Tinker Bell chimed a laugh at Wendy for thinking it was necessary to add the please, though Wendy wasn't sure why that was supposed to be funny. Then Tinker Bell circled over Wendy's head, powdering her with glittering golden dust.

"So?" Peter asked. "You ready to go?"

Wendy felt the tingle of the magic seep into her skin and burrow its way to her heart and mind.

"Think a happy thought," Peter coached.

Wendy considered. Was she happy? Happy enough to fly? How happy did a thought need to be before it was effective? Her mother probably thought she was missing and was frantic with worry.

That was *not* a happy thought.

She thought about what she would be doing if she were in London at that moment. It was midday. She would likely be forced to take callers and sit through insipid conversations while pretending to be riveted by her company.

That was not a happy thought, either.

Except delight filled her with the knowledge that she'd managed to skip one of those wretched afternoons. If she never went back, she'd never have to endure another afternoon of listening to some caller or another tell her about *his* plans and *his* ideas. She wouldn't have to wish she could share some of *her* ideas and *her* plans. Here in Neverland, she was free.

She thought about the moment she'd turned and looked down at Neverland after scaling a rock wall, *in a dress*, she might add, and had seen the whole of it all at once with the sights like a work of art and the sounds like a lullaby. And now she was here, with Peter, and he had not forgotten her after all, and—

"There you go!" Peter said, bouncing up into the sky. "I told you. Easy."

Wendy looked down at where she was now hovering above the ground—maybe only a few feet, but she was flying! She hadn't forgotten how! That thought sent her up several feet more. She frowned slightly, though, because try as she might, she couldn't seem to get any higher. Why was that?

"So? You ready?" Peter took her hand again.

"For what?" she asked.

"An adventure, of course."

"What kind of adventure?"

"Aw, one of the lost boys got caught by the shadow conjurer. I've got to go rescue him." Peter said all of this as if it were just another morning of tea, but the news alarmed Wendy. It stirred up the nightmares from when she'd slept and left her cold and trembling. She felt herself sinking back to the ground under the weight of those nightmares.

"What's a shadow conjurer?" she asked, hating the quake in her voice.

"Aw, it's just a story that frightens the lost boys."

Wendy sank a little more. She had things she needed to tell Peter about Hook and Hook's nephew. She also had many questions she wanted to ask. Why hadn't he come back for her for so long? Why did he have more lost boys? Where had he gotten them from? Was Mr. Blackwell right when he said Peter stole children?

She squeezed Peter's hand, refusing to let herself sink all the way to the ground. Of course Mr. Blackwell wasn't right. This was *her* Peter. Peter would never steal children. Mr. Blackwell was wrong. And if the shadow conjurer was just a story, she didn't need to worry about it.

"Away we go!" Peter called to her as he shot up into the sky, dragging her along with him. Wendy hadn't been able to fly very high without him, but with Peter holding her hand, Wendy could touch the sky once again.

The ground shrank away beneath her, and a sense of etherealness buoyed her up, allowing her to shrug off the weight of the world. For a moment, Wendy floundered against the dizzying height, but Peter's firm grip reassured her that she was safe.

They soared higher, the wind tousling Peter's hair like a mother might do to her small child. Wendy's dress and overcoat flapped behind her, and her hair unraveled the rest of the way in the wind. The sky was Peter's playground, and he wanted to play. Tinker Bell and Peter—dragging along Wendy—zigged and zagged around each other in the sky.

Peter crowed out a laugh, forcing a laugh of her own to bubble out. "I'm home!" she thought. But then another thought struck her.

Peter had said he would come often to bring her back to Neverland, but it had been so long.

"Peter," Wendy said, trying to think of a diplomatic way to bring up the subject. Upon not finding any way, she decided to just be out with it. "Why did you not come back for me?"

"What do you mean?" He dove them into a little loop.

"You said you would come to get me so we could clean house together." It was silly now that she was saying it out loud. Clean house? Why would she even want such a thing?

"I don't know what you're talking about. I only took you home a few days ago."

"Peter, that was years ago."

"Was it? Well, that can't be right."

Wendy glared at him for discounting the truth she knew. "You abandoned me," she said, determining to say what she felt. Her heart pinched a little that he seemed not to see it that way at all, that he dismissed the very notion that time had passed. "What have you been doing the whole time since you saw me last?"

"We've been warring with the shadow conjurer. She makes these terrible shadow snakes that bite the lost boys when we're walking through the jungle. Those bites cause the worst nightmares you've ever seen. They dream about monsters with sharp teeth and fiery eyes. They wake up crying an awful noise. And if that wasn't bad enough, she sends her dream reapers out to corner the lost boys and then touch them on their foreheads with their cold-clawed fingers so that they can feast on their hopes and dreams and make it easier for the shadow snake venom to let the nightmares in. So I've been busy."

Wendy had to admit that all of that did make Peter sound terribly busy. "I thought you said the shadow conjurer was just a story that frightened the boys. Are you trying to tell me that it's real?"

"Sure it's a story. Why should that mean that it's not real?"

It was hard to tell if he was being cheeky with her or if he was showing real insight. "How do you war with a shadow conjurer?"

she asked, deciding she didn't want to know if he was being cheeky or not.

"We have to use neverflowers."

She had no idea what a neverflower was and worried that he might think she was stupid if she had to ask. Gratefully, he continued on with no prompting from her.

"The stars got tired of just looking at humans doing things all the time, so some of them decided to fall and plant themselves in the earth, where they could influence the way things went here. Every place a falling star landed is where a neverflower grows. They make light that dissolves the shadow conjurer's creations. But we're running low on neverflowers. So we're creating some other things that might work as well."

Tinker Bell chimed something that sounded low and mournful about the shortage of neverflowers.

The odd thought of Mr. Blackwell entered Wendy's mind. Did he know about this shadow conjurer? Was he in league with the creature? Or perhaps he was fighting against it, too. She hoped that he was fighting it. For reasons Wendy didn't understand, she felt her heart would break if Mr. Blackwell and this shadow conjurer were on the same side.

They soared higher over the patchwork landscape with silver river ribbons cutting through its patterns and the lush jungles looking like velvety green carpets. Peter seemed to think there wasn't anything more to say, but Wendy still had so many questions.

"Where is the shadow conjurer?" she asked when it became obvious he wasn't going to add to the narration.

"Skull Rock," Peter said. Tinker Bell nodded her agreement.

"I didn't see any shadow anything when I was at Skull Rock before."

Peter shrugged and did another loopy twist, dragging Wendy along with him and making her stomach roil. She was suddenly glad she hadn't eaten, or she would be sicking out all over everything.

"Peter," Wendy chided, trying to keep him on the topic at hand.

"Was the shadow conjurer always there? And if so, how have I not seen it?"

"I don't know where she came from. She was just there one day. She keeps to her shadows on the dark side of Skull Rock in the shadowlands where the jungle is so deep that light doesn't ever touch the ground. She rules the caverns there. But she sends out the snakes and the dream reapers. They're her eyes."

Wendy shuddered at the idea of this creature and then considered again how Neverland felt off somehow. Was it this creature that had disrupted the balance of the island? She didn't get the luxury of pondering the question too deeply because, at that moment, Peter let go of her hand so that he could scratch behind his ear. Wendy immediately began to fall.

Tinker Bell chimed what sounded like an alarm. When Peter noticed Wendy was falling, he dove down to grab her hand again.

"You're not flying very well, Wendy," he said with a grimace as if she had stepped in something foul.

"It's been a long time, Peter," Wendy said, feeling foolish for not flying well. Could one forget how to fly? Perhaps. But she hadn't forgotten exactly. She hadn't fallen nearly as fast as she might have without pixie dust and her happy thoughts. Pixie dust just didn't seem to be enough, though. At least not to keep her from falling without him.

It didn't sit right with Wendy to have to depend on Peter, especially when he was so forcefully reminding her that he wasn't the sort who could be depended on.

She didn't think Mr. Blackwell would have let go of her hand if he knew she would fall without him.

But that thought was plain silly. Mr. Blackwell was a pirate. Of course he would let her fall. Wasn't he the one who let her be locked up on the *Jolly Roger*? Wasn't he the one who tricked her into coming to Neverland in the first place?

Was *tricked* the right word?

Wendy wasn't sure. She'd made the choice. But he knew that

was the choice she'd make if he gave her the right clues. He'd known what to say. It felt tricky.

A distant rumble of thunder pulled her from her thoughts of Liam Blackwell. Wendy searched the sky to see where the sound had come from since it felt like it had rolled over and around them from all directions. Black clouds shrouded the blue sky straight ahead.

Gooseflesh pimpled the skin on her arms, and an icy chill shivered up her spine and prickled her heart. She'd never seen a storm like this in Neverland. Something was wrong on the island. Terribly wrong.

"The storm." Wendy pointed in case Peter had missed the obvious. Since he was trading silly faces with Tinker Bell, he probably had.

"Aw, we'll go up over it."

The growing mass of clouds seemed to swallow the sky into its dark maw. How were they to go up and over something that had taken over everything?

The wind, which had been playfully pulling at her hair and clothes, tugged with greater insistence. The faint metallic smell of the earth far below and the charge of lightning in the clouds mingled together. Petrichor was Wendy's favorite smell in the world, but as the sky turned to a charcoal-colored bruise, she couldn't think why she had ever liked the smell of a coming storm.

Lightning forked across the sky in jagged blazes. Thunder boomed in response.

Rain filled the air, and the wind whipped it into Wendy's face with a force that stung as she was tossed wildly through the sky. If Peter hadn't been holding on and if Tinker Bell's light hadn't been so easy to follow, Wendy would have feared getting lost in the storm. As it was, she felt like her stomach had lodged itself in her throat, and her heart beat so rapidly that Wendy could barely hear the thundering tempest over it.

"Peter! The storm!" Wendy shouted again just as another flash of white-hot lightning zipped past them, blinding her and making her jolt back.

Her fingers slipped from Peter's hand, and Wendy plummeted toward the earth like a raindrop destined to splatter on the ground.

"So let us watch and say jaggy things, in the hope that some of them will hurt."

CHAPTER TEN

"Happy thought!" Wendy shrieked to the torrential sky in the hope that she could compel a happy thought to the front of her mind just by saying the words.

Nothing.

How close was the earth? Thirty seconds? Twenty?

"I'm happy to not be in London pretending to find Mr. Hurst vastly intelligent!"

Not good enough, though she *was* happy about it.

"I'm happy to have escaped Hook!"

Again nothing.

"I'm happy to be with Peter again!"

She was sure that one would work and was surprised when not only did it *not* work, but it also felt *not* exactly true. The ground loomed larger.

"I'm happy to be in Neverland!"

Her rapid fall slowed, though not enough to keep her from slamming into the ground with a great whump that knocked the wind out of her. Wendy didn't move for several long moments, even though it felt like the rain was trying to drown her where she lay in a crumpled heap of limbs on a rather impressive pile of leaves.

She wiggled her toes and fingers, hoping they still worked. They did, miraculously. She moved various parts of herself to check if anything had broken in the fall. The leaf pile must have softened the crash because, other than some soreness and shock over the entire experience, nothing seemed to be wrong. The leaf pile made no sense, though she was grateful for it. Leaves just didn't fall from the trees in Neverland. The verdant jungle remained lush and green always. But here, the trees above her had all shivered off their leaves and stood stripped against the stormy sky.

Wendy frowned as she crunched a handful of the ashy leaves and let the sickly ash turn to a grey mud in her palm as it mixed with the rainwater.

She scrambled to her feet, her skirts heavy and sloshy around her ankles. She squinted up, blinking against the fat drops of rain for any sign of Peter or Tinker Bell, but if they were there, the storm had dropped a curtain over wherever it was they'd hidden in the sky.

The buckets of rain had soaked Wendy to the skin, leaving her shivering with cold and quivering with anger and sadness over having been abandoned by Peter. Again. She was drenched in fear of being struck by the charges of white-hot lightning arcing from the clouds. Even that, however, was not enough to keep her from attempting to jump into the sky to find Peter.

She kept jumping up but then landing back in the mud with an irritating squelch. "Happy thought! Happy thought!" she chanted to herself.

When a crack of thunder split the sky, Wendy had to look away from where the lightning flash burned a hole in her vision for several moments. She blinked away the spots but then frowned. Was someone approaching her?

"Just my imagination," she murmured to herself. She looked back up to the sky and gave another jump.

"Well, well, well. Who could this flooded figure of distress be, I wonder?"

She knew that voice. Liam Blackwell. Wendy lowered her head sharply from where she'd been staring into the sky, her eyes squinting to see through the raindrops. She hoped everything on her face revealed she was not happy to see him. "So you caught up with me," she said flatly. "How . . . unlikely."

Mr. Blackwell raised an eyebrow at her before he could bring himself to vocalize a response. "No reason to be rude."

She narrowed her eyes at him. "I feel I have every reason in the world. You should move along. Peter will be coming to get me any moment, and it would be a tragedy for any other members of your family to get a hand thrown to the crocodile." She jumped into the air again and hoped he didn't hear her muttering, "Happy thought. Happy thought . . ."

Mr. Blackwell leaned against a tree and watched her attempt to fly two more times before he said, "Would it help if I gave you a boost?"

The glare she turned on him could have melted sand into glass. "I'm glad to see this side of you. You'd been so charming at the ball that it's good to see the truth."

Mr. Blackwell straightened to his full height. "Oh, you're one to talk. One of the reasons I thought you'd be happy to help us with our Pan problem was that you had me fooled into thinking you were possibly the nicest person I'd ever met. I cannot wait to get back to London so I can tell Mrs. Connolly how entirely wrong we were regarding your character so she doesn't recommend you to any other poor unsuspecting man."

"Of course I won't help you. And I am nice!" she insisted, furious to have been accused otherwise.

"Says the lass threatening to feed my hand to a crocodile."

They both stood glaring at one another until he said, "It's my terrible misfortune to have to return you to the *Jolly Roger*. You can come quietly, or you can come loudly. I don't care either way, but you will be going back."

Was he serious? One look at his face told her that yes, he was. She steadied her stance, bracing herself for a battle. "I dare you to try to make me."

Mr. Blackwell clearly hadn't expected that response because he also steadied his stance as he said, "How were you so disarmingly charming in the ballroom when you are nothing more than brazenness held together with spit and venom?"

She lifted her shoulder in a half-shrugged response. "You thought I was charming?"

"A mistake, I assure you. One I won't make again. But please remember you *did* dare me to do this." Mr. Blackwell lunged for her.

Wendy easily ducked his grasp and scooped up a tree branch she'd spied while he was talking before rounding on him and swiping at his legs. He jumped the branch before it could connect with his shins. The force of her swing connecting with nothing unbalanced her. But she recovered and held the stick like a cricket bat, ready to swing again.

The confident look in his eye gave way to uncertainty. "Now, Wendy, let's be reasonable."

She tightened her grip on the stick. "That's another thing. When did I ever give you permission to call me anything besides Miss Darling? You insult me with your casual inference."

"We're in Neverland," he insisted, dancing back several steps to escape the swing of the branch that whistled past his nose. He nearly slipped in the mud but managed to keep his balance. A pity. "Not a London ballroom. You can call me Liam if you'd like."

"I would *not* like!" She took another swing.

He spun out of the way of her branch and then pivoted sharply on his back foot, his body twisting as he lowered his center of gravity, bringing his leg around in a sweeping arc. His foot hooked behind Wendy's ankle, pulling her legs out from under her.

She went down with a cry and a sludgy splash into the mud. She dropped the branch, which he quickly kicked away from her reach so she couldn't use it against him. Not that she could have. The wind had been knocked out of her once again.

"I don't want to hurt you, Wendy." He held out his hand to her to help her up. She slapped it away and scrambled to her feet on her own in a rather undignified manner as she slipped in the wet grasses and mud. He took hold of her arm so she couldn't make a run and grab for another branch.

"You? A pirate? And not wanting to hurt someone? Please tell me another joke, Mr. Blackwell. You're really quite hilarious." She tried twisting out of his grasp until he locked both of her hands behind her in his.

"I really don't want to hurt you. Taking you back to my uncle is the only way. I don't have a choice."

"You always have a choice to do the right thing." She tried to pull away again but to no avail.

"But I *am* doing the right thing. Protecting those boys Pan kidnaps *is* the right thing. How can you not see that?" He shifted so that he held both of her hands in one of his. She had to strain to see what he was doing so she could prepare for anything, but he merely dragged his free hand down his face to clear away the rain from his eyes.

"In the first place," she said. "I don't believe that they were kidnapped at all. In the second place, if you were so filled with your righteous cause, then you would be helping me save a lost boy caught by the shadow conjurer, not dragging me off and making me Hook's prisoner."

Liam spun her around so she faced him. "What about the shadow conjurer?" he demanded to know. "That creature has one of the boys?" His face darkened with dread. "How do you know this? And how long ago was the child taken?" He gripped her arm tighter than he'd probably meant to because, when he saw her wince, he relaxed his hold.

"Peter told me," she said. "He was taking me there when we were separated in the lightning storm—*a lightning storm* . . . in Neverland . . . Have you ever seen such a thing?" She shook her head. "Anyway, I think the child had just been taken because Peter was on his way to attempt a rescue when we crossed paths." She stopped, and, rather than moving away from him as she might have expected she would want to do, she peered into his face. "You're seriously worried, aren't you?"

"Of course I'm worried. A little boy should not be in the power of something so dark. If we don't get to him by nightfall, he'll be lost to the nightmares of the shadows." Mr. Blackwell sighed and looked in the direction of Pirate Cove. Then he looked in the opposite direction toward Skull Rock. Then, as if there were nothing to be done for it, he dropped Wendy's arm and started off toward the shadow conjurer's lair. He turned to Wendy and gave a jerk of his head to encourage her to follow him. "Come on then. Skull Rock is a long way away, and since you clearly can't fly, and neither can I, we should get started immediately. The boy doesn't have much time."

Wendy stared at him for several long moments, confusion and suspicion fighting for space in her mind when she finally gave in and followed, trudging along behind him in silence; the only sound between them was the patter of rain against the leaves of the trees.

"Why are you helping me?" she asked after a silence that felt like it had stretched into a day.

"You said one of the boys was in trouble. You can think what you like about me, but the boys are always my first priority."

Wendy nodded, but the frown on her face felt permanent. The rain slackened and then just as suddenly as it had started, it stopped.

"What made you decide to believe that I was helping you?" Mr. Blackwell asked. "For all you knew, with the way the jungle spins people around and makes it difficult to get one's directional bearings, I could be marching you back to the *Jolly Roger* with every step we take."

She hesitated but decided she might as well tell him. "I saw you before we left the Westridges' property. At the line of motors and carriages. One of the drivers had been about to strike a boy, and you stopped him. Most wouldn't have intervened." She glanced at Mr. Blackwell out of the side of her eye. "I've just never seen a pirate who helped a child. It makes you a puzzle."

Surprise crossed his expression. He probably hadn't expected her to be so forthcoming. "I must admit you're a puzzle to me as well. Everything I heard about you from my uncle led me to believe that you were another of Pan's victims who was under his thrall. But at the ball, everyone talked about you like you were some sort of national hero, and after spending the evening with you, you seemed like a woman who knew her own mind. I'm still not sure what to make of it."

They fell silent again. The sun had come out fully. The sounds of birds, shaking off the water and calling to one another, filled the silence between them.

Mr. Blackwell opened his mouth to begin a conversation of some sort but then closed it each time. Coward. Not that she fared much better. She couldn't think of anything to say either.

Wendy broke the silence. "How did you know?"

"Know?"

"That I'd follow you to Neverland."

"When I went home to check on my affairs, I visited Mrs. Connolly. She told me of a guest she'd recently entertained—a young lady by the name of Wendy Darling. She wanted me to call on you, but as soon as I heard the name *Darling*, I knew who you were. Your reputation for being an adventure seeker was well-known among my uncle's crew. You weren't afraid of the crew, according to their stories. Someone like that would crave the sight of Neverland's shores once again." He held aside a large pricklebush out of her way so she could pass by without getting stuck. It was just the sort of gentlemanly thing that one of her suitors would have done. It bothered her to think of it that way.

"What if I hadn't understood your hints? They weren't exactly forthcoming," she asked once she'd edged past the bush.

"You're clever. I knew you'd figure it out."

"You have something nice to say to me? That's unexpected."

Mr. Blackwell rolled his shoulders, looked from her hair that hung down in tangled curls to her ripped gown, which was filthy in spite of being soaked with rain. For a moment, there was a heat in his eyes that made her think he had something else to say, but he shifted his glance away from her.

Apparently, he had no other compliments for her.

She swiped at the foliage in her path, not knowing why she felt vexed by the man. She focused on her surroundings to distract her mind.

A red bird landed on a nearby branch, and the leaves shimmered red. Some of the trees had chameleon leaves that changed to whatever color touched them. Each time Wendy or Mr. Blackwell brushed past the chameleon trees, the leaves shivered and changed to match the charcoal of Wendy's father's overcoat or Mr. Blackwell's jacket, making the leaves look somber. Reminding her of the way so much of the plant life appeared to have shriveled.

There was evidence of dead foliage in the underbrush and the grasses. Wendy frowned as her feet crunched against the lifeless vegetation. She didn't remember Neverland having any dead growth. It had always been lush and alive.

Perhaps she remembered wrong?

Perhaps. But she didn't think so.

Mr. Blackwell didn't complain even though his feet had to be aching. Wendy was certainly tired, but if he wasn't going to complain, neither would she.

Mr. Blackwell reached into his satchel and pulled out a biscuit and some dried plums. He held them out to her. "We don't have time to stop to get you anything more substantial, but I imagine you're hungry."

Wendy almost gave a stubborn retort that she could fend for herself, except her stomach growled loudly enough to be embarrassing. Why be prideful? She needed her energy. There was no weakness in admitting when you required the help someone offered. She accepted the offering with a grudging thanks.

She ate while scanning the skies continually until Mr. Blackwell blurted out, "He won't come back for you. He's probably forgotten he was on his way to anything of vital urgency and forgotten that he'd had anyone with him. Pan is like that."

"Peter would not forget me." She didn't believe herself. She'd already assumed he *had* forgotten her. It certainly wouldn't be the first time, as Hook had so tactlessly pointed out.

Mr. Blackwell scoffed and pulled out his cutlass to hack away a bloodshade plant that crossed the path so neither one of them accidentally brushed against the poisonous flower. "So why hasn't he come back for you the last several years?"

"It's not me he forgot," she huffed. "It was the time. It's hard for him to keep track of time."

Mr. Blackwell huffed too. Wendy suspected it wasn't because he was feeling indignant but because the steep hill they were climbing felt like it might go on forever. It was certainly enough to wear her out.

"I don't know why you make excuses for that monster," Mr. Blackwell said.

"And I don't know why you hate him so."

Mr. Blackwell whirled on her and pointed to the scar on the side of his temple. "The first time I met him, I was just a boy. He might have looked like a boy, but he was an eternal being. And he gave me this."

Stopping short at the sudden nearness of him, Wendy said, "He wouldn't have done that to another child."

"Keep telling yourself that, lass, if you feel like it might help you sleep better at night."

Wendy drew herself to her full height and frowned. It bothered her that she still had to look up at him. "Well, what did you do to him? It takes two to fight, you know."

"I asked for one of his lost boys to be handed over to me so that I could take him home."

The stab of his words hit their mark. Mr. Blackwell had wanted to take home a child and received a scar for the request?

Emboldened by her obvious distress over the information, Mr.

Blackwell continued. "Pan didn't want to give up one of his lost boys. Starkey was a favorite of his on account of the boy being such a good hunter. When I asked for the boy, Pan challenged me to a duel for him. I had been trained well enough that I felt confident in an easy win against this other child who grinned far too much to take seriously. That was before I realized the truth."

"What was the truth?" Wendy put her hands on her hips. The jungle seemed to go quiet as if waiting for Mr. Blackwell's response.

"I wasn't fighting another boy my own age and skill level. I was battling an ageless creature with experience and time on his side. When he disarmed me, he made sure to cut my face so that I'd remember I had lost. He told me he would never give Starkey up and that if he saw me again, he would kill me like the pirate he now knew me to be."

Wendy was already shaking her head and stepping back as if she could remove herself from the truth he had given her. She felt sick but could not deny how plausible it was that Peter would do such a thing. She grasped at excuses—any excuse. "But you did get Starkey back. You told me at the ball that you had spent the day before with your good friend in London. The two of you had been helping Mrs. Connolly with some management of her affairs or another."

"That's true. I did manage to get Starkey back, but only because Starkey had decided he was homesick and wanted to leave Neverland. He got so homesick, he refused to play games with Pan. Pan doesn't like it when the boys get too old to play. He thins them out on occasion. Growing up is against the rules."

Mr. Blackwell could likely tell that she was thinking that through, remembering Peter's reaction to her own exodus from Neverland with all those little boys in tow. She recalled those lost boys from long ago telling her that growing up was against the rules. She had thought it a silly little game they played. But were there darker meanings in the words?

Mr. Blackwell kept talking.

"We take a lot of the boys when Pan abandons them to the

beasts of the island. We took Starkey and kept him working on my uncle's crew for a short time while we made preparations to return him to London. When we finally took him there to meet his mother, we realized how confusing it would be for Mrs. Connolly to have her son show up on her doorstep as a young man instead of the toddler she'd lost, so Starkey and I agreed to introduce him to her as my friend."

Wendy's head snapped up. Her hand covered her mouth, but she wasn't sure if it was to hold in the scream or to hold back the sickness she felt was sure to erupt out of her. No. No, no, no! "Mrs. Connolly? Your friend is Mrs. Connolly's son?"

Mr. Blackwell nodded.

She took several more steps back. "No. No, I don't believe it. I don't believe you." He had to be lying. He had to be. Poor Mrs. Connolly, who mourned for the child she had lost every day since it had happened. That was when her own word choice struck her. The child she had *lost* . . . a *lost* boy.

Mr. Blackwell shrugged and began hacking at the path before them again. "Whether or not you believe doesn't change the truth. Wendy, Pan stole the happiness of both mother and son for his own selfish purposes because he was bored and lonely. He's a devil."

She remained where she stood for a time, but Mr. Blackwell didn't wait for her.

"We need to reach Skull Rock before nightfall," he called over his shoulder.

Wendy didn't move, needing a moment to process what he'd told her. When she scrambled to catch up to him and then passed him just to prove she hadn't been holding him back, she felt everything she had once believed about the world unraveling and falling at her feet.

Her Peter really might be a villain.

No words of mine can tell you how
Wendy despised those pirates.

CHAPTER ELEVEN

Liam had to be lying. He was a pirate, after all, and pirates were notorious liars.

But Mrs. Connolly? Would he lie about her? Wendy had seen him at the ball with Mrs. Connolly. She'd seen how gently he treated her, how he had led her through the dance forms with the care and love of one who considered her a mother figure. Would he use that same woman to sell a lie to Wendy?

She knew Mrs. Connolly's story. The nanny had taken Mrs. Connolly's small son out for a walk in the park. She'd come home without him. A frantic search was made, but no trace of the boy existed. And for all of Mrs. Connolly's bright smiles and witticisms, the pain of mourning dogged her every moment.

Wendy's head shot up at that thought. She halted, forcing Liam—no, she would not think of him that way—*the pirate*, to stop as well. "You're monstrously cruel," she told the pirate.

"Me? You just learned that your hero, Pan, stole a child from your dear friend, and you call me cruel?"

"If what you say is true—and I'm not agreeing that it is—then you keeping this truth from her is the cruelest thing I've ever heard. Do you know nothing of mothers? She deserves to know that she still has a son. She deserves to see him and hold him and kiss his cheek.

Leaving her suspended in her mourning is the cruelest thing I've ever heard." She crossed her arms over her chest and leveled a look that would rival her mother's sternest. At his silence, she narrowed her eyes. "You hadn't even given it a thought, had you? Foolish boy, thinking you know what is best. You will tell her the instant we return to London. You will if I have to drag you over by your ear!"

"Yes, ma'am," he responded, hanging his head in a pitiable show of repentance. He frowned, probably because she'd called him a boy.

She startled at the thought, however—no longer thinking of him or even Mrs. Connolly. Her words, "the instant *we* return to London," confused her. We? How had she begun to think of her and this pirate as a *we*?

"Let's keep going," she said, her voice shaky. "We've a long way yet, I'd imagine. And you said we were in a hurry."

"Aye. We are at that. We're almost to the land bridge that will take us to Skull Rock. This close, make sure to stay in the light. Avoid shadows. The shadow serpents slither all through the underbrush in these parts, even in the daytime."

Wendy scanned the ground to make certain her feet stayed in the light of the path instead of accidentally stepping a toe into the shadow. "Shadow serpents. Peter said something about them. Shadow snakes anyway. He said they bit the lost boys, causing them to hallucinate the most terrible nightmarish things."

Liam nodded. "They do the same to the crew."

"Why? What do they get out of that?"

He hacked at the underbrush in front of them to give them more space on the path that had light. "I honestly couldn't say. It feels like the creatures are feeding on our energy somehow. Uncle James said Pan controls the conjurer and that it's trying to unravel the magical barriers between the lands so that it can go to our world and have a feast of the energy there."

"That's awful." Wendy felt sick at the thought of anything malignant finding its way to her world, where her brothers and mother lived. "But Peter is most assuredly not controlling it. He would never."

"Like he would never take a child that doesn't belong to him? Something's controlling the thing. And whatever it is, it needs to be stopped. A single bite is enough to make a hideous torment. If a boy is kept overnight in the conjurer's lair? He won't come out the same person. He'll never be in his right mind again."

The trees began to thin, and crashing waves sounded up ahead. Wendy and Liam broke through the tree line to a view of the beach and the large rock formation jutting out of the water in front of them. The surface of the rock face had been weathered by wind and waves; the gaping cave entrance looked like the maw of a skeleton. Liam pointed. "We'll need to cross in line with the mouth."

"Cross? Do we have a boat?"

"No. But see?" Liam took out his spyglass and pointed again while handing it off to Wendy. "See how the water appears to be shallower there? We go by foot on land. The tide is going down. Soon it'll be low enough to let us pass without getting smashed over the rocks by the waves. Once we get across, we need to go to the back side of the island."

"I thought you said the shadow conjurer lived inside the cavern," Wendy said, taking the spyglass and pressing her eye to it. She scanned the distance, worrying at how desolate the rock island seemed to be. Where was Peter?

"It does, but there are too many dark passages from the front. We would be dragged down one of them and that would be that. The back entrance takes you in and bypasses all that."

They settled on the beach and waited for low tide to reveal the narrow stretch of sand that would take them across. Wendy openly viewed her companion, noting the way he tapped his fingers against the spyglass. "Are you nervous?"

His eyes met hers and the dread was written there plain as his nose. "Hardly. Just ready."

"For what?"

"Skull Rock is a dangerous island. Even my uncle chooses to stay away if he can help it. It's haunted, you know."

She scoffed at that. "I don't believe in ghosts."

"You will."

His intense look sent a shiver down her spine, though Wendy couldn't be sure if it was from fear or excitement. And not just excitement from the adventure of it all, but because the man was attractive and having his gaze settle on her so completely left her breathless—even if he was a pirate she was determined to loathe.

But that wasn't right either. Wendy was not as determined to loathe him as she had once thought. Liam Blackwell had proven to be fairly likable when he wasn't rowing her over to imprisonment. She admired his fierce protection of children. His story regarding Mrs. Connolly's son unsettled Wendy. How could it not? If it was true . . . She shook her head. It couldn't be true. She wouldn't believe it. Not her Peter.

"Why are you shaking your head at me?" Liam asked.

"I'm afraid I was shaking it at the conversation I was having in my own head, a conversation totally irrelevant to you. I would like specific reasons as to why we should, or should not, be nervous."

Liam splayed out his legs in front of him, crossing them at the ankles. His leather boots were scuffed and scratched after chasing her through the caverns and then following her through the jungle. Wendy felt some satisfaction in knowing she hadn't been easy prey. The games she played with her brothers and her previous time in Neverland had sharpened her skills. If the lightning hadn't happened, he would never have caught her. Liam rested back on his arms. "Skull Rock used to be a place where the lost boys and my uncle's crew—"

"Pirates, you mean," Wendy interrupted.

"His *crew*," Liam insisted. "It was a place where they both had equal ownership. Pan even built a labyrinth—a game of truths we will have to play in order to get to the back entrance. My uncle's crew always used the front because of the labyrinth. I've never been in it. But I'm told no lies can exist in it if you want to get out through the cave entrance."

"The truth doesn't sound so bad."

"That's not how those who've been through it tell it. They say it's a flaying of the soul. Regardless, the shadow conjurer owns all of Skull Rock now—even the labyrinth since the only way out is through Skull Rock. The front entrance is where she and her shadow creatures reside. We'd never get in that way without being encircled by the monsters. We have to go through the labyrinth."

"But I've entered through the front. There was no creature then."

Liam nodded and sat up, picking up a pile of sand and sifting it through his fingers. "True enough. Shadow magic has always existed in Neverland. But something happened a few years ago. It was as if the shadows had gone feral. We don't know where the conjurer came from, only that she has disrupted the balance of this place. If she has captured a boy, the nightmares she would inflict on him are unspeakable. Retrieving him quickly is necessary."

Wendy considered again how wrong Neverland felt. Like it was sick. "How are there no creatures in the maze?"

"Wait until you see. There are no shadows in the maze. Only light."

She took a deep breath and stared out at the ocean. The waves breaking against the rocks looked dangerous. If high tide came in while she was crossing that thin stretch, she would be dashed against those rocks. Wanting a shift in the conversation, Wendy changed it entirely. "You've spent years of your life on the sea. Do you ever worry that Poseidon will one day tire of allowing us mortals access to his waters and rise up and drown us all under a mighty wave?"

"I cannot say that I've given much thought to mythology in the real world."

She turned to face him, her face scrunched into a look of incredulity. "I thought all sailors believed in mythology."

"Not this sailor. There's no place for fairy tales in the real world.

I simply don't believe in them. And I don't have time to waste on thinking about them."

"That's awfully cynical. What do you call Neverland?"

"I certainly don't call it the real world. How is being reasonable cynical?"

Wendy toyed with the acorn button under the neck of her dress before she dropped her hand and smiled at him. "The real world has all sorts of fairy tales in it. Every twilight, as the stars come out, do you not see the magic in their shine? When the morning sun rises and there is dew sparkling on the blades of grass and flower petals, do you not feel the electric charge of the enchantments the night left behind? And if you cannot see that, then I must ask, what *was* your childhood like?"

She was glad he laughed because, in a certain light, she'd insulted him. But he hadn't taken offense.

"My childhood with my mother was like a fairy tale. I will confess that much. My childhood on the sea, on the other hand, was definitely more like a nightmare. Long days. Longer nights. Under the whip and backhand of every other person aboard the ship because you are the youngest and the smallest and the easiest target. But they did find that I was not so easy a target as they first believed. Uncle James—"

"Hook, you mean," she said.

"If it makes you feel better to say it that way. He trained me in all the ways I could defend myself. It was how I rose in rank even though I came from a relatively humble background. It gave me status, economically as well as socially."

"Were you sad to have chosen a life on the sea?" She pitied him. She had so few choices in her own life, but it seemed that Liam Blackwell had fewer still.

But he shrugged. "Sometimes I was. But not so much anymore. I've grown strong enough to defend others as well as myself, and I cannot regret that." Liam clapped his hands together and wiped away the sand, then he moved to his feet before holding out his hand to her. "It's time." He gestured with his chin to Skull Rock.

Wendy hesitated a moment before she took his hand. When their fingers connected, she almost gasped at the steadying warmth of his grasp. As soon as she had her feet underneath her, she hurried to let go and look away toward the passage they were to take. She would not let him distract her.

As he'd said it would, the tide had withdrawn to reveal a narrow strip of sand that would allow them to cross over without being knocked into the rocks by the waves. Tide pools teemed with orange sea slugs, pink starfish, and bright blue crabs. There were also things Wendy didn't recognize. The sand and rocks were soaked, making them slippery.

Try as Wendy might to tread carefully, her slippers betrayed her precision, and she slipped several times. Liam finally took her hand again in his. "Safer together," he said. The warmth of his hand enveloping her own with such gentle firmness made her breath catch in her throat. She looked to where they were connected by their hands and wondered that she was not afraid of him, that she trusted Liam completely. How could that make sense when he was Captain Hook's nephew? And when had she decided to think of him as Liam, not Mr. Blackwell?

"Safer together," she echoed. And felt the truth of it sink into her bones.

She slipped twice more with Liam catching her from falling into the rocky ocean both times. He slipped once, and she managed to keep him upright. She didn't much like that she'd slipped more often than he had, but she reminded herself that not everything was a competition. No one was keeping score.

"I'd say that I owed you one," Liam whispered as they exited the sandbar onto the rocky beach of Skull Rock Island. "Except I saved you three times, so you owe me two."

All right. So someone *was* keeping score. She dropped his hand with a shove that nearly sent him tumbling back into the ocean. He chuckled softly and then straightened and shrugged.

"Avoid the shadows," Liam reminded her as he crept around the jaw of the rock. Then he pressed his fingers to his mouth as if she were talking when the only one who had been talking was him.

Infuriating man.

They circumvented the forested area of trees and underbrush to avoid the shadows and kept to the shore as they wound their way to the back. Wendy gasped aloud when she caught her first glimpse of the maze. Iridescent walls that were too tall and too sheer to climb jutted out of the rocky ground. Light bounced off the walls in a kaleidoscope of colors as if the walls were made of diamonds.

"It's . . . otherworldly, isn't it?" she whispered. Maybe this thing was why the island felt so wrong. It didn't look like it belonged.

"It is."

"How can such a thing of light exist next to a place of shadow?" The split of light and shadow was visible, even to Wendy.

"Some of my crew—"

"—Pirates—"

"My crew," he continued as if she hadn't interrupted, "says that the shadow was drawn here because of the light. Whispers among the inhabitants of the island say that the balance of the island is off somehow. Skull Rock is the epicenter of that balance shift."

"When you say the inhabitants," Wendy asked, "are you talking about the pirates again?"

Yes. She was just trying to vex him, which was why it surprised her when he answered, "No. I spend time with people other than my crew. If you must know. I meant Tiger Lily and her people. In fact, it was Tiger Lily who taught me half of my fighting skills."

Wendy sniffed in irritation. "Remind me to thank her."

"Oh, I will."

He sounded entirely too pleased with himself, so Wendy turned back to the gleaming walls of the maze. "Why would Peter build it?"

Liam clicked his tongue. "Rumor has it that he believes he was betrayed by one of his friends once. Pan makes all the lost boys go through the maze to reveal treachery."

A soft laugh bubbled up and escaped Wendy. "You say that as if Peter's paranoid."

Liam leveled a look at her and traced his fingers over the scar at his temple. "You say *that* as if he isn't."

The smile froze on Wendy's face. She didn't want to see Peter in a negative light, but it was hard to think of him any other way, with Liam twisting her thoughts the way he did. She took a deep breath. Her Peter was not a villain. She would not believe it.

"We should wait for Peter," she said.

Liam shook his head. "If a boy is in there, every moment we wait is a moment he's in pain and torment. I will not idle my time away out here while that is going on in there."

Two glass pillars—at least Wendy thought they might be glass—flanked the arched opening of the maze. "Remember," Liam said. "You can only tell the truth inside the labyrinth. Any falsehood will send you back to the beginning and deny you entrance ever again."

"Have you ever been here before?" Wendy whispered.

"No, but most of the lost boys I've met have."

"So you don't really know what to expect?"

He frowned. "Well, no, but we'll figure it out."

They shared a look of agreement and passed under the arch.

A whispering swish fell behind them and Wendy turned to find that the entrance had been closed off. There were no seams to indicate where the entrance had been. It was just gone. Inside the maze, the air that had been thick with humidity cooled considerably and felt drier. The sound of the waves hushed to a distant, pulsing murmur. Wendy pressed her hand to the cool, smooth glass wall that shimmered various forms of her reflection back at her.

She'd already been told that the maze contained no traps or dangers, only truth. She couldn't explain why that thought frightened her more than if the maze hid a chimera or a troll. Hadn't she been the one to say the truth didn't sound so bad?

"Here we go," Wendy whispered. She went first, choosing to turn right at the first passage, her hand brushing along the wall as she moved. She wound them through until they came to a dead end. She frowned at it. "Another way then."

Feeling foolish for having led them to a dead end so soon into the maze, she waited for Liam to take the lead. They'd barely walked fifteen feet before they came to another dead end.

The farther in they ventured, the more the air seemed to be electrified like the sky before the lightning that had separated her from Peter. It was charged with an energy that made it difficult for Wendy to focus on direction. All of her focus seemed to turn inward, and her reflection in the shimmering glass shifted. Crackling static whispers that hinted at faint splashes and cold fragility and reminded Wendy of stepping in slushy snow vibrated and echoed through the corridor. The corridor opened up into a small room.

"Share your pain," the slushy whispers said.

Alarmed, Wendy whirled to see who had spoken. Liam did the same. She was glad to see he looked as startled as she felt.

"Share your pain," the whispers said again.

Wendy squared her shoulders. This must be the first truth. "All right. I'll go first." She took a deep breath. "My pain comes from the loss of my father. His passing left a hole I don't know how to fill. A gloom in moments that should be joyous. That is my pain."

"No. No. No," the whispers said. Wendy could almost see a collection of phantoms shaking their heads in disappointment with her. *"That is pain. But not your deepest pain. Deepest. Deepest."*

Deepest? Whatever could that mean? What could hurt worse than her father being gone? Liam reached up and swept the back of his finger gently against her wet cheek. Was she crying? Yes. Why? Then the words poured from her. "My mother hardly smiles any longer. I am not enough to give her joy. All of her joy was swallowed up in the loss of my father. No matter what I do, I cannot fix it. I am inadequate at every turn. Not strong enough. Not good enough, or well-behaved enough. I am a disappointment in every way. I have failed her." As soon as the words were out, she knew them to be not just a truth, but *the* truth.

She heard the sound of a stifled sob and realized the sound was coming from her. Her legs shook from the exertion of saying the words out loud.

Liam lifted his hand and swept away more of her tears when the slushy voices began. *"You. Now you. Share your pain. Pain."*

Liam's hand froze and then slowly lowered. He turned away from Wendy as if hiding his face. "My mother had to raise me on her own in a society that judges women harshly for things beyond their control." His voice shook.

"No. No. No. That is pain. But not your deepest pain. Deepest. Deepest."

Liam swallowed hard, and for several long moments, Wendy worried he wouldn't answer, and they would be forced to go in through the front. But then he said, "My father served in the military and was stationed in another country. He never returned. Not because he had been wounded or killed in battle, but because he didn't want us. Didn't want *me*. My mother tried to hold the pieces of our lives together, but she was so shattered by the gossip and the financial strain. If it hadn't been for my uncle, we would never have survived. Even so . . . I didn't know how to be the man of the house. I was born into a role for which there was no role model. When I received my commission, I was so angry that he was not there to share the news with me. It was like a part of me was ripped out and left on some distant shore out of my reach, and I will never be able to recover myself. My own father didn't even want me born. I am unlovable."

An arched opening appeared with a soft swish.

Liam didn't move toward it. His hands were at his sides, clenched into tight fists. His jaw worked like he was grinding his teeth, and his breathing came in rapid, shallow puffs. He didn't cry like she did, but she wondered if he wanted to.

She took his hand in hers and tugged lightly to force him to open his fist. She smoothed his fingers out and said, "I know what we've revealed is the truth, or the door wouldn't have opened. But it is only a type of truth—the way we see ourselves. It isn't how others see us. These truths are only in our heads. Not reality. That is what I am seeing in these twisting, dancing reflections around me. I am seeing myself in all the ways I fear myself to be, but when I look at your reflection, it is solid. Strong. Steadfast. More, I have seen the truth of a person who loves you. Mrs. Connolly's face shone like a sun when you danced with her. She loves you very much. And her opinion is unimpeachable."

He squeezed her hand, his eyes never leaving her face. "Thank you, Wendy. Thank you." He bowed over her hand as if they were still at a ball and not in some bizarre maze. His breath teased across her skin as the gentle press of his lips to her hand sent shivers coursing along every nerve in her body. His thumb brushed the tips of her fingers in a way she could not help but respond to as she traced her pinky over his thumb.

Why could she not breathe? Why did she not even want to? *This is what it means to swoon,* she thought.

The moment was over too fast as he straightened. A slight frown creased his forehead as if he were confused, but the crease quickly disappeared. "We should continue."

He released her hand, taking with him the electric current that could have powered every light bulb in London.

Wendy finally remembered how to breathe.

She also said she would give him a kiss if he liked, but Peter did not know what she meant, and he held out his hand expectantly.

"Surely you know what a kiss is?" She asked, aghast.

"I shall know when you give it to me."

CHAPTER TWELVE

Wendy led the way this time, which she regretted because it meant she had to feel his gaze on her. What must he think with her hair in tangles and the bulky man's overcoat that she had managed to hang onto during the entire adventure through the jungle?

Wendy felt foolish admitting the pain of being incapable of repairing her mother's sorrow. She felt ashamed of such weak whimpering. But was her pain any different from his? Not really. She hadn't considered his pain weak whimpering. The longer they moved through the labyrinth while they talked and shared other small details about themselves, the easier it became to forget the burn of shame over her confession. At least, it was easy to forget until, after three or four wrong turns and dead ends, they found themselves in another small room.

"How many of these do you think there are?" Wendy asked, feeling as pale as he looked over the idea of doing more of such emotional unveiling.

"I don't know. I'd like to say that there won't be any more, but I would be lying, and then we'd be expelled from the maze and not be allowed back in. Best get through it quickly. I'll go first."

The slushy voices issued their command immediately after Liam declared himself willing to go first. It was as if they were responding to him. *"Share your fear."*

Liam cast a glance at Wendy. She saw his thoughts as clearly as if he'd spoken the words aloud. They had to hurry. The boy could go mad under prolonged nightmares. Liam dove into the new revelation of fear. "My father had no loyalty to anyone. Not to Mother. Not to me. Not to his country. How can I ever trust that I am not like him? How can I ever have a family of my own if I cannot trust my loyalty? What if I *am* just like him?"

The confession felt like an oil slick in her stomach. Did he want a family? Did pirates want such things?

The voices didn't ask him to dig deeper, which Wendy took as a sign that, yes, he really did want a family.

Interesting.

She didn't have long to ponder the new revelation since the whispers directed the request to her.

"You. Now you. Share your fear. Fear."

Wendy licked her lips and looked up as if trying to speak to the voices directly. She did not want to look at Liam for this one. "My mother wants me to marry to secure my place in society and to honor my father's memory, but I don't want to marry. Not yet. Not for a while. I want to be just Wendy Darling, not Mrs. Somebody-or-other. I'm afraid that I will be forced to marry and end up with someone I don't respect or love or even like. I'm afraid of being trapped."

Her cheeks burned.

Another arch hissed open. Liam moved to hurry through it when he noticed Wendy trembling where she stood. Following her previous example, he took her hand. "No weddings in Neverland," he said with a smile and a shrug. "You're safe for a bit. But if I may be so bold as to offer some advice. You should not marry to please others. I believe marriage is the one choice where we should allow ourselves to be selfish when we make it."

She sniffed. "You say that because you're a man."

WENDY'S EVER AFTER

141

"I say it because it is true. For everyone. Wait to marry until it's something you want." He pushed back one of the tangled curls from her face. "With *someone* you want. Then you won't be trapped. You'll be whole."

Wendy nodded at him. She made no move to let go of his hand, and he didn't pull it away. She was glad. Glad to have someone walking with her through this emotional upheaval. Glad that the other person was Liam Blackwell.

"How long do you think it has been since the boy was taken?" Liam asked her as they hurried to find the next room or, more hopefully, the exit.

"I don't know."

He released her hand. She would have thought his reaction a response to her answer, except he scrubbed his fingers through his hair in panic. "What if we're not in time to actually help him?"

"We'll be in time. Let's talk while we search. It'll help take our minds off our worries."

So they did. They talked of books. Jules Verne and the secrets the world could possibly hold inside of itself. L. Frank Baum and the possibility of worlds in other spaces. Sir Arthur Conan Doyle and the mystery that existed in the world as they knew it.

They talked about music. He was a fan of Chopin, and she was a fan of Tchaikovsky. She admitted that she found the latest ditties to be charming even if they weren't the works of great composers.

"All right," Wendy said. "Art, music, and literature are all fine and good, but let's talk about really important things."

"Such as?" He'd led them into another dead end.

She felt her panic rising with each wrong turn. "Such as weather," she said, keeping her voice light and pushing her panic down.

Liam laughed at her unexpected response. "You want to talk about the weather? The very thing that we've been trained our whole lives as the only true polite topic that's safe for people who don't know each other at all to discuss? It almost wounds me to think that we are no better than a weather conversation."

"But that's just it," Wendy insisted, also laughing and relieved that she could still laugh even with her insides coiled in fear of what was happening to the little boy. "It really is the only way to decide whether or not people are capable of friendship. Someone who loves the winter is unlikely to have any genuine fondness for someone who is fond of summer. They simply cannot spend time together in the same space."

"Never before has the idea of a weather conversation made me quite so nervous. So if I declare my favorite, and it is not in alliance with your favorite, you're saying we could never be friends?"

"Oh, not at all. I'm merely stating that if we are not compatible in that way, we would need to find a way to compromise. I believe all mature adults can compromise, don't you?"

"Certainly. And with that in mind, I will tell you that my favorite time of year is autumn. I like the crisper weather. Where the heat of summer has given way to cooler days and the world turns into a riot of color. Being on the sea for most of my childhood where my views consisted of varying blues and grays, I yearn for a vibrant color palette. Neverland has been good to me that way."

"Well, for the same reason you stated, I prefer spring. The world is finally free of the drudge of winter, and flowers are everywhere—even in the trees."

"I cannot abide winter," she said at the same time he said, "I detest winter."

They both laughed again. Some of the tension left her shoulders.

"So, I assume this means we're meant to be friends." He quirked his head to the side, awaiting her answer.

"Perhaps. It depends."

"On what?" he asked.

"We have yet to discuss which is better. Pies or cakes. The answer to this one is terribly important to me only because I have strong feelings regarding the answer."

WENDY'S EVER AFTER

"The answer is obvious, isn't it?" he asked.

"It's cakes," she said at the same time he said, "Pies."

"How can you say pies?" Wendy didn't bother hiding her revulsion.

"For many reasons." He ticked the reasons off on his fingers as they hurried down another corridor. "The contrast in texture is a surprise and delight to the senses. You get the flaky, buttery crust alongside the various fillings." Even as Wendy made a face, he went on ticking off another reason on his fingers. "They're visually appealing. The lattice work and clever designs in the crusts are beautiful. But most importantly," he lifted a third finger, "they can be whatever they want to be. Savory or sweet, apple, cherry, or meat. It hardly matters what ingredients you have; you can almost always make them into a pie of some sort or another."

"Hm," Wendy mused. "That was almost a convincing argument." She had to avoid looking too closely at the walls because she hadn't been wrong before. Her reflections within the walls felt skewed somehow. She didn't like it.

She noticed he avoided looking at the walls as well.

"Almost? What argument can you give for cakes?"

"You talk about the versatility of pies, but cakes are truly versatile. They can be made to fit any occasion. They can be grand or small, one tiny little cake for a single person or multi-tiered for a grand event. And you talk of latticework as beautiful, but pies are flat, boring little things. Cakes have true dimension. And they are synonymous with celebration. Weddings, birthdays, anniversaries, celebrations of any kind really."

"I can celebrate with a pie," he said, frowning as they hit another dead end and had to turn around.

"Certainly you can, though the celebration might be a little lackluster. I confess mostly it's the crust I don't like. I usually just scrape out the middle and eat that. I seldom eat the crust."

His mouth hung slack before he finally shook his head. "You're a monster."

She shrugged and gave a small laugh. She'd pretty much suspected that about herself all along.

"Thank you," he said after another wrong turn.

"For what?"

The glance he sent her way could have been called tender. "For working with such dedication to distract me from my worry."

"It's as much for me as it is for you." Still . . . she felt her ear tips warm from the appreciation.

They had to backtrack several more times before hitting the next room.

"Share your hidden desire," the voices whispered.

"Oh, for heaven's sake!" Wendy cast a terrified glance in Liam's direction.

For the briefest moment, she almost said that her hidden desire might be *him.* She was, after all, holding his hand again, though she wasn't quite sure when that had happened. She shoved the thought aside and labeled herself a fool for allowing the thought to surface.

"Control," Wendy said before Liam could answer. "I desire control over my fate."

They didn't ask her for her deepest desire. So she must have told the truth.

Relief flooded her mind since she wasn't sure she *had* spoken honestly, whether her answer was accepted or not.

The voices interrupted her emotional spiral and addressed Liam. *"Now you. Share your desire. Desire."*

Liam looked at her. The cool space of the labyrinth suddenly felt stiflingly hot. The heat of his gaze on her made it impossible to catch her own breath. She knew what he wanted to say. Hadn't she wanted to say something similar? Would he do it? Or would he come up with some other acceptable truth? He couldn't run away, nor could he lie. She wasn't sure she wanted to hear his answer. But she couldn't run away either. A child was at stake.

Liam closed his eyes. "Wendy Darling," he whispered.

"What did you say?" Wendy asked.

He opened his eyes and turned to her with a look that said he intended to apologize, but no apology came. How could it when he wasn't able to lie here in this place? "I have something I think I need to tell you," Liam said slowly. "I desire to be your friend. For you to care about me the way I'm coming to care for you." He looked like he wished the voices would stop him from speaking, but they seemed content to let him continue rambling. "I know we haven't known each other for very long, barely the work of two days, but—"

She interrupted him by placing her hand on his chest. Her touch wasn't meant to stop him from speaking, only that she meant to touch him in some way, and the impulse had been too strong to resist any longer. His heart pounded beneath her fingertips.

Liam swallowed hard, his Adam's apple bobbing. His hand curved over hers, and his head bent achingly closer. "What I mean to say is I think I—that is to say that I feel—"

She closed the distance, pressing her lips gently against his, silencing whatever declaration he'd been about to make with a declaration of her own. *I care about you too,* the kiss said. *I feel it too.*

Liam's other hand cradled her face, his fingertips trailing up her cheek, his fingers lingering over her skin, the warmth of him sending a shiver through her. She felt as though she had been breathing him in from the first moment she saw him. Now she was drinking him in, his lips so much softer than she'd ever imagined. Every movement deliberate, speaking aloud the words they had yet to say.

She melted against him as their kiss became a shared breath, a shared heartbeat.

He finally pulled away and rested his forehead against hers. "Yes," he said. "That was precisely what I wanted to say to you."

Another arched passage revealed itself.

Wendy stepped back, her eyes wide as she stared at him as if she couldn't quite believe what she was seeing. "We should go." She turned on a heel and quickly swished out of the room and into the new corridor.

"Are you all right?" he asked. Part of her wanted him to take her hand and pull her to a stop so they could talk. So that maybe he could kiss her again. Though he probably wouldn't because surely he wasn't a cur. At least she didn't think he was. Maybe he was. Maybe *she* was. Could a woman be a cur? Probably, since Wendy was certain if the chance was given to kiss him again, she'd take it without hesitation.

"I'm fine," she said.

Was she? Was she simply saying that to make him stop asking? London society would declare them practically engaged at such an occurrence as a kiss. Since she had no intention of marrying anytime soon, and since he'd declared he had no intention either, she was glad they weren't in London. Neverland didn't have those sorts of rules. At least, she didn't think it did. Oh dear, she hoped it didn't.

"I'm sorry if that confession came as a surprise to you," he said. He frowned. "Curses. Why can I never stop talking?" He shook his head, clearly startled to have said the last aloud. "It's just that I've never met anyone I can talk to so easily as you. I've never met anyone so determined and capable and charming, really."

He glanced around to the crystal walls with an evident hope they'd seen the last of the labyrinth's questions. Wendy agreed entirely. Three soul-flaying truths were quite enough, weren't they?

The maze, apparently, did not agree. After they raced through more tunnels, compelled by their need to find the boy—and probably more compelled to not have to discuss their emotions any further—they came upon another room. Though they made no wrong turns this time, they would never reach the boy if they kept having to stop and answer these infernal questions. The child would be a husk of deranged nightmares and shaking bones.

"Speak your regret." The voices demanded. The request felt different somehow from all the others.

As soon as the request was made, Liam's eyes met hers. His shoulders slumped. Why did he look like he hated admitting this new truth out loud? Was he going to say he regretted kissing her?

He opened his mouth. Only a puff of air came out. He tried

again. "I regret going to Neverland with my uncle that first time. I regret that that one decision has chained me to this island ever since."

"No. No. No. That is regret. But not your deepest regret. Deepest. Deepest."

Liam heaved a deep breath. Wendy lowered her head, sure he was about to say he regretted kissing her, but then he said, "I regret that I cannot go home until I complete my mission."

"No. No. No. That is regret. But not your deepest regret. Deepest. Deepest."

"I regret that I must kill Peter Pan."

Wendy's head shot up. Their gazes locked. After everything? He still planned to kill Peter? Her eyes clouded with tears she refused to let fall. She thought that he would change his mind, that getting to know her would stay his hand in this matter. But how could it when he was Captain Hook's nephew?

He held out his hands as if pleading for understanding. "It can be no surprise. You know what I must do."

"Now you." The voices prompted Wendy. *"Speak your regret. Regret."*

Her chin lifted. Her mouth flattened into a slash. Wendy held his gaze as she said the one thing she'd been afraid he would say. "I regret caring for and kissing Liam Blackwell."

Neverland had always begun to look a little dark and threatening by bedtime. Then unexplored patches arose in it and spread, black shadows moved about in them, the roar of the beasts of prey was quite different now, and above all, you lost the certainty that you would win.

CHAPTER THIRTEEN

The arched doorway whooshed open to a tunnel that was a black pit in contrast with the bright maze. Conflicted emotions swirled in Wendy. She truly cared about Liam Blackwell. She felt all the ways he was a good man. But it must have been true that she regretted those feelings, or the arched door wouldn't have opened and let them out.

In spite of that, it hadn't felt true exactly, even as she said it. It felt sad.

That was what she was now: sad.

Sad because Liam still intended to go through with his plot to kill Peter. She thought that trekking across the jungles of Neverland with him had shown her he was not the pirate, but deep down, that was all he was. A pirate.

She couldn't think about that now, not when she heard crying coming from inside the tunnel. A child's cry.

"Wendy," Liam started, but she lifted a hand to silence him and pointed into the tunnel. They couldn't talk about it now because their feelings didn't matter at the moment. Only the lost boy inside mattered.

Liam reached his hand into his pocket. "We need light," he whispered, which made her furious because *obviously* they needed light. Did he think she was incapable of coming up with that thought without him spelling out the details to her?

She tamped down her anger. She didn't have time to be furious with every little thing Liam said or didn't say. If only they had Starna with them now or Tinker Bell. The pixies could give off enough light to help them get through the passage.

That was when Wendy heard another noise, barely audible but there. Tinker Bell.

Tinker Bell was inside, which meant . . .

"Peter," she breathed in relief.

"Pan?" Liam did *not* sound relieved. His entire body tightened and straightened as he scanned his surroundings to see where Peter might be hiding.

"He's inside. You see? He did not forget what he was doing. He's here to rescue the boy. The least you could do at this point is try to forget that you're a deplorable pirate, find some semblance of honor, and help him."

She hated herself for being the one to make his face fall the way it did. The shock and hurt at her words were evident in the furrow of his brow and the downturn of his mouth. But she didn't take the words back or try to smooth them over with apologies. He was a pirate. She would do well to remember that.

A pirate you care about.

That thought wasn't going to be very helpful. She shoved it out of her mind. "If he's inside with Tinker Bell, it means they have her light. We only need something with a little light to get us to them."

"That's what I was saying before when you silenced me." He pulled his hand out of his pocket to reveal glowing moss.

"Where did you get that?"

"The cave where you left me to stumble around in the dark where I could have broken my neck. How do you think I made it out of there alive? And you call *me* a pirate." He mumbled the last.

"We don't have time to bicker. We need to get the boy. You were the one who said we had to do it before nightfall. And look." She pointed up. "The sun's setting."

"Then let's stop wasting time." He broke the handful of moss into two sections and handed her half of it before he plunged ahead into the darkness.

Wendy hurried after him, worried over what might happen if he reached Peter first. Liam could not be trusted where Peter was concerned.

But was he wrong? She thought about Mrs. Connolly and her son. Was *Peter* a pirate, too, pillaging the hopes and dreams of a young mother? The child in the cave cried out again. Wendy quickened her steps. She couldn't think about Peter's possible piracy now. She had to focus on the boy. Not Liam. Not Peter. Not pirate. Not villain. The lost boy was all that mattered at the moment.

The soft purple glow of the moss gave enough light to see the passage they were in. The walls were slick with water sweating through. Patches of damp moss clung to the stone, and the smell of musty decay filled the air. Wendy kept a quick but quiet pace—rushing toward the faint glimmer and the soft chime of Tinker Bell.

She turned a bend in the passage. There he was. Peter.

She thought she would be relieved to see him, but she only felt anger and confusion. *Had* he stolen those boys?

She had to set aside that question, that worry. She was there for the lost boy.

"Wendy." Peter had been crouching down and talking to Tinker Bell who was standing on a rock. He straightened and said much too loudly, "How did you get here?"

"Shh, Peter," Wendy whispered. "You'll alert the shadow conjurer that we're here."

Tinker Bell nodded her agreement.

"You brought a pirate?" Peter asked, seeing Liam ahead of Wendy. At least he said this more quietly.

"She brought *help*," Liam said with a low growl in his tone.

Peter shrugged. "That's a different kind of game, but okay. I guess."

"Do you have a plan?" Wendy asked before Liam could beat Peter for calling saving the lost boy a game.

"Sure I do."

"Well, don't wait for an invitation, mate," Liam said. "Spill it."

Peter made a face at Liam.

Wendy didn't know why that display of childishness embarrassed her, but it did. "Just tell us, Peter."

"Okay. Okay. So I'm going to be a distraction, flying around and causing a ruckus and stuff. That'll get the shadow snakes and dream reapers to go after me. Then Tink'll get Theo, and we'll be on our way."

"A little overly simplistic," Liam whispered with a scoff.

"Scared?" Peter asked, his mouth quirked to the side in a smirk.

"Not hardly," Liam said. "There's a difference between fear and intelligence. I'd like us to have a genuine strategy. What about the shadow conjurer? Who gets *her* out of the way?"

"I'm supposed to make a trade. She wants my flute, but Tink says she'll use it to try to control the pixies. So we're going to use the sunlight and this." Peter held out a silver casing with a cracked pocket mirror inside it.

Liam made another noise low in his throat. It didn't seem to matter what Peter said, Liam was determined to be annoyed by it. "So we have no strategy," Liam said. "There's no time to make one now. The sun is setting. We don't have much time before it's gone entirely, and then the real nightmare starts for that poor boy."

"Then we should hurry. Okay, Tink. You heard the pirate. Let's go." Peter lifted off the ground and flew behind Tinker Bell.

Determined not to be left behind in the dark passage, Wendy lost no time in following. Liam kept step with her. Peter stopped suddenly. "Tink, hide your light and wait here 'til it's all clear," he said. When he held out his hat to her, Tinker Bell ducked beneath it. Then, with a vibrant crowing sound, Peter flew out into the open cavern and began flying erratically around. He called several taunts to the shadows. The deepest, darkest parts of the cave slithered forward to give chase. Peter flew into the passage off to the left. Tinker Bell vacated her hiding place and flew to an alcove. Once she was there, her light shone brightly on what had been hidden in that alcove. A cage with a small boy huddled inside.

Tinker Bell pulled at the latch but couldn't get it to come free. She chimed a pixie's version of cursing and tugged harder.

"It's stuck," Wendy whispered and dashed forward, hurtling over a small pool of standing water. She grabbed the latch and yanked with all her might until it opened. A large lumbering creature of shadow that Wendy could only assume was a dream reaper peeled away from the darkness of the cave walls and wrapped its clawed hand around Tinker Bell, pulling her to the ground where she struggled in vain to free herself.

Desperate to free little Theo from his cage, Wendy reached in to grab the boy, who had yet to even look up from where he huddled, when a gong vibrated through the air. The deep thrum hurt Wendy's ears even as it felt familiar. It was like a darker, corrupted tone of Tinker Bell's or Starna's chimes. It sounded like a warped music box. Unsettled, Wendy scanned the darkness to try to find the source of the noise.

Another shadow peeled away from the wall and began flying toward the cage.

A pixie?

Could a pixie be all darkness and shadow like that?

"Wendy!" Liam called as he hurled his glowing moss at the flying shadow. He struck it dead on. A squealing trill echoed through the cavern as the creature was swatted to the side. "Get the boy!" Liam yelled.

Wendy seized the boy and pulled him out of the cage. She cradled him in her arms and stood to run when the dark pixie caught Wendy by her hair and pulled her back. "Peter!" Wendy cried out. He still had the mirror. She needed him to use it to reflect light into the cave. "Peter! Help!" The dark pixie yanked harder on Wendy's hair, pulling her down to the ground. Wendy managed to keep the boy in her arms without dropping him, but the dark pixie had flown around her and seemed to be diving for her eyes.

Taking her lead from Liam, Wendy reached into her pocket where she'd shoved the glowing moss and hurled it at the creature.

Another squeal of anguish and then a snarl came from the creature as it gnashed its teeth and called forth another reaper. This one slid toward Wendy, holding out a clawed finger as it approached. What was it Peter and Liam had said? The dream reaper would feed on her hopes and dreams. The reaper came from one direction while the dark pixie came from the other, diving again for Wendy, determined to make her let go of the boy. Wendy had nothing else to fight back with, and Peter still hadn't returned from where he'd led away the other creatures. The sun was surely setting by now. They were too late. And now they would all be caught in the nightmares of the shadows.

The dream reaper stretched out his clawed finger to Wendy's forehead and sliced a line down to her nose. Her hope leaked out of her through the open wound like blood. She felt herself emptying of all light. She wanted to put her hands up on her forehead to stop the leak, but the boy. The lost boy Peter had called Theo. His tiny body lay in her arms, completely defenseless. She couldn't let him go. She *wouldn't*. Wendy trembled until her body shook violently. So much darkness! No hope. No light. Just swirling nightmares and despair. And something hiding in the shadows—something that made the tick tick tick sound of a clock measuring seconds.

She couldn't think about what that sound might mean. Wendy felt herself crumbling, caving in, when a flash of light appeared from the mouth of the cavern. She let out a stifled sob at how impossibly bright and joyful that pure light felt to her. Peter had returned at last to save her. The flash beamed in, straight like an arrow, until it struck the dark pixie's back. The shadow fairy staggered forward under the impact, momentarily stunned. The light illuminated her face, narrow and perfect but shrouded in a mask of fury and hate. It really was a pixie. How could a pixie go dark? The light spread out from her back, encompassing the rest of her body all the way to the tips of her delicate wings. The dream reaper crumbled in a fall of ashy smoke, releasing Wendy's mind.

Had they done it? Had they won? But no. The dark fairy's form trembled. She howled, then she shook off the light in golden flakes and turned back to Wendy with a look of savage wrath.

Wendy shrank back against the outside of the cage and clutched the little boy tighter. Her eyes were wide, and she felt her lip trembling. The fairy approached her with murder in its eyes. Wendy's mind raced. This wasn't possible. Fairies were good and light and hope and joy. She couldn't believe this was how she would meet her end.

That was it.

She couldn't *believe*.

The fairy was almost to her. She had only moments.

"I don't believe in dark fairies!" Wendy shouted at the top of her lungs.

The fairy stopped midair as if she'd run into an invisible wall. Then she fell to the ground dead.

They'd done it. Because Peter had saved her, she'd been able to defeat the dark fairy once and for all.

Except when Wendy turned her smile on him, it was Liam standing there. Peter was nowhere to be seen.

Disappointment shook Wendy to the core.

The pirate had saved her, not Peter. Wendy puffed out a breath. "Is it dead?"

"Aye, that it is. Don't anyone dare clap for that little beast," Liam said. He clambered over the rocks to Wendy, his hands at her shoulders and his eyes searching her face. "Are you all right?"

She felt her forehead for any sort of wound but her skin was unbroken. "No. Yes. I will be. You saved me. Thank you."

"What I did didn't work. Rather useless, this." He held up a shiny silver case. "It's a fine compass, but not much for a weapon, apparently."

"But it did work. It slowed the fairy down and melted the reaper. It freed my mind and gave me the time to think of what I could do. Thank you."

"Of course. I'd never let anything happen to you." His eyes finally fell to young Theo in her arms. "How's the lad?"

She looked down into the small face and felt her heart constrict. "He's not awake. I don't know if he's all right or not. He's breathing, so that's good, and he has no visible wounds."

"We need to get him out of here." Liam held out his hand to her.

Wendy stood with Liam's assistance and readjusted the boy in her arms so she could more easily hold him. They made their way to the mouth of the cavern and exited around the sharp rocks that made up the teeth of the skull shape that gave the small island its name.

"Do you think all the shadow creatures are gone?" she asked Liam.

"It seems probable. You saw that reaper disintegrate when its master was damaged."

"But a dark pixie? How is that even possible?"

"Choices. I can't say what the creature's reasons would have been, but it clearly chose darkness. And I think my choice, in the future, is to be nicer to pixies. I don't want my choices to influence another plague of shadow spawn."

Wendy gave a tired chuckle. "Starna will be glad to hear it." The weight of the child felt heavier by the moment. Wendy was so tired, having gone with little sleep and even less to eat. She was spent. "I'll never be able to carry him back to the lost boys from here."

"Tinker Bell will take him." That came from Peter, who'd flown out of the cavern with Tinker Bell, who still looked dazed from her time with the reaper.

"She's not in good enough condition to fly with the lad," Liam said with a tone that said he felt that should have been obvious to everyone. "I'll carry him." He gently took Theo and turned him so the boy's body was tucked against his shoulder.

"Flying's faster." Peter put his hands on his hips, looking like a defiant and small child, especially compared to Liam. "And you can't fly. The rest of us can."

"I can't right now." Wendy hated admitting such a thing to Peter, who would see it as weakness. But the reaper had done its damage. It would take time to recover.

"As if I would trust a boy to you," Liam said.

"I don't see why not." Peter looked insulted by the very idea.

Liam pointed to his scar. "Did you forget what you did to me when I was just a boy?" Liam looked like he wanted to pull a sword on Peter. "Besides," he said instead. "Flying with the boy is dangerous. He needs a doctor. We have one on the *Jolly Roger*." Liam gave a look that dared anyone to argue with him.

Arguing was exactly what Wendy intended. "You're absolutely *not* going to take a lost boy onto a pirate ship. That's the worst sort of mischief I've ever heard."

"He needs a neverflower," Peter said. "It'll heal him."

Tinker Bell chimed her little bells.

Wendy turned to Peter. "I thought you said they were running low, not that they were all gone."

Peter frowned. "They're not all gone. I know where one is. It's by the forget-me-not pools. I can fly him there."

"I dare you to try to take this boy from my care." Liam leveled a look at Peter that said Peter would lose that fight. And though Wendy believed in Peter's skill, she didn't doubt that Liam would win.

She thought about what he'd said to her in the labyrinth. Mrs. Connolly's son was stolen.

"Flying's faster," Peter puffed out his cheeks and scowled.

"Not arguing is faster," Wendy interrupted whatever Liam had opened his mouth to say in response. "We have to walk. Lead the way."

Tinker Bell took the lead. The tide was rising again, but a sliver of land still existed, though the waves crashed in and soaked their feet on occasion. Well, they soaked Liam's and Wendy's feet. Tinker Bell and Peter flew above them.

Everything Liam had told Wendy about Peter taking children marched through her thoughts as if on parade. She tried not to focus on that and instead on keeping her feet under her and moving forward. Wendy was hot, thirsty, exhausted, and furious. Furious that Peter hadn't been the one to save her. Furious that she couldn't stop thinking about Liam and the warmth and tenderness of his kiss. Furious that she doubted Peter.

How could she doubt him?

She glanced up at him, confusion soaking her soul more than the ocean had soaked her feet.

She was angry with him, but that didn't stop her heart from leaping with a certain type of joy at being with him again. That made her angry with herself for being so muddled in her thoughts.

Peter finally landed lightly next to her and began walking by her side. "Why, Wendy," he said. "It seems like you're angry with me."

"I *am* angry with you." She glanced up at Liam, who was following closely behind Tinker Bell. She slowed to let him get farther ahead. "Oh Peter, how could you have?"

"I can see why you're confused by some of the things that I do. I'm pretty complicated."

Wendy would have once laughed at such a saying. Peter was not at all complicated. He was just a silly little boy. A selfish, horrible, wretched little boy. Liam had been right. Liam, of course, was not right about trying to kill Peter. There were far better ways of dealing with children. Sending them to bed without supper. Making them pull all the weeds in the garden. Having them do pages and pages of mathematics. Of course, the best way to teach a child how to treat people, next to setting a good example, was to have them read a book that showed examples of compassion and empathy.

"Is it true that you stole Starkey from his mother? Did you know that she still cries for her son all the time because you stole him from her?"

"That doesn't sound right, Wendy. I never steal anybody." He looked quite cross to be accused of such a thing. "I didn't know you could tell lies." Peter looked as scandalized as she felt.

She shook her head sadly. "It's *not* a lie. I've met his mother. I've seen her sadness. He had a home. And you took him from that home."

Peter waved a hand. "How can she still be crying about him being gone? Starkey hasn't been here for . . . well . . . for forever. He decided he needed to grow up and then went off and joined the pirates. He tried to blow a hole through my middle with one of those cannons." Peter lifted his shirt as if to show her the evidence. Of course, there wasn't any evidence because if Starkey had *actually* blown a hole through his center, Peter would no longer be breathing.

"Peter, stop being such a child!"

"You're being awful mean." His cheeks grew red, puffing out just like she imagined a toddler's would when throwing a tantrum.

Wendy stamped her foot, even while she walked, and pointed a finger at him. "How dare you? How dare you accuse me of being cruel when *you* were the one who stole a child? And not just one. You stole many children! You stole *me*."

Peter was shaking his head hard. "Nuh-uh. You were crying. They're all crying when I go to them. They all want me to help them. *You* wanted my help."

"I was not crying! *You* were the one crying when we first met. *You*. Not me!" she shouted. "Neverland was supposed to be magical." Wendy was ranting and marching forward faster now, swatting at the big glossy leaves around her and pretending it was either Liam's or Peter's head. She vacillated which one she wanted to punch more. "Neverland was supposed to be fun and joyful. But now I know it

160   JULIE WRIGHT

to be nothing more than a place of shadow and nightmare. A pixie went dark! You're a child stealer! How can that happen?"

Peter flew up in front of her, keeping just ahead on his bed of air. His scowl was deep enough to be a chasm. "You've got it all wrong."

"Do I? Then enlighten me. What is the alternate story to you snatching children away from their mothers? Tell me how you ended up with my dear friend's son, Starkey."

Though it seemed impossible, his scowl actually deepened as if, for the first time, Peter Pan was trying to think hard about something. "I can't remember. But I know what can help. You'll see. Let's get going."

"I'm not going anywhere with you. Child stealers do not make very good companions." She hated how childish her own behavior was becoming, especially since she was, of course, absolutely going somewhere with him. She was going with him to help Theo get better.

Peter didn't seem to mind that she was acting petulant and throwing her own version of a tantrum. He grabbed her hand anyway and started tugging her along faster. "But you'll understand once you see. We have to go there anyway to get the neverflower."

Wendy pulled away and folded her arms again. She wouldn't be tugged along.

Peter shrugged. "Suit yourself. Well then, you best catch up since you can't fly."

The insult struck her hard, but she nodded. She felt a spark of something in her that said she could fly if she could find the right happy thought, but her mind was a jumble. The spark seemed to flare whenever that jumble tried to settle on the moment she and Liam had truthed their way into a first kiss.

No. Not first kiss.

Only kiss.

There would never be another one.

Wendy would have to be all right with that. She told herself she was perfectly fine and completely indifferent to the idea of kissing

Liam, but her burning cheeks told her what a liar she was. And then the spark of flying would blow out again, confirming the truth that Wendy was not fine at all with not kissing Liam ever again, which made Wendy feel heavy and rooted to the ground.

Time does wear on in the Neverland,
where it is calculated by moons and
suns, and there are ever so many more
of them than on the mainland.

CHAPTER FOURTEEN

Liam had to readjust the boy on his shoulder several times. He continued on in silence as they scrambled over rocks, hiked up one side of a mountain, and slid back down the other side. Even though he didn't admit it out loud, Wendy knew he wouldn't last much longer. She tried to take custody of Theo to give Liam a break, but he wouldn't hear of it. Annoying, irritating man.

Night had fully settled, but Tinker Bell's light shone brightly enough to guide their steps. Though the dense jungle teemed with noises and life, no shadow serpents slithered through the plants to bite at them. Had they truly solved the shadow problem that had plagued the island? She wanted to believe it, but the wrongness of the island polluted every breath she took of Neverland air, every step she made on Neverland soil. The island's balance had tilted precariously, so any breeze or whim could send it crashing in on itself.

They went deep into the jungle, every now and again spying a pixie glowing in the underbrush before it darted away. Some of the giant ferns emitted a soft glow, and, when Wendy almost stumbled into a fairy ring, Peter pulled her back. "You don't want to do that," he insisted.

"Why not?" she asked.

"It's a gate ring. It'll make you appear somewhere else on the island."

"You mean to tell me we could have taken a gate to wherever we're going?" Liam snapped. Wendy couldn't help but agree.

"Of course not. This is a one-way gate. It only goes *from* here. It doesn't come *to* here. There aren't gates where we're going."

Liam harrumphed at that, clearly not believing him. But Tinker Bell chimed her agreement.

When Liam stumbled again, Wendy was about to insist he relinquish his charge, but Peter finally pulled back a screen of vines and revealed a clearing tucked into the forest. Luminescent plant life glowed all around the clearing. At the far end, a waterfall trickled over a tiny cave and fell into a group of three pools that flowed one into the other. They took up the center of the clearing and held the bluest water Wendy had ever seen in her life. They reminded her of Liam's eyes.

In her awe and reverence for the ethereal beauty, Wendy must have forgotten that she was angry with Peter because she asked, "Where are we? What is this place?"

"Forget-me-not pools. Whenever I've forgotten something really important that I need to remember, I come here. The water tells me all I need to know. You wanted to know about Starkey."

"We'll heal the lad before we do anything else, Pan," Liam said, the warning evident in his tone.

Pan flapped his hand in a wave of dismissal. "Oh sure. We can do that, I guess."

He guessed? Was he not concerned for the welfare of one of his own lost boys? She thought of what Liam had said. He'd called Peter a child thief. Could she really expect a child thief to be concerned with anything but his own selfishness?

"The neverflower's around here somewhere. We'll have to look for it," Peter said.

"What does it look like?" Wendy asked.

Peter smiled at her. "It's pretty."

Was Peter meaning the flower or her? The look he gave left her unsure of the answer. Not sure why she cared what he thought of the comment, Wendy glanced over to Liam to find him glowering at Peter. "What does it look like *specifically*, imp?" Liam asked Peter.

Peter didn't seem to notice that Liam clearly wanted to strangle him right then and there because he went into a matter-of-fact description. "It has long petals that look like Tinker Bell's wings. They're clear and shiny and bright. And in the center, there's golden liquid like starlight. Well, I mean, *like* starlight because it *is* starlight." He turned and went to work looking with the rest of them.

Wendy felt as though she'd looked everywhere. It was hard to locate one glowing plant when it seemed they were all glowing in their own way.

Theo had been laid out in a patch of soft grasses. He'd begun shivering and crying out like he was fighting monsters in his sleep. His nightmares had begun in earnest. They had to hurry.

Wendy gave a quick inspection to every glowing flower and shrub in the vicinity and had almost lost hope, but then Liam moved aside a large green leaf and gasped. Wendy, who was searching close to his location, went over to see what could elicit such a gasp from the pirate. She couldn't help herself. She gasped too when she saw the tiny, iridescent flower, which had been bent at a strange angle, as if someone had already tried to scoop out its center.

Liam leaned down to inspect it, and as he touched the petals, some of the golden center spilled out onto his fingers and over the several cuts and bruises on the back of his hand. And just like that, his cuts closed up.

"Healing," he murmured.

For a moment, Wendy worried he would dip in his finger and rub the golden liquid over all the scrapes on his face and arms. She couldn't deny the temptation of the pull toward the flower—the desire to heal her own aching body swelling inside her chest.

Liam cleared his throat and stepped back. "This healing is for the lad. I would never do what you're thinking." He said this as if he knew her thoughts but also in a way that was more like he was speaking to himself.

So he had been tempted too.

"We found it!" Wendy called to the others with a relieved laugh. "If we didn't need it, we could bottle this up and open up an apothecary shop in London. We'd be wealthier than the king within a week."

Liam opened a flask and collected the rest of the center of the flower. "Thank you, little blossom," he said. "It's a generous gift you give."

He held up his flask to show Wendy his intentions were pure and promptly took it to Theo. They all converged on the boy at the same time. "Do we pour it on him? Into his mouth? What?" Liam asked, clearly hating that he had to ask Peter for any information.

"He doesn't have any injuries to pour it on." Peter said this like Liam was a fool for having asked. Theo didn't have external injuries, but he was convulsing now, his body reacting to the nightmares in his mind.

"His injuries are all internal," Wendy said. "He should drink it." She wasn't sure that was really the right idea, but when Tinker Bell made a noise that sounded like agreement, that apparently decided it for Liam. He opened the boy's mouth and poured.

Nothing happened.

"Did it work?" Liam asked, echoing the question ricocheting through Wendy's mind. Anxiety gnawed on her stomach. If it didn't work, Liam was likely to cut Peter down right then and there.

"Look," Wendy said.

The boy stopped convulsing. His whimpers and cries subsided. Theo's features, which had been pinched and tense, softened and relaxed. He opened his eyes briefly, blinking up at the group surrounding him, and murmured the word, "Better." Then he smiled, rolled to his side, and went to sleep.

"It worked," Peter said as if he'd never doubted it would.

"*How* did that work?" Wendy asked.

Peter shrugged. "It always does."

Wendy sat back and heaved a sigh of relief. Then she fixed Peter with a look.

"What about that other thing?" she asked. "You said you can show me proof that you didn't steal Mrs. Connolly's son."

"I can," Peter said and went to the side of the largest pool. Wendy followed. Liam did too, compelled by curiosity. Tinker Bell was either bored or unconcerned because she flew away.

"How does it work?" Wendy asked. It was just water. How could it prove or disprove anything?

"It's a lot like pixie dust," Peter said. "You gotta think about it. You think of the thing that's bothering you. The memory that itches at the back of your mind that you can't quite reach to scratch. And then the water shows you what you want to remember."

Wendy took a few tentative steps closer to the water. "Does it have to be my memory, or can I access somebody else's memory?"

Peter made a face. "Why would I want to be scratching around in somebody else's memories? How boring. That's not fun at all. Nobody else is as interesting as I am."

"Arrogant hobgoblin," Liam said.

Peter didn't seem too bothered by the insult. He seemed to actually take a little pride in being called arrogant. He smirked at Liam. "If you say so." Then he said to Wendy, "If you're so keen on rooting through another person's memories, go ahead and try it."

Wendy crept closer to the water's edge until she was looking down at the smooth, mirror-like surface. Nothing happened.

Peter also looked into the water, clearly curious about this new experiment they were trying. "Are you thinking of something? Or are you just sitting there? It's hard to tell."

"Of course I'm thinking of something. I thought of my mother's wedding day. I wanted to see her in her dress, see the look of happiness as she and father joined hands and became a family. But nothing." Wendy slumped her shoulders. She had so hoped to see that memory.

Peter nudged Wendy over just a little bit, not enough to be a shove exactly, but certainly enough to be impolite. Wendy glowered at him. But he didn't seem to care as he closed his eyes for a moment before popping them open again and staring into the water.

"Naw. I guess it doesn't work for other people's memories."

"Who did you try to see?" she asked.

Peter's expression darkened. "Hook on the day he decided to betray me."

Liam scoffed at that.

"Anyway, it's not important," Peter said. "You're here to see my memories, and because I'm here with you, the pool will show you." He closed his eyes again for a moment and then popped them open and peered down into the water. Wendy did too. So did Liam.

The brilliant blue surface rippled until it flattened out again and an image appeared. Wendy saw everything as if through Peter's eyes. She saw the earth below her since Peter was flying at the time of this particular memory. It took Wendy a moment to recognize where Peter was. Hyde Park. It was strange to see it from this point of view but also exhilarating. She felt fairly certain no one else had ever seen it from above this way, except maybe people who flew hot air balloons.

Down below, near the water's edge, Wendy saw a small child toddling alone without a mother or a father or a nanny or an older sibling to hold their hand. Farther from the child, an older woman in a nanny's uniform leaned against a tree and slept while her charge had gotten away from her. The little boy was crying as Peter had told Wendy they all did.

Wendy gasped aloud and covered her mouth with her hand in alarm when she realized the child was toddling straight toward the water. Liam shared her terror and frantically looked around but could see no one else who would help the child. And then the child was in the water, bobbing for a brief moment before disappearing beneath the surface. Peter dove in after the boy, pulled him back up out of the water, and looked down into the child's dripping face.

"You're not breathing." An echoey voice came from the pool. It was Peter's voice from the past. "Well, that won't do at all. But I know someone who can help." Peter bundled the child up in his arms and flew away with him. He flew over oceans and through clouds. He arrived at Neverland a great deal faster than seemed possible. When Wendy had traveled between the worlds, it had taken an age. Peter gently landed on a rock in the mermaid lagoon where the mermaids were busy fussing with their hair and laughing about the sailors that they had teased that day. Mermaids were a bunch of terrible gossips.

"He breathed water but without a mermaid's help," Peter from the past said to the mermaids. "When they're little like this, they don't always know that that's not how it works, so now he's broken. Can you fix him?"

The mermaids practically tripped over their tails to be of service to Peter—the flirts. It was no big secret to anyone that all of the mermaids felt Peter loved them best and would do anything to stay in his good favor. The mermaid with silky green hair and silver eyes took the boy in her arms and pressed her lips to his mouth.

After a moment, she pulled away, and the little boy sputtered out water and seemed to be breathing normally again. Wendy watched with fascination.

"Is that child Starkey?" Wendy asked softly.

"Yep," Peter said. "I remember now that he was an awful lot of trouble 'til he got big enough to stay away from the water. I was always having to scoop him out of one disaster or another." Peter glared as if irritated with the child from his past.

"You saved his life." Wendy frowned, revisiting her own memories of the night Peter had taken her to Neverland. Had she been crying like he'd said? She looked down at the memory of the tiny boy breathing again. Maybe she had been? Liam had been wrong about Peter. He looked like he hated being wrong. Peter really hadn't stolen the child. He'd saved him. Had he saved the others as well? Had it gone in much the same way?

Would Liam tell Hook and the rest of the pirates? They deserved to know the truth. Then they could end this feud. They could go back to their lives. Liam had said Hook intended to kill Peter so he could stop Peter from stealing children. But now that they had proof he'd been rescuing them, would Neverland become a place of peace?

Liam had also said he wanted his own life in London. This new revelation meant that Liam could live without the burden of defeating his uncle's greatest foe. It meant Liam could leave.

That thought filled Wendy with something like joy—relief to think Liam would go back with her to London.

Wendy's vision blurred with unshed tears. "You heard him crying, and you saved his life, just like you said."

Peter put his hands behind his head and fell back without hitting the ground, the air catching him as if cradling him in a hammock. "Course I did. I'm a hero. Not everyone thinks so, though. Do you know that Hook has been telling people that I never grow up because I steal the youth of my lost boys? Isn't that silly? Why would I need to do that when I can just use the time-twister vines?"

Liam shot a guilty look at Wendy. In an obvious attempt to change the subject, he asked, "What's a time-twister vine?"

The question had merit. Forget-me-not pools, healing flowers from starlight, time-twister vines. What else was there here in this magical clearing?

"Hook knows about the time-twister vines. I swore him to secrecy, but I'm surprised he didn't tell you. He broke every other promise he made me, so I figured he probably broke all of them. But maybe he just forgot, like he forgot to keep his promises. Anyway, it's the vine that climbs the trees around the forget-me-not pools." Peter pointed to a creamy orange vine that twisted around the trunk of an evergreen tree.

Wendy cocked her head to the side and stood, brushing the dirt and leaves from the tattered remnants of her skirt, though it did little good. "Do you eat it?"

Peter made a face. "Blech! No. You just touch it. It only pulls away a few seconds at first, but the longer you touch it, the faster it twists time away. I visit the vines every year on my birthday."

"When is your birthday?" Wendy asked.

Peter shrugged. "Beats me." He eyed her for a moment, clearly not approving of what he saw. "You should give it a try, Wendy."

"What? No. I shouldn't."

"But if you did, we could be the same age again. You could stay here with me." Peter actually looked vulnerable to be making such a request, and Wendy considered all the reasons why she wanted to do as he asked.

Liam looked like he wanted to smack that request right out of Peter's mouth.

Even so, Wendy's fingers stretched out toward the vine. To touch it and take away some of her years . . . to remain young and not have the burden of adulthood looming over her . . . pretending to be a mother and being one in truth were not the same thing at all. Her vision seemed distorted. Everyone else faded into the background until she saw nothing but the vine.

Liam straightened and tensed, his movement bringing her back to herself.

Wendy pulled back just as Liam began to spring forward. Was he planning on snatching her hand away? Was he going to stop her?

She shook her head clear of the trance.

"Bad form, imp," Liam said. "Dangling a curse in front of a person and calling it a blessing."

"I wasn't inviting *you*, pirate." Peter took Wendy's hand, making Liam growl low in his throat. Wendy shot him a disapproving look. Why did he keep growling at Peter? Liam wasn't an animal. But it seemed Peter brought the worst out in Liam.

"Come on, Wendy." Peter tugged on her hand. "We need to get Theo back to the lost boys so he can sleep in his own bed. And pirates aren't invited to the lost boys' hideout."

Wendy looked down at her hand in Peter's and gently pulled it away. Wendy gently picked the boy up.

"I can do it," Liam offered.

"I'm quite refreshed," she said coolly, thinking of Liam's confession that he intended to kill Peter. Did he still feel that way?

When Liam didn't move, Wendy raised an eyebrow at him. "Kindly step aside so I may pass."

She wasn't sure why she was mad. Was she angry at Liam? Sure, he'd told her that he thought Peter was a villain. And sure, he'd told her that he intended to kill Peter. And then she had actually accused Peter to his face of being a monster and basically forced Peter to defend himself—all because Liam had made her doubt herself. But had Liam done that? Should she be angry with herself for doubting more than with Liam for instigating that doubt?

But it wasn't just that she was angry. She could handle that emotion. It was the confusion she couldn't handle. She had told the labyrinth that she regretted kissing Liam—that she regretted caring for him. Obviously, that was true, or they would never have made it out. That truth did not erase the other, more inconvenient, truth. She *did* care for Liam. For a while there, she had thought they were both fighting on the side of right. Were they on the same side now?

Wendy glanced back to discover that Liam was not behind her as she had expected him to be.

That was the problem, wasn't it?

He was not where she expected him to be.

And she wasn't sure if he ever would be.

Wendy still felt uneasy about everything she had seen, but more, she felt uneasy about everything she had felt while she'd been within that clearing.

I love Peter. That had been her driving thought as her fingers stretched out toward the time-twister vine. Having Peter bring her back to Neverland had once been the only thing she'd thought about for years. The problem was that she was not *in love* with Peter. She'd grown up enough to know the difference between those two things.

Peter remained trapped in his childhood while she'd moved on. They were no longer the same. Not like her and Liam. As much as she felt betrayed by the fact that Liam had made her doubt Peter and, more importantly, doubt herself, he had truly believed the lies Hook had told him. He'd believed that Peter was some demon kidnapper who needed to be stopped before he struck again. Liam had been wrong, and now he knew how wrong he'd been, though he hadn't apologized. Peter was guilty of absurd amounts of bravado and an overabundance of self-importance and childish selfishness, but he was no villain.

Liam was not the villain either.

Hook was the one who had created all those lies and spread them like malicious poison.

Hook was the villain.

"Build a house?" exclaimed John.

"For the Wendy," said Curly.

"For Wendy?" John said, aghast. "Why, she is only a girl!"

"That," explained Curly, "is why we are her servants."

CHAPTER FIFTEEN

Wendy and Peter had not gone too far from the forget-me-not pools when Liam finally caught up to them. Peter scowled and rolled his eyes while muttering, "Pirate."

Wendy tried not to notice. In an attempt to ignore the tension between Liam and Peter, she focused on her feet and the coral-colored stones making a bridge across the stream. Hoping to introduce a lighter and happier form of conversation, she was about to remark on how lovely and flat and perfect the stones were for stepping on when the color revived a memory. A coral-colored mermaid held captive in Hook's ship.

"What would Hook want with a mermaid?" she asked Peter.

"Oh, there are lots of reasons a pirate like him would want one." He said the word pirate a little louder than necessary and turned to Liam so Liam would know he was being called a name. He then turned back to Wendy. "Hook probably thinks the mermaids know how to find me, which they do, but no mermaid worth her salt would ever give me up. And then there's the magic. A mermaid has a voice of enchantment so that she can mesmerize and control anyone who can hear her. Hook could get her to charm his crew to be more loyal, or charm his enemies so they don't want to fight him." Peter laughed. "That'd be something a pirate like him might be interested in since his fighting skills aren't much to brag about. It's how he ended up losing a hand."

Wendy didn't have the patience to listen to Peter boast over the times he'd bested Hook. "Wouldn't she be able to charm him to let her go?"

Peter shook his head and started to fly instead of hop over the boulders they'd come across. "He'd keep his ears plugged if he ever got too close to her. Hook might be an evil, rotten pirate," he turned to Liam again to make sure Liam knew that was what he thought of him, "but he isn't stupid."

Wendy considered this before saying, "I saw a mermaid locked up in a glass case on his ship. She was the color of those rocks there." Wendy pointed.

"What?" Peter landed on the ground with a thump. "Why didn't you say so before?"

"I forgot. I'm sorry. There's been quite a lot happening."

"Mira's been missing for . . . well for forever. Her mother and father have been devastated. We've all looked for her." He whirled on Liam and pointed his dagger into Liam's chest. "What do *you* know about this, pirate?"

"Nothing." Liam's eyes met Wendy's. "I swear it, Wendy. I know nothing of any mermaid. I'm never invited into my uncle's quarters."

Theo stirred in her arms, making Wendy nearly stumble under his weight. He murmured something, and Wendy halted in her tracks. Peter and Liam were bickering, which meant surely Wendy hadn't heard right.

"Would you two be quiet?" she yelled at them. They both fell silent immediately. Wendy looked down into Theo's little face. "What did you say?"

Theo's eyes were still closed, and his face was crumpled in a look of pain. "He controls the shadows. Turn the pixie to shadow. Turn the mermaid to shadow. Turn the boy to shadow. He controls the shadows. Turn the pixie to shadow. Turn the mermaid to shadow.

WENDY'S EVER AFTER

Turn the boy to shadow." Theo repeated it a third time before he fell silent again.

"Theo?" Wendy jostled him gently to try to make him wake up and explain his bizarre chant. But he'd gone into the deep sleep he'd been in before.

"Did you hear that? Hook turned the pixie!" Peter shouted at Liam.

"That's not what the lad said!" Liam insisted. "The boy never said who did what. The term *he* could refer to anyone. *He* could be *you*."

"That's ridiculous. Why would I make a dark fairy? That *he* could also just as easily refer to you."

Wendy had had enough of the two of them. "Be quiet. Both of you. You're making my head ache."

"You hear that, pirate? You're making her head ache," Peter said.

"You're *both* making my head ache," Wendy hurried to clarify before Liam could interject his own comment. "And I need to think."

"What's there to think about? We've gotta get Mira back," Peter insisted before he twisted his face in disgust and pointed at Liam. "Not you. You can't come. We're not taking you where you can warn Hook that we're there. Wendy, tie him up."

"What?" Wendy's eyes widened.

"What?" Liam's narrowed.

Wendy was not going to do any such thing. "He can just go with Tinker Bell to the lost boys and deliver Theo to his bed."

"Now just wait a second," Liam argued at the same time Peter shook his head and said, "Nuh-uh. No pirates allowed at the lost boys' hideout. Everyone knows that, Wendy."

"I'm not tying him up, Peter," Wendy said.

"You gotta. You heard Theo. Turn the mermaid dark? Hook has a mermaid! Hook could be turning her dark like he did to the fairy. We can't have the pirate sounding any alarms that we're there."

Liam's jaw worked. "In the first place, you have no proof that my uncle did anything to that fairy. But in the second place, I promise not to sound any alarms. I, too, hate to think of a mermaid wrongfully imprisoned. I'll help so that no one is aware we're even there. You have my word."

"The word of a pirate!" Peter sneered.

But Wendy was looking at Liam, taking in his expression and the truths she'd learned about him in the labyrinth. He wasn't the villain. She'd already decided that. He would help. She was certain. "He's coming with us. We'll need a lookout who doesn't appear out of place on the *Jolly Roger*."

Peter looked like he might argue, but Wendy gave him the look her mother had always used on her when they weren't in agreement over something.

"Fine," Peter pouted. "But I'm the leader."

"No. *I'm* the leader," Wendy said before Liam could interject his own opinions. "We leave as soon as Theo is safe."

• • •

Tinker Bell had shown up with a woven mat that she used to cradle Theo and carry him back to the lost boys. Wherever she'd gone had revived her so she had the strength to make the journey without any issues.

The rest of them arrived at the shore near where the *Jolly Roger* was anchored. The ship creaked, and the lanterns hanging from the decks swayed as the waves gently rocked them. Peter flew up into a tree to get a better vantage, and Wendy scrambled up the trunk so she could see everything he saw with her own eyes. Liam elected to stay on the ground, grumbling something about not giving "that imp" any opportunity to push him out of a tree.

Wendy crawled out onto the thick branch where Peter had perched. They both fixed their eyes on the ship. She shivered at how frightening it appeared—like a dark stain leaked out over the sky. It reminded her of the dark fairy. Wendy glanced over at Peter. "Are you ready? Remember, Peter, we need to be as quiet as shadows."

"Have you met my shadow?" Peter replied, jabbing a thumb behind him. "He's always bumping into things. The guy is noisier than a thunderstorm."

"Well, keep an eye on him then," Wendy scolded as she slid out of the tree and landed on the ground next to where Peter had already landed.

Wendy and Liam started toward a group of jolly boats lashed to the sand anchors on the shore, but Peter stopped her. "Let's be quick about it. Try to fly."

She looked at Liam, feeling foolish for making the attempt with him watching. But when their eyes met, she thought of their shared kiss.

"See," Peter said. "I told you to think about the mermaids."

Wendy realized she was no longer held down to the ground like her feet were made of boulders. She was flying and had the feeling she could fly as high as she wanted to go.

Only she hadn't been thinking of mermaids. She glanced again at Liam.

Not at all.

Sensing something had happened that he didn't quite understand, Peter also looked at Liam. "Maybe you should stay here."

"Hardly," Wendy said. "What good is a lookout on the shore?"

"While I agree with Wendy and will absolutely not be staying behind, it doesn't seem like you'll run into much opposition," Liam said.

"Why?" Wendy asked.

"Look." He pointed to all the jolly boats tied up on the shore. "I'm betting they've sent out a search party for me. And for you." He grimaced and sent her a look of apology.

"Well then," Wendy said. "Let's not waste a perfect opportunity. Follow us in one of the boats." She then shot up into the air and laughed with the sheer joy of flying on her own. She hadn't forgotten how to fly, after all. The tension in her shoulders relaxed even though they were on their way to do something dangerous. But she couldn't help it. *She was flying.*

Flying through a Neverland sky, where the stars seemed closer and the wind seemed gentler. The pit of emptiness that had been gnawing at her gut back in London was suddenly filled and content. She was home.

The flight was over much too quickly. Peter glided over the balustrade and landed softly on the deck with Wendy settling next to him, though not nearly as gently since she was out of practice with such things. Liam was right. There was no one keeping guard over everything. The crew that was left were all below deck. Their raucous laughter and sea shanties echoed faintly from below the wooden planks.

"Look, Wendy, I'm a captain!" Peter's loud whisper nearly gave Wendy a heart attack. She turned to find him wearing one of Hook's hats and gripping the ship's helm as if he were sailing it off to some new land.

Liam arrived on deck just in time to witness the whole spectacle. Wendy burned with embarrassment over Peter acting like such a fool, especially when Liam shot her a look that said, *Really? Why do you want to spend time with this infant?*

Wendy growled inwardly. She didn't have the patience to explain to Peter that there was a time for silliness and a time for seriousness. *This* was *not* the time for silliness. She stalked over, knocked the pirate hat off his head, and grabbed Peter by the hand, dragging him away from the helm. "Behave, Peter. I'm not here to be your nanny." Wendy let go of Peter's hand and waved for him to follow her and Liam. Thankfully, he did so while he put his own hat back on his head. She wouldn't have known what to do if he'd refused. Why had Wendy thought bringing a child into such a dangerous environment was a good idea?

Liam led them to the door to Captain Hook's quarters. Wendy

tried the gold handle. Locked. She'd guessed that would be the case. "Do you have the key?" she whispered to Liam.

"No. He's only ever invited me into his quarters three times in my whole life. It's been over a year since the last time I stepped foot inside. Maybe we should leave. I can ask my uncle about it later."

Peter blew a raspberry that was not at all quiet. "I told you we should have left him on shore." At least he whispered.

"No, we shouldn't have. And the locked door is not a problem." She reached her hand into the pocket of her father's overcoat and pulled out the lockpicking set Michael had given her for her last birthday. She'd never tried it on something as fancy as Hook's door but hoped for the best. She slid in the tension wrench and pick and began pushing up the pins until she had them all set. She opened the door.

Peter gaped at her. "Whyever didn't you tell me you had magic?"

Ignoring the comment, since she was unsure if he was making fun or not, Wendy peered cautiously inside. Just like she had ignored his comment, Peter ignored the idea of caution and walked through the door as if he hadn't a care in the world. Except he stopped dead when he saw the glass cage used as a centerpiece to the dark elegance of the captain's quarters.

"Mira's crying," he whispered.

"How do you know?" Liam asked, clearly skeptical.

He had a point. The mermaid was in water. How could Peter tell the difference between tears and sea water?

But as Wendy looked closer, she realized there were glimmering trails of shadow leaking from the mermaid's eyes.

Were mermaid tears always shadowy, or was Hook already in the process of trying to turn the mermaid into a creature of shadow like the fairy? The mermaid didn't look past saving the way the fairy had, but how was Wendy to know?

Mira met Wendy's gaze. Wendy took an instinctive step back. The mermaid's eyes were dark orbs, like the pupil had expanded to fill the entire eye. The darkness seemed to swallow all light, reflecting nothing back.

"We're too late," Wendy murmured.

As if hearing the fatalist tone in Wendy's voice, Mira shook her head, placed her hand on the glass, and then pointed to her wrist.

"What's she saying?" Wendy asked.

"I may not speak French," Peter said with a grin, "but you gotta admit, speaking mermaid is much more useful."

"What is she saying, Pan?" Liam was obviously losing patience.

"She said we're not too late and that we shouldn't give up on her because she's held the shadows off with her voice. If we get her to the water, her people will know she's there. They can pull the shadows from her entirely."

Liam frowned. "What if we let her go, and instead of getting herself healed, she goes off and causes the same sort of trouble as the dark fairy?"

When Wendy shot Liam a look of horror, he held up his hands and said, "What? You had to be thinking it, too."

"We're letting her go, Liam." Guilt squeezed Wendy's heart because she had been thinking it, but still. . . . Wendy shook her head and inspected the glass box. "How do we get her out?"

Mira said something more, and Peter translated. "Hook locked the cage with the spiral shell charm she kept on her bracelet. She said we need to find the key. But we don't need a key. Do your magic, Wendy, and let's go."

Honestly, Peter could be infuriating at times. "My lockpick set won't work," Wendy said. "It's the wrong kind of lock for the tools that I have. We need her shell key. Let's find it quickly."

They began searching, though Liam murmured that he would be keelhauled for being there, and Peter grumbled that Wendy's magic wasn't very interesting because she could open only certain kinds of locks. They opened drawers full of maps and charts and navigational equipment. They opened chests full of jewels and gold. Wendy looked behind the several portraits Hook had of himself and one portrait of a beautiful lady smiling serenely for the painter. But there was nothing that resembled a shell.

Liam said he heard a noise and went to the door to make certain no one was coming.

Mira pressed her hand to the glass again and began to speak. Peter listened for a moment before saying, "She said he always plucks the harpsichord when he comes in to see her before he opens the top. Though she doesn't think he tunes it because the noise it makes is awful." Peter made a face to illustrate.

Peter and Wendy inspected the harpsichord. Wendy didn't dare actually touch the strings in case it made enough noise to alert the pirates below that they were in the captain's quarters. Peter had no such inhibitions. He twanged several strings and then strummed his fingers over all of them. Awful didn't begin to describe the discordant noise.

"Peter!" Wendy whispered, wishing she could shout. "No!"

Liam popped his head back into Hook's quarters, his eyes wide with horror, his hands in the air as if saying, *Control the imp.* Liam then left again, likely to verify that no one was moving their direction.

Peter shrugged as if he hadn't just alerted an entire ship full of pirates that they had some uninvited guests. Wendy opened her mouth to further scold him when he said, "Lookee here." He tugged another string, but instead of making noise, it released a latch that opened a hidden compartment.

Inside was the small shell.

Wendy bit back her previously planned scolding, tucking it away to use later since he would undoubtedly get into some sort of mischief that would require her to give him the rough side of her tongue in the future. She pulled out the shell, hurried to the lock, and inserted the shell into the impression. A whirring sound came from within the mechanism. The lock clicked open.

Peter shoved the glass top to the side. "You're free to go, my lady," he said gallantly, sweeping off his hat and bowing to Mira.

But Mira didn't move. Instead, she looked from Peter to Wendy and then down at the water that filled up her cage.

"You're free," Peter said again as if trying to coax her out of the cage.

"She can't leave," Wendy whispered. "It's not like she can swim across the deck."

Mira nodded at Wendy's understanding.

Peter snapped his fingers. Wendy wished that he didn't have to do everything so loudly. They'd been lucky no one had come up to investigate the brief musical interlude he'd provided. "We can take her out in these." Peter crossed the room and held up an edge of the scarlet-colored draperies. He gave it a solid tug, and the whole curtain rod, drapes and all, came down around him.

The scowl Wendy hurled his way bounced right off of him for all the attention he paid to her, but she agreed with him. "That's a good idea."

Mira must have agreed because she finally moved to action, pulling herself up enough to slide out of the cage where Wendy and Peter wrapped her in the draperies so they could carry her out. "I wish Liam were back already," Wendy said softly.

"Why?" Peter asked.

"He's stronger than both of us together. He could help."

Peter flexed his tiny arm. "I'm strong."

"Yes, you're strong for a boy, but this is a job for a man." She went to the door and peered out. Liam was still not back, and she didn't dare wait. "Apparently, we're all we have."

"Are you going to help or not?" Peter snarled the question at her. He seemed extra waspish when she mentioned Liam, evidently not liking the idea of sharing his friends with any other person. Peter acted as if, over the last several hours, Liam's presence had become a pebble in his shoe.

Together, Peter and Wendy pushed and pulled, dragging the draperies and the cargo they held out of the captain's quarters and across the deck.

"What are you doing?" a voice from behind demanded to know. Wendy whirled to see it was only Liam.

"You scared me!" she hissed at him.

"What are you doing?" he repeated.

"You left. We had to get her out of there." Wendy explained, exasperated that everyone felt it necessary to continue conversing.

Liam took both sides of the draperies and lifted it. Peter scowled at having to relinquish his side. Liam carried Mira to the balustrade. Once they reached the edge, Mira grabbed hold of the railing and pulled herself up until she was looking at the water.

Mira turned back to Peter and said something.

Peter grinned. "Aw, I know, Mira. I feel the same about you."

The mermaid raised a hand to touch Peter's cheek.

Peter recoiled, then straightened as his face went slack and he spoke in a monotone voice. "He controls the shadows. Turn the pixie to shadow. Turn the mermaid to shadow. Turn the boy to shadow." Like Theo, Peter repeated the phrase twice more before he shook himself and said in his normal voice, "That was . . . odd."

"Are you all right?" Wendy asked, alarmed.

Liam had his cutlass out, ready to strike but seeming not to know what at.

With a shrug, Peter said, "I'm all right. But Mira," he turned back to the mermaid, "you gotta get someone to sing healing to you fast. That shadow swirling in you is getting bigger."

Mira nodded, then pulled herself a little higher.

"Are you sure about this?" Wendy asked. "It's a long way down."

As if to answer, Mira hefted herself over the side and dove headlong into the ocean below. Wendy had expected a mighty splash from a fall at so great a distance, but Mira's dive seemed to slice open the water, allowing her to enter the ocean before it folded her up inside it again. The mermaid's head popped back up, her coral-colored hair glowing in the moonlight. Several other mermaids were with her. Wendy released a relieved breath. They would help heal her. Mira waved a hand in thanks and then was gone.

"I best be off too," Liam said. "It'll take me longer to reach the shore, and getting caught up here will not end well for any of us. So leave immediately. Both of you." The last bit was clearly meant for Peter by the look Liam shot him.

Peter did not leave immediately. "I think I want that hat," he said once Liam had lowered the jolly boat to the water.

"Don't you dare," Wendy said.

The grin Peter flashed helped Wendy understand why Liam continually called Peter an imp. "But I *do* dare."

"I mean it, Peter. No!"

Listening was not one of Peter's finer qualities. He'd gone back to the ship's helm, tucked his own hat into his belt, put the pirate hat on his head, and strutted back to Wendy. She couldn't help herself. She covered her mouth to muffle the laugh.

But Peter never got the chance to enjoy the fact that he'd made Wendy laugh. He shoved Wendy to the side. "Look out!" A woosh over her head told her Peter had saved her from a pirate's blade.

Peter threw the hat he'd been wearing at the pirate who'd attacked. Then, with his dagger in his hand, Peter engaged the pirate in a fight, steel clanging on steel. A quick glance around told Wendy there were no weapons readily available for her to join the fight in the usual way, but there were hoists hanging from ropes. The pirate cornered Peter and was striking again and again. Wendy grabbed the hoist and swung it hard, knocking the pirate in the head and giving Peter the time he needed to fly out of reach.

The pirate set his murderous eyes on Wendy. "You grubby little girl!" The pirate bellowed, which was just insulting. She was *not* a little girl any longer. She was a grown woman.

"Jump, Wendy!" Peter called from the rigging.

Three more pirates thumped up the stairs to join the fight, likely having heard the commotion. Wendy was surrounded on all sides except the ocean.

"Jump!"

But Wendy had seen how far down it was to the water's surface.

Were her thoughts happy enough at the moment? Her worries over Hook trying to turn Neverland into a shadowland made happy thoughts feel mythical. Her chances might be better with the pirates. There were only four of them, after all. If only she'd had a blade of her own.

"Jump!" Peter insisted again.

He was right to insist. She had no weapon. Better to live to fight another day. She turned to climb onto the bulwark when one of the pirates latched onto her father's overcoat, making her fall to the deck.

Maybe it was the way they laughed at her. Or maybe it was that Peter was watching the whole thing, but when the one with the red scraggles that he passed as a beard stopped laughing so that he could swing his sword at her, Wendy rolled out of the way and, like Liam had done to her, swept a leg at the pirate's feet, knocking him off balance and sending him crashing to the deck. She leaped to her own feet and grabbed at one of the ropes hanging down. As the other three lunged for her, she used the rope to swing herself off the deck and over the water.

She had to let go.

Swinging back into the pirates on the deck would get her killed. She *had* to let go.

With a whimper, her hands released the rope, and she fell.

There hadn't been time for her to even try thinking happy thoughts, even though it felt like she'd been falling for forever.

When she hit the water, it was not with the gentle slice that Mira had managed. It was with a great splash that slapped at Wendy's skin. She would have cried out except she was under the water. Her feet kicked, but the dark water had disoriented her. Which way was up? Her lungs burned. Where was the surface? Her father's overcoat weighed her down, dragging her farther and farther from safety. Wendy squiggled out of the overcoat and struggled once again to orient herself in the direction she needed to go.

A hand took hers. Liam's? She didn't know why she would think it was him. What would Liam be doing out in the middle of an ocean? He had to be to shore by now. But at that moment when she needed someone, she realized the one she needed most was him.

When her head broke the surface of the water, Wendy gasped in the delicious oxygen. The hand that had hold of hers pulled her to the shallows, where waves gently lapped at the sand. She rubbed the water from her eyes and saw that it was Mira's steadying grip on her hand. Her eyes were no longer black pools. Mermaid healing evidently worked fast.

"Thank you." Wendy's voice cracked. "Thank you."

Mira nodded and dove back under the surface in the direction of the deeper waters, leaving Wendy to trudge up onto the shore on her own, her skirts heavy with water and sand.

"There you are!"

Wendy looked up at Peter. "I almost drowned." Her teeth chattered.

"I knew Mira would help you. Mira would never let you drown."

While Wendy believed that was true, she was still upset with Peter for not catching her hand and helping slow her fall when she'd jumped from the ship. He could have prevented her from ever hitting the water if he had wanted.

Wendy sat on the shoreline and looked for Liam. He was nowhere to be seen.

Peter babbled on with no concern over Wendy's almost drowning or that they'd lost their personal pirate. "There's only five of them, Wendy," he said. "On the whole ship. Five pirates. That's all. I'm going back to the hideaway to tell the lost boys. With all of us, we can take on five and then take the ship." Peter hooted. "Won't that old codfish be surprised when he comes home? No more making shadow creatures for him. I'll be right back. Wait here."

"But Peter—didn't you hear yourself just—"

Peter was gone before Wendy could finish the sentence. When Mira had touched him, he had said, "He controls the shadows. Turn the pixie to shadow. Turn the mermaid to shadow. Turn the boy to shadow."

Wendy was certain that the boy Hook meant to turn was none other than Peter.

Instead of listening to her explain, he left Wendy soaking, shivering, and alone in the cove. Why hadn't Liam shown up yet? Had the pirates who'd attacked her and Peter gotten to Liam before he got away? Frowning, Wendy searched the darkness. Was he lying crumpled in a bludgeoned heap somewhere or sinking to the bottom of the cove after having been tossed overboard? The thought made her feel like throwing up. What if he wasn't safe? She picked up a large branch, intending to use it to start a fire to warm and dry herself—pirates be hanged.

A crack sounded behind her, like the breaking of a twig underfoot.

All are keeping a sharp look-out in front, but none suspects that the danger may be creeping up from behind.

CHAPTER SIXTEEN

Wendy whirled, holding the branch like a club when she saw the person she'd been equal parts dreaming about and worrying over.

Liam.

She flung herself at him, nearly knocking him over as she clutched him close to her. He returned her embrace, the thrum of his heart against her own as steady as the second star to the right. He hadn't been taken prisoner.

She knew she'd been the one to say she regretted kissing him, but now with her relief so raw and her emotions so intense and with the knowledge that her happy thought that enabled her to fly had been him, Wendy did the one thing she'd sworn not to do ever again.

Pushing up on her toes, she pressed her mouth to his. His lips fell open in surprise, but he recovered quickly and kissed her back. His kiss trailed to her cheeks and her eyelids and the tip of her nose.

Wendy felt grounded for the first time in days, even while knowing she could fly forever on the joy of his embrace.

"Are you all right?" He pulled away long enough to ask. "I heard swords clashing but had no idea what was going on." He demanded to know everything even as he crushed her to him in an embrace that seemed as much relief as it was affection. He traced his lips over every inch of her face, which made answering him difficult.

"We were ambushed by a few of your friends, but we got away. No harm done." Wendy's words broke as her teeth chattered with cold.

"Where's your coat?"

Her eyes filled with tears. *Her father's coat.* "In my panic, I couldn't manage to hang on to my happy thoughts. I fell into the ocean, and the coat was so heavy it nearly drowned me. I had to get out of it." The loss was a knife to her heart.

Liam removed his own jacket and swept it over her shoulders, rubbing her arms to keep her warm. "We need to get you dry."

She couldn't argue with that. They navigated the craggy path rather than the easier sand so they wouldn't leave tracks of any kind as they moved. The bright moon cast long shadows, making the terrain difficult to see as they stumbled and bumbled their way to the stream that divided the rocks and the sand. Once they reached it, Liam guided them through the water.

They trekked a long time through the stream that had only been ankle deep when they started but was now past their waists. Wendy's teeth chattering was the only noise that kept beat to their journey.

"We're far enough away from the ocean." Liam pointed to the trees. "Let's press into the jungle."

Once he'd found a clearing surrounded by dense brush, Liam called their march to a halt. "We need a fire, or we'll both freeze." It wasn't strictly true. The night air was cool, certainly, but not freezing. But being wet made it seem as though frost had descended on the island. Liam and Wendy gathered wood together and made a small firepit, building up the wood inside the pit with tinder and larger branches.

Liam approached Wendy, who was still wearing his naval coat. He reached for her, and her breath caught as her eyes met his. "I need to get my flint and steel. It's in the pocket there." He pointed to where the pocket was located on the inside of the coat.

"Oh." She blinked as if pulling herself from a daze. "Of course."

He reached forward again as she pulled the coat open to reveal the inner pocket. His eyes never left hers as he retrieved the military-issued flint and steel, his hand brushing hers as he pulled the small pouch from the pocket.

Was she cold before? Looking at him as he gazed down at her made her feel like a fire had already started. Liam cleared his throat, and his hand went up. He absently raked through his hair as he stepped back. "Good thing the military gives us these flint and steel kits, or we'd never get dry."

"Yes," she whispered. "Good thing."

Liam worked with the flint and steel until he had the tinder burning. They'd purposely built it small to keep the light of the flame concealed as much as possible. Once it was burning steadily, Liam sat next to Wendy who had huddled close to the warmth. He put his arm around her to help retain their body heat.

"This was not at all what I expected when we first met at the ball," Wendy said.

Liam laughed. "No. I would imagine not."

"I mean . . . I knew you were trouble the moment I laid eyes on you. That domino mask hid nothing of your mischief. It was written on the curve of your lips when you smiled at me."

"Oh really? I'll have you know," he said as he pulled back and shot her an indignant look, "your blue feather mask did nothing to hide your unconventional way of doing things. The very set of your shoulders said you didn't want to be there at that masquerade. If you could have set fire to the building so that you'd have an excuse to leave, I think you would've done it."

"I suppose this is where you tell me that your bad influence was doing me a favor by inspiring me to leave the way I did."

"I probably should have just asked you outright to come with me," he confessed.

"Yes. That probably would have been better. I would have, you know. If you had said, 'Come away with me to Neverland,' I would have gone. Not just for the sake of Neverland but because I liked you from the first moment. I respected you from the moment I saw you dance with Mrs. Connolly. I held you in high esteem after I saw you protect that stable boy from the motor driver. Such a short time to determine you were worth knowing."

"I went to that masquerade expecting to despise you." He laughed when she twisted her face at that news. "But I confess, I liked you from the first moment, even though I had been misinformed about the person you were. I must be honest in this. Your beauty had a lot to do with my initial decision to like you. And I fully admit that it does not speak well of me to be so shallow. However, I learned to respect you when the society ladies were all clamoring about your compassionate heart. I held *you* in high esteem when Mrs. Connolly told me how often you called on her just to say hello. And I knew I had completely met my match when you escaped me three times in less than a day." Liam reached up and wrapped a still-damp tendril of her hair around his finger. "They must be drawn to the fire," Liam said, pointing to fireflies fluttering in the foliage around them.

Wendy sighed and leaned against Liam. "No, they're attracted to contentment and happiness. They're always flying around the lost boys' encampment and Tiger Lily's village. This is the closest I've ever seen them to Pirate Cove."

"I *am* happy," Liam said, turning his focus back to her. "Even with my uncle behaving with such bad form." He traced the path of a water drop that had rolled out of her hair, over her forehead, and across her cheekbone. "You know, I should have been afraid of all those gentlemen clamoring for your attention at the ball. I've never been much for competing when it comes to matters of the heart."

Her eyes fluttered closed at his touch. It was the first time that Neverland felt balanced since she'd arrived. "Oh, there was no contest," she murmured. "I confess that on the very day we met, I told my mother I intended to respond to the many bouquets of flowers interested suitors sent me with sprigs of hemlock so they understood how improbable their chances were of gaining my affections."

"Hemlock?"

"Mm-hmm," she sighed.

"That's the best thing I think I've ever heard." His fingers traced the outline of her lips. Her eyes were still closed, but she felt his nearness as his breath washed over her lips.

"There you are!" Peter's shout shattered the moment. Wendy and Liam jumped apart, each of them reaching for some sort of weapon with which to defend themselves.

"Peter! You found us." Wendy cast a furtive look to Liam.

"Just in time too," Peter said with a glower, which Liam reciprocated.

"Where have you been? Are the lost boys with you?" Wendy adjusted her hair and hurried to remove the jacket Liam had placed on her shoulders.

Liam frowned, looking between her and Peter.

Hadn't Liam just confessed to her that he didn't believe in competing for hearts? And now here she was, locking him into a contest he would never understand. She could have sworn he muttered, "Curse that imp."

Peter wrinkled his nose like he'd tasted something sour. "What were you two lovebirds kissy-whispering about?"

Wendy straightened to her full height. "We were having a private conversation. There's no need for you to be vulgar." She felt like she'd spent more time scolding Peter than anything else.

Imp indeed. Peter had interrupted a perfectly good kiss. Or what would have been a perfectly good kiss, had he not interrupted.

"Where are the lost boys?" Wendy asked Peter.

"Aw, I haven't gotten them yet. I ran into Starna, and she gave me an earful about leaving you alone. I told her you broke your ability to fly and would slow me down, but she didn't care. So I came back for you. We can go to the lost boys together."

A short while later, Wendy stood on the edge of the clearing where she and Liam had doused their fire as they waited for Peter to return from checking to make sure the coast was clear. He'd been delighted to scout ahead. Liam stood next to her, unusually quiet. Wendy peeked over at him, but his expression was intense and unreadable.

Was he feeling the same excitement and dread she felt? Probably not. It made no sense that she should feel such things. But she hadn't seen the newest additions to Peter's little family and felt eager to meet them.

Liam opened his pocket watch and used the moonlight to read the time. A *pocket watch*. Here. On Neverland.

What must his uncle think of that since all watches or clocks were outlawed in Neverland? What thoughts went through Liam's head as he stared into the inky darkness? Did he feel ashamed that his uncle was such a man? Did he understand now that his uncle was the villain on this island? She wanted to push away the nagging thoughts of Liam's possible loyalty to Hook, but how could she when Hook was Liam's family? She would not be able to turn her back so easily on her own family.

She decided to shift her focus to Peter, who'd returned from scouting ahead. "Is it all clear? Can we safely get to the home under the ground?"

Peter blew a raspberry at her. "Psh. We don't live there anymore. We had to move, on account of Hook finding it and blowing it all up after Tink drank the poison he'd left for me. He was awful mad that I didn't drink the poison. He threw one of those tantrums you always told us to be mindful of, Wendy. Hook is an awful baby."

Liam stiffened. Wendy wasn't sure what his reaction meant but hoped it further solidified that his uncle was a bad, bad man. Only bad men ran around poisoning pixies.

They began their journey through the jungle. Starna joined them to light their way, flying near Wendy and chattering as if she were competing for the longest sentence ever spoken all at once. Starna informed them that Captain Hook and his men were located on the east side of the island. Wendy was glad they were so far away but worried, too. Was he trying to turn some other creature to shadow? Why would he do such a thing? What could he gain? And then another pixie flew in like a shooting star streaking across Wendy's vision.

"What did it say?" Liam asked after Tinker Bell chimed her bells for quite some time.

"You mean what did *she* say," Wendy admonished, not able to shake her role of mother in this place.

"Yes. Yes. That. Of course. What did *she* say?"

Peter answered before Wendy could. "She said the mermaids are moving. They're gathering at the edge of their lagoon."

"Sounds like they're seeking revenge for their stolen daughter," Liam said.

Tinker Bell chimed again and then flew up to join Peter.

Translating that new bit made Wendy blush. "She says you're very handsome."

Liam's posture seemed to soften, but then Starna chimed as well.

"You don't have to translate that one," Liam said. "I could tell from her tone that she wasn't paying me a compliment."

"Well, you *did* lock her in a lantern," Wendy said.

Casting a furtive glance up ahead to where Peter and Tinker Bell were telling jokes to one another, Wendy whispered, "Liam?"

"Hm?"

"Do you think Hook is the shadow conjurer? Everyone seemed to think it was the dark fairy, but now . . . well, I'm not convinced."

"I understand why you think that, but my uncle has complained about the shadow conjurer on several occasions. You must remember that many of our crew have been plagued by the bites of the shadow snakes. A few were lost irretrievably to the darkness."

"But he had a mermaid. He was trying to turn her."

The uncertainty in his face made her stomach drop. Did he not believe his uncle was the villain in all this? How could he not?

Liam chewed the inside of his cheek. "We don't know that's what he was doing with the mermaid."

Wendy couldn't believe what she was hearing. "Mira said her song kept the shadows at bay. What other way can you interpret that?"

His eyebrows knit together and he let out a breath in resignation. "You're right. I know you're right. It just seems so fantastical to imagine. My uncle has a temper to be sure, but he isn't a bad man."

"Except he's a pirate." Wendy pointed out.

"Yes . . . except that."

They had fallen far enough behind the others that Peter was certain to get suspicious. Wendy walked faster to catch up even as she whispered, "I think he means to turn Peter into one of the shadow creatures."

Liam blinked in surprise. He'd obviously not considered who the boy could be in that strange monotone repetition that both Theo and Peter had given.

The truth was that Peter had his own form of darkness in him. His shadow was never far from him and always instigating mischief. It was often in the form of pranks, but once Peter had told her that there was a saying in the Neverland that every time you breathed, an adult died. Peter confessed that when he felt extra churlish, he breathed rapidly in and out to hurry along the extinction of adults.

"Pan is a troublemaking imp at his best. If you're right, Wendy, then we're all in for a lot of trouble. If Pan were to ever become a shadow creature, I don't know that Neverland would recover."

Children have the strangest adventures without being troubled by them. For instance, they may remember to mention, a week after the event happened, that when they were in the wood they had met their dead father and had a game with him.

CHAPTER SEVENTEEN

They walked through the night until morning lightened the skies and Peter announced, "We're almost there. The lost boys will be so happy to meet you, Wendy. You can tell them a story!"

"Ah, the storyteller returns," Liam said.

Wendy shrugged. How to explain her role among lost boys? She was mother, friend, advocate. She had loved playing at being a mother. It was something she hoped to do for real someday. Not any time soon, of course. Someday, though. But that was quite a lot for her to admit to a pirate, no matter how much she liked him.

The narrow path they'd followed opened up into a clearing with a grove of several large trees. "We're here," Peter said.

"We're where?" Wendy asked.

"Home above the ground." Peter edged Liam out of the way and put his arm around Wendy's shoulder as he pointed. "Look up."

Wendy looked and felt her mouth drop open in shock and wonder. Above her, the trees were filled with small houses built into the branches. The houses in the various trees were all connected by wooden bridges. Peter grinned at Wendy's gasp of delight. "Tootles and Nibs would have been proud of us if they could have seen it. Do you remember the house we built for you, Wendy?"

"They would indeed be proud, and of course I remember," Wendy murmured.

Peter began to sing, "We've built the little walls and roof and made a lovely door. So tell us, mother Wendy, what are you wanting more?"

Wendy blinked away the tears. She remembered the song but was surprised that Peter remembered it. Responding to him with the rest of the song was impossible without her heart breaking a little. Instead, she asked, "How do we get up to your treehouse city?"

"We fly," Peter said.

When Wendy gave him a look, he laughed and pointed to Liam. "He'll have to take the stairs." Peter pulled aside the ivy on one of the trees to reveal the staircase that had been carved into the hollow of the tree.

"I'll go with Liam," Wendy said.

"Suit yourself." Peter then flew up to the largest of the treehouses and crowed for the children inside.

"Peter!" came the cry of several young but strong voices. Wendy felt a pinch in her heart. She remembered that crow and the greeting the lost boys always gave when Peter returned. The cry of joy filled her with equal parts joy and sorrow that she was determined not to give in to. Tinker Bell chimed some instructions.

"Oh. Thank you."

"What are you thanking her for?" Liam asked.

"She said I'd find a change of clothes upstairs." Wendy stepped through the arched ivy doorway and into the tree Tinker Bell had indicated. She'd anticipated having to adjust her eyes to the darkness, but the interior proved to be well-lit with lanterns that glowed with something that wasn't exactly flame. The sides of each step were lined with tiny glowing mushrooms in blue and green hues.

"See?" Wendy whispered to Liam, who had followed behind her. "Notice there aren't any pixies in their wall lanterns."

"If they'd used pixies, they probably wouldn't require the floor

WENDY'S EVER AFTER

203

mushrooms," he murmured back, to which Wendy socked him in the arm.

"I'm only teasing," he said. "I am now friend to all pixies who don't control shadows." He put his hand over his heart like he was giving an oath.

Wendy rolled her eyes at him and continued climbing the steps.

The stairs wound up through the tree's interior, each step decorated with intricate carvings of leaves, flowers, animals, and fairies, beckoning visitors onward to enjoy the inviting artistry.

As they ascended, Wendy traced her fingers along the carvings of more art in the smooth, dark walls of the tree. A picture of the *Jolly Roger* with the words *No Pirates Allowed* carved into the wood, mermaids, stars, more flowers. These works of art intermixed with the whimsical decor of twine dreamcatchers and strings of acorn caps.

They neared the top. The air grew sweeter with the scent of pine and blossoms. The stairs opened up into a cozy little room with windows of various shapes and sizes, which allowed Wendy to catch glimpses of the lush forest outside. The floor was lined with woven rugs and the furniture was made from branches, twisted and bent and lashed into place. Colorful hammocks hung from the branches, and a ladder woven from vines led up to another series of rooms.

"I've never seen anything so ingenious and charming as this little tree home," Liam said.

"Nor I. Even the home under the ground wasn't quite this grand. The little house they built me seems like a sad shadow of this new home they've created."

As Tinker Bell had said, there was a change of clothing that would fit Wendy in the little side table made of planks and driftwood, likely salvaged from old shipwrecks that washed in with the tide. Wendy pulled a curtain made of woven leaves to change and came out feeling much better about herself. The red tunic and brown trousers were loose, but the belt kept everything held together well enough. She rooted through the various sizes of makeshift boots from animal hides until she found a pair that fit perfectly. She snugged them onto each foot with a leather cord. Her feet could not have withstood another moment in those dancing slippers.

"Ta-da!" she said, stepping out from behind the curtain. "Shocked to see a lady in trousers?" she asked.

"Not at all," Liam said, eyeing her in a way that suggested he appreciated her new look. "You are lovely no matter what your attire." As if forcing himself to turn away so he didn't gawk for too long at her new clothing, Liam asked, "Where is everyone? With all the noise, I'd expected an army of children up here."

"They'll all be outside greeting Peter now that he's returned to them. That's how it usually is." Wendy followed the noise out another little arched doorway of ivy and found herself on a wooden bridge that connected to one of the other houses. Now that she was up high enough to see, she discovered that there were many such bridges all woven and intersecting one another like a spider's web. Lanterns hung along the bridges, and it seemed everything led to one central platform that spanned between the large branches of three different trees. A long wooden table with a mismatched collection of small chairs took up the bulk of the space on the platform. Peter stood on top of the table surrounded by a dozen little boys of various ages.

"Lost boys, meet Wendy. She tells the best stories. She likes to tell one about a glass slipper, but the best ones she tells are about me and my adventures fighting the evil Captain Hook." Peter pantomimed a hook as he twisted his face into a snarl and curled his back so that he looked like a predator about to pounce.

"Boo!" the boys all said when they heard Captain Hook's name.

"Who's the other one?" one of the boys asked. His skin was so pale he looked like he'd never seen sunshine, and Wendy wondered if perhaps he might be ill. He wore a vest that seemed to be made entirely of pockets with all sorts of odds and ends sticking out of them.

Wendy smiled at the boy. "This is my friend Liam." She didn't mention that Liam was also Captain Hook's nephew. No reason to start an unwanted commotion. "And who are you?"

WENDY'S EVER AFTER

205

"Firefly," the boy said, squinting large, inquisitive green eyes at them. "Where are you from?" The question was directed to Liam.

"London," Liam answered, kneeling down so he was eye to eye with the boy. "And where are you from? Do you remember?"

Firefly shook his head. "I'm not from anywhere. I've always been here."

"Surely not always," Liam insisted.

But the other boys were now clamoring for attention and talking over Firefly so they could have a turn speaking to their new storyteller. Firefly tried showing Wendy all the things in his pockets, which consisted mostly of various colored stones and a few feathers.

"I'm Bookworm," said another boy with warm brown skin and even warmer brown eyes. A small notebook and the tip of a pencil peeked out of the top of a belt that had several pouches in it. "They call me that since I'm the only one who can read."

"Not that we have any books," another said, sweeping a cap off his head like a proper little gentleman. "I'm Flint." He kissed Wendy's hand and grinned with a wide mouth full of crooked teeth. He was tanned as if he spent all his time in the sun. Flint popped his cap back onto his mop of brown hair. A small scabbard hung around his waist with the bone handle of some sort of knife or blade sticking out the top.

"You're quite the charmer," Wendy said.

Liam laughed. "You must have learned such good manners from your mother."

"What's a mother?" said a boy with wild curly red hair and freckles dotting his cheeks like constellations. He had a bright yellow scarf around his neck, and goggles rested on his forehead as if he needed them ready to pull down in a hurry.

"Surely you know what a mother is," Liam said, echoing something Wendy had said a long time ago. A pang of . . . *something* struck her so forcefully that she had to grab hold of a branch overhead to steady her. If Peter had rescued Starkey from drowning, what had been the reason he'd brought the others? Years ago, he had told

Wendy that the boys had fallen out of their prams and become lost. It hadn't occurred to her to wonder what that meant or to inquire further. She'd been too busy feeling the compliment of Peter telling her that girls were much too clever to fall from their prams. Under what circumstances had these boys come to Peter? Had their stories been equally frightening? Equally sad?

"Are you crying, Storyteller?" the boy with the red hair and goggles asked.

"No. Just some dust in my eyes."

Liam took her hand and gave a reassuring squeeze. He might not know exactly why she felt sad, but he was paying enough attention to her to understand that a little rain cloud had descended on her emotions. He looked down at the boy with curiosity. "What's your name?" Liam asked.

The boy straightened his scarf. "They call me Jinx. Pleased to meet you!" He jabbed out his hand for Liam to shake. Liam untangled his fingers from Wendy's, which was disappointing, but she didn't want him to be rude to the boy by ignoring the greeting.

The other boys leaned forward, watching the handshake intently.

When Liam grasped Jinx's hand, a little buzz sound came from where their hands joined. Liam instantly yanked his hand back with his eyes wide. The boys fell over themselves laughing at the prank as Jinx held up his hand to reveal a tiny metal buzzer on his palm.

"Very funny," Liam grumbled.

Peter took that moment to clap his hands. "Fun time is over. Now it's time for battle! Hook was the one who stole Mira."

The boys gasped, which made Peter grin. He loved to spin a story as much as he loved to have one told to him. "Don't worry. I rescued her." He went into the details of the rescue, making himself out to be the hero, and then he said, "When we rescued Mira, we found out Hook was trying to turn her into one of those shadow creatures that have been causing all kinds of trouble. Mira said he's doing it to defeat me. But can anything defeat me?"

"No!" the boys shouted in unison.

"Can Hook ever be allowed to win?"

"No!"

"Because what is a Hook?"

"A creepy, over-coddled codfish!" The joy in the boys' faces as they shined their adoration on Peter made Wendy smile. They really did love him.

"They worship him," Liam said from next to her as he still shook out the tingles from his hand. Liam was *not* smiling.

"Of course they do. He's Peter Pan." She couldn't keep her own affection from her voice.

"And you're all right with all of this?" He waved a hand at the boys listening intently to Peter unfold a plan to take the *Jolly Roger* and defeat Captain Hook.

"What do you mean? Hook has to be stopped. Why wouldn't I be all right?"

Liam staggered a step back. "I agree something needs to be done about my uncle. I just don't agree with the idea of going into a battle using children as soldiers. Pan's going to get them killed."

Wendy tried to tug at Liam's sleeve because he looked like he planned on jumping on the table and dueling Peter right then and there. "What would you have them do? Wait for Hook to attack? It isn't as though Hook has given them many options over the years. And with this new threat, you can hardly blame them. Besides, they'll be fine. Fighting pirates is a common game." Her cheeks burned the instant the words were out of her mouth. She knew better than anyone that there were consequences to actions. None of this was a game, and she felt ashamed of herself for having said as much.

Liam looked shocked that she could say such a thing, which made her cheeks burn all the hotter. But how had he lived on the island and never come to understand how it all worked and what was required to put the fighting to an end?

"A game? They're living like animals in the woods." His harsh whisper was quickly turning to a shout. Wendy was glad Peter and the boys were too caught up in their revelry and plans to notice.

"Just a moment ago, you called their living conditions ingenious and charming."

He ignored that comment as he continued. "They don't know where they came from. They don't know who their mothers are. Wendy, they don't know *what* a mother is. Maybe Pan doesn't steal them, but honestly, Wendy, what kind of monster makes one forget their own mother?"

"That's not Peter's fault. It's the island. Neverland makes you forget. It swirls away memories. Surely, you've been here long enough to notice. The island takes memories from everyone, even if they live on a pirate ship or in Tiger Lily's village or with the fairy king and queen. It's the island that casts the spell of forgetfulness, not a boy. Quit making him out to be a monster."

At that moment, Theo crept out of a nearby hut. He approached Peter at the table and said, "Peter, I want to go home now."

All of the boys fell quiet.

"You *are* home," Peter answered.

"No, my other home. The one with my mother."

Wendy forgot that she had been discussing anything with Liam under the weight of that small request. Her heart pinched, and she wanted to sweep him up into her arms and take him immediately to his mother.

"Today's a battle day. I don't take requests on battle days," Peter said.

Theo's face fell. He shuffled back a few steps as the other boys erupted again with questions regarding the battle plan.

"Peter!" Wendy scolded.

Peter looked more annoyed with her for interrupting than he did repentant, but he said to Theo, "We'll talk as soon as the battle's over, okay?"

Theo nodded.

Liam grunted, clearly not impressed with Peter's response. "He doesn't let them go, Wendy. You say the island makes you forget. Did the island make you forget he *is* a monster after all?"

She hated that she agreed with him. But his comment made her feel small and stupid and angry. "Let's compare monsters, Liam," she said, feeling defensive. "The one you call a monster saves little children who would have otherwise died. He keeps them fed and sheltered and entertained. The one I call a monster keeps a mermaid locked in a small box away from her family and friends. He threatens little children all the time and on occasion has tried to kill them." She held up her hand to stop him from interjecting. "*I* was threatened, Liam. Hook tried to have *me* killed. If Peter hadn't saved me, Hook would have succeeded. So if you ask which monster I will side with, then you're a fool if you don't already know my answer." Why was she always so hot and cold around this man? She'd never been so irrational before in her life.

"Curses, Wendy, I don't know why we're fighting. We want the same thing," Liam said.

She was sure he was right about that. Mostly sure.

He'd paused, probably so she could agree with him, but when she stayed silent, Liam blew out a long breath. "If your theory is correct, and my uncle means to turn Pan to the shadow, then we need to take precautions. If I already think Pan is a villain, I would hate to see him fully facing the dark."

Hope flickered in Wendy's chest. "So you'll help us?"

He shook his head. "Not like this. We don't know what my uncle is planning. We don't know that we shouldn't be joining forces with him instead of fighting him."

Irritation bubbled up in Wendy all over again. "Why are you so quick to defend that pirate?"

"He's my family. Why are you so quick to defend the imp?"

Wendy crossed her arms over her chest and narrowed her eyes at Liam. "The *imp* hasn't tried killing me, for one. But fine. If you're so certain Hook is saintly, why don't you go talk to him and have him tell you his whole plan? I'm certain he'll be incredibly forthcoming and tell you every little detail."

"Maybe I will."

Wendy waved her hand as if shooing him faster on his way. "Fine then. Go. I'm certainly not stopping you."

Before Liam could respond, Bookworm grabbed hold of Wendy's arm and yanked her to the table where the boys prodded her until she stepped up onto its surface—a thing no lady would ever do under normal circumstances. Peter grasped her hands in his. "Today, we go to war with the pirates once and for all. Today, we show that codfish who rules this island. Today we win!"

The boys cheered and whooped as they danced around the table.

Through the crowd, Wendy met Liam's eyes to try to convey to him that she needed him with her on this. The boys would need her and Liam both to help protect them.

Her heart sank when Liam looked away.

She should have gotten down from the table, but with all the boys pressed in, how could she? Soon, tactical plans and questions regarding the layout of the ship had her sidetracked. When she looked up again, Liam was gone.

She was not a little girl heart-broken about him; she was a grown woman smiling at it all.

CHAPTER EIGHTEEN

"He left." Wendy sat on one of the vine-twisted chairs in a slump of mixed astonishment and dejection. "He just left."

Starna chimed her response, to which Tinker Bell laughed.

"Yes, I know I told him to. But that doesn't mean he should do it. Does the man not recognize sarcasm? It wasn't an invitation for him to actually leave. It was an indication that he should stay and come to my way of thinking."

Starna and Tinker Bell both had a lot to say on the subject. And most of it was commentary on how Wendy wasn't very bright. The lost boys and Peter Pan, however, had nothing to say at all. Solemn eyes watched her as she tried to make sense of what had just occurred in her life.

So he left. So what? She didn't need him. She knew she didn't.

She knew it.

She hoped she knew it.

But what she actually knew was that she missed Liam profoundly. Even though she was furious with him for siding with his uncle. Even though he'd only been gone a short while.

He was just so nice that he made it easy to forget he was a pirate.

Peter slowly approached Wendy as if she were a wild animal who was injured and might attack at any moment to protect itself from further injury. He held out his hands. "Lost boys, continue making preparations. Wendy and I are going to fly."

"Peter, you know I can't fly right now. Where would I find a happy thought in any of this?"

Peter didn't answer but instead pulled her out of her chair. "Think of your freedom. Of the Neverland wind in your hair and the stars in your eyes," he whispered.

She closed her eyes and found she was able to picture it.

"Think of soaring so high that you can hang from the crescent moon." He paused for a long time, and Wendy opened her eyes again to see his grin. "And there you are."

She looked down. Her feet no longer connected with any solid surface.

Peter took her hand, and together, they flew up high above the tall trees. "Sometimes I find I feel better when I get looking at things from a different point of view," he said to her.

"I don't think this method of yours is going to change anything. As lovely as this view is, it doesn't make anything better. Liam told Starna he was going to find his uncle. Do you know what that means? That means he's chosen to follow the most ridiculously evil man I've ever known. And we're supposed to be making preparations. I really do believe Hook means to do something awful to you, Peter. I think he means to turn you to shadow like he did that fairy."

"Not possible."

They circled the conversation several times, with Peter insisting that nothing could turn him to shadow because he was a hero and never did anything wrong. Memory told Wendy that he was wrong, of course. She recalled him doing several sinister things in her time of knowing him. Strange that she hadn't once thought about those things during her years of missing him. But now? How could she not think of them when he seemed determined to remind her? She tried a different tactic to get him to see the urgency of their situation.

"We need to get back. We don't know how long it will be before the rest of Hook's crew returns to the ship." She didn't add that they

WENDY'S EVER AFTER

215

might have less time because, surely, Liam was returning to warn Hook.

Peter swept close to the waterfall, close enough that the mist left them damp. Wendy tightened her hand around his. He looked down at her. "It'll all work out. Everything always does. Besides, we can't go to battle if you're feeling bad. That wouldn't be any fun."

Fun? Going into battle should never be considered fun. Peter flew higher, and when he decided to land, he touched gently down on a large, flat rock that was perched atop a cliff. The rock was well hidden as it was surrounded by trees, vines, and flowers on all sides except the one with the edge. Wendy landed next to him and gasped at the sight. The view of the ocean and a portion of the island was enough to make her forget her worry for a moment. "You know," she said, "my mother always says that life is extraordinarily hard, but it also comes with extraordinary views. If only she could see this. I feel like I can almost see London from here. Where are we?"

"Starry Cliff. I come here when I need to think and be alone."

"You need to think?" That seemed like a foreign activity for Peter to be engaged in.

"What? I think a lot." His defensive tone made her want to laugh.

"I'm sure you do," Wendy hurried to say so as not to hurt his feelings, though she didn't exactly believe herself.

"It's not the tallest point on Neverland, and it doesn't give the best views of the whole island, so it's not much good for keeping an eye on things, but at night, it gives the best views of the stars. Since they're always looking at us, I figure it's nice to look back every now and again." Peter sat on the ground and leaned back on his elbows to look at the bright expanse of blue.

Wendy sat next to him and looked up as well, trying to imagine the view at night instead of midday. Her gaze eventually lowered. Wendy frowned at the bit of forest down below. Swaths of the jungle looked ashy grey as if someone had wrung out a wet newspaper over the trees. Were those parts of the jungle dead? "Does Neverland feel . . . wrong to you?"

He just looked at her. His face pinched in confusion.

"You know," she continued. "Broken somehow?"

He peered over the ledge as if he could catch the island getting into mischief. "Nope. It feels like Neverland."

She tried and failed to put it into better words. A tremor had caused a cave-in. Plants were dead—turned to ashy dust. Even the air Wendy breathed felt topsy-wobbly. Peter waved away each example Wendy gave as if she were unreasonably paranoid. But even with the shadow conjurer gone, the island *was* sick. How could she make Peter see the truth of it?

Peter rolled his head to the side and surveyed Wendy. "I'm glad you're here."

A sigh escaped her lips. In spite of herself, Wendy responded, "I'm glad I am too." And she was. Even with everything, she would rather be here than in a London ballroom, pretending to care about the supposedly important men of society or in a drawing room, pouring tea and making polite conversation rather than interesting conversation.

"Good, then it's settled."

Wendy blinked and straightened. "What's settled?"

"You'll stay here this time. With me."

Wendy sat up straight. Here it was. The thing she had wanted him to want from her for years.

"You can help me find lost boys. We can give them homes here in Neverland and play games. It'll be great fun. Think of the adventures we'll have!"

For a moment, Wendy crawled into the daydream with him, allowing herself to imagine living in Neverland forever with Peter, flying on the crisp wind above the mermaid lagoon, and never getting older. Never having her heart stop like a watch that wasn't wound. Like her father's heart.

It was a beautiful moment, living in that daydream. But when she looked over at Peter, her smile sagged. She shook her head. She'd been here before in this sort of moment. She could've stayed years ago if she hadn't been tired of Peter's childish and reckless behavior. She hadn't stayed exactly because she *had* been tired of it.

Since then, Wendy had done a considerable amount of growing up. And Peter hadn't changed at all. "I can't stay with you, Peter. Less now than I could have before."

"Why not?"

"Well, look at you. You're a child. I'm a grown woman. I'm afraid it would not work at all."

"I'm older than you," he said, puffing out his chest in defiance.

Liam had said as much about Peter as well. "Yes, well. That may be. But you do not *act* older. You do not *look* older."

"But I could. If I had a reason . . ."

Wendy smirked. "And what reason would ever induce you to change?"

"*You're* a good reason." Peter stood up, brushing off his clothes, and then he began to shimmer and glow, a light so blinding she had to shield her eyes against the glare. When she dared look again, Peter was no longer standing there. That is to say that Peter, the little boy, no longer stood in front of her. Instead stood a tall, handsome young man—someone her own age.

"Peter?" Wendy jumped to her feet, feeling equally alarmed and charmed by the man in front of her.

"It's me, Wendy," the man said. "The me you've always known I could be."

He was wrong. If she had known the handsome man Peter could grow to be, she would have forced him to grow up a long time ago. His facial features were strong and defined. Instead of looking pointed and sharp, he looked chiseled and rugged. The clothes were an echo of his usual garb. The green color deepened into the darkest shades of the forest. His tunic was a fine-cut coat with embroidered leaves and vines along the lapels and cuffs. The tunic was paired with dark brown, well-fitted trousers and dark brown boots. Over his shoulders hung an emerald-green cape that billowed softly in the breeze. His tousled hair remained charmingly unruly, a perfect blend of boyish lack of concern and manly handsomeness. He leaned in close, so close that his cheekbone grazed hers as he whispered in her ear, "I can be anything you want, Wendy. All you have to do is ask."

Wendy closed her eyes at the nearness she had hoped for and imagined for years.

"You once promised me a dance," Peter said, stepping back enough to offer her his hand.

She shook her head in disbelief. "You know how to dance?"

He nodded. "The pixies dance. Tiger Lily's family and friends all dance. They've taught me."

Wendy tentatively slipped her fingers into his, and she slid into his arms. The bright blue sky dimmed, and they were suddenly under a canopy of stars as he began a simple box step. Music came from behind them as if the flowers and trees and even the stars were applauding this dance that everyone had waited years to see happen. He took her into a natural turn and then an underarm turn.

"It's hard to imagine pixies waltzing. How did they ever learn?" She had to ask questions to try to force her mind out of this daydream. It had to be a daydream. How could it be real?

"Pixies are fascinated by humans, though Tink would never admit such a thing. They watch humans sometimes when they're sure they won't be caught. Then they come home and teach us what they learned. I hated learning, but Tinker Bell said she wouldn't play with me anymore if I didn't."

Peter hummed with the tune, then sang the words out loud, words that Wendy had never heard before but that she somehow knew by heart all the same.

> *Once upon a time*
> *Underneath the starry sky*
> *We found a place where hearts stay young*
> *And wishes never die.*

Stay with me and let's pretend
For just a little time
That you and I are forever young
And you are forever mine.

His movements were fluid and graceful as he guided her effortlessly across the surface of the stone, and then they weren't on the ground any longer. They were dancing in the air as he twirled her through clouds, and the stars sighed, echoing her contentment.

Peter's eyes were fixed on her, and they stopped dancing. Wendy and Peter hung suspended against the starry backdrop. "You also owe me a kiss, I believe," he said as he tilted his head down. She tilted her head up, her heart racing. She had waited for and wanted this moment, and yet . . . And yet.

Liam's face was the one she pictured.

Liam, whose soft blue eyes and easy smile made her heart warm just to think of him. Liam, who was misguided and ridiculous, but who was also kind and generous. She cared about Liam. She could not pretend anything different.

Wendy shook her head and pulled away. "No, Peter."

Bewilderment flooded his handsome features. "No?"

Though they had been hanging suspended, she and Peter now slowly spiraled to the ground, where they landed gently on the cliff.

"This isn't you," she continued. "Not the *you* you want to be. And honestly . . . this isn't me either. You were a beautiful dream. But that dream isn't my reality any longer."

In a flash of light, Peter was himself again, the boy with the ragged-edged, emerald tunic and the bycoket hat with a red feather. The stars had given way to blue skies. "Well, that's just plain silly," Peter said, his cheeks red and puffed out in anger. "Reality is whatever you want it to be."

"Peter, saying such things is what's plain silly. Emotions are more complicated than flashing pixie magic at them to make things the way you want."

"You've ruined a perfectly good game!" Peter threw his arms in the air to punctuate the tantrum he was now throwing.

"How would you even know how to play that game?" Wendy demanded to know, feeling like boxing Peter's ears.

"I watch the fairy king and queen when they have the royal festival of lights. I was just imagining that I was the king opening up the beginning dance with my queen and imagining how he always looks at her and behaves, and you ruined it. Now I can't be the king. You're being awfully disagreeable right now."

"You're the one being disagreeable. Honestly, Peter, you need to grow up!" She hated that she shouted at him. How could she be shouting at him—her Peter Pan?

"It's against the rules to grow up!" Peter shouted. Then his shoulders slumped. "That's the problem with you, Wendy," he said softly. "That's exactly what you've done."

Wendy's irritation diminished at that. She gently touched Peter's arm. "I'm sorry that it hurts you that I grew up. But I'm not sorry to have done it. Giving up childhood means opening yourself to compassion for others. It's the chance to become a better version of yourself every day. To not change and progress would be a nightmare for me, not a dream."

Peter sighed, but that was the last sign of distress he showed. "Well then. We should get back. We have a ship to take!"

Wendy wanted to talk more, to make sure Peter really was okay, but ignoring his emotions was his way.

They traveled back to the boys. The world of Neverland flew past underneath her. Liam was down there somewhere with his uncle. Definitely plotting against Peter. Possibly plotting against her. But she found she couldn't really be angry with him.

She hated how much she understood his reasoning for thinking the way he did. Hook was his family. Besides, Liam believed that Peter was harming children, and she had already seen that Liam was a child's greatest defender. In her mind, that meant he should be Peter's greatest defender. For wasn't Peter a child?

WENDY'S EVER AFTER   221

She looked up at Peter with the wind ruffling his hair as he flew over Neverland and knew he wasn't.

Now that she had seen what Peter could be as a grown man, she understood that Liam had been accurate when he had said that Peter was older than the sky itself. He had been able to age himself without giving the matter a second thought. She wondered if that meant that Peter had traveled through his time-twister vines to the end of what his life would be. Had he stared into the forget-me-not pools and seen the face of a weathered, lined old man? Had that frightened him and been the moment Peter decided he didn't want to grow old after all? Or had it been something else? What had made Peter Pan decide to be Peter Pan?

She couldn't ask him. Peter didn't answer questions like that. Those were far too serious for a boy who only wanted to have fun and play games.

Regardless of all the things Liam was wrong about, he was right that Peter was not a child. Not really. Wendy was not angry and hurt with him for viewing Peter as an adult and considering him a fair target in the rules of war. She was hurt and angry that he took his uncle's side and not hers.

But why should he take hers?

Their time together was the work of what? A few days? She expected to command loyalty over family on so short an acquaintance? Of course not. She was as great a wantwit as Hook.

She was glad when Peter landed back with the lost boys. It meant she no longer had to be alone to think her thoughts. She could drown them out with action.

While they'd been gone, Bookworm had created a detailed map based on the things Wendy had told him before she'd left. She marveled at his accuracy and commended him on a job well done. Jinx had created several whiz-bang explosives and smoke bombs. And there was a stockpile of grappling hooks and ropes.

"Where did these come from?" Wendy asked.

"We've been making these for forever," Flint said.

Wendy's gaze fell upon a lock-picking set. "And where did these come from?" she asked.

"Those are mine," said a boy who had earlier introduced himself as Ollie. He'd been quiet aside from his initial introduction, but now that Wendy was looking into those dark gray eyes, she understood that he was not to be underestimated. She had no doubt that he could pick locks as well as she could. Probably better. His slight, nimble build and muted clothing made him nondescript enough to be a wonderful sneak thief.

Milo and Sparks were excited to show off several pairs of gloves that magnetized to the metal of a sword so the wearer could never be disarmed in a fight. If Liam had been there, she might have teased him that he wouldn't be permitted such a tool while fencing with her on the outing he owed her. But he wasn't there to tease.

Peter crowed, calling the boys to attention.

They were ready to take the ship.

Theo slipped a hand in hers. When she looked down at him, he whispered, "I don't want to play anymore. I want to go home. You could take me without him knowing. We could get away while they're all busy."

Wendy's mouth hung slack. If he was willing to sneak away, he must have been much more desperate than she'd known. Had she been so blind to Peter's faults that she hadn't really seen what Liam had seen?

Peter might not have been stealing children, but if he didn't let them go when they wanted to leave, perhaps he was a villain after all.

"To die will be an awfully big adventure."

CHAPTER NINETEEN

After Theo's request, Wendy fretted and stewed over what to do. She finally decided that her best option to help the boy was to find Liam and do it his way. They needed to put an end to battles between children and pirates. While everyone was busy preparing, Wendy crept into the jungle far enough away to not be visible from the encampment. She closed her eyes and imagined Neverland—not the discordant Neverland in which she stood, but the bright, hopeful place she'd remembered. Her feet left the ground, and she scanned the world beneath her until she spotted what she'd been searching for.

Liam.

He stood close to the enclosed grove that hid the pool of pixie magic that showed memories. Hook stood with him. So did several other pirates.

Was Liam revealing the time-twister vines and forget-me-not pools?

She watched as Liam sent the rest of the pirates ahead, down a path that steered them clear of the bluff that afforded a strategic view of the island. At least he wasn't leading them to the other populated areas of the island. The island's other inhabitants didn't need to be pestered by pirates.

226   JULIE WRIGHT

Wendy flew closer and landed in a tree that was almost directly above the pair of pirates. No. She didn't really think of Liam that way. Hook? Yes. Liam? No.

Liam pushed aside the vines that led to the pools. "Uncle, I need to speak with you privately for a moment." He beckoned Hook within the confines of the vines.

With a grumble about time and not letting those cockroaches of a crew get lost again, Hook followed Liam.

Wendy glided to the ground and crept through the vines as well, hiding herself among the leafy shrubs. Once Hook and Liam were by the pools, Liam said, "Tell me how you came to be in Neverland."

"What is this? Why would you waste my time with such a question?" Hook snarled as he raised his hook threateningly. The pirate had always been quick to temper and suspicion, but it seemed so much worse than she remembered. His behavior had gone from villainous to pure, deranged malevolence.

"I need to know how we are tied to this place."

Hook's eyes glazed, and he seemed to look past Liam as if focusing on something very far away. "There was a storm. Then the stars shifted and the air was thick with enchantment. Suddenly, I was in a place where time stands still, and magic is as common as salt in the water."

As Hook spoke, the pool's flat surface rippled and flattened again, images appearing of a storm that made it seem as if the pool had taken on the violent twists and rolls of waves in a turbulent sea.

"What is this? What witchery are you doing?" Hook looked down at the memory reflected on the water's surface, clearly alarmed by what he saw.

Wendy had expected to see Hook as he was now, an older man. But the person at the center of the storm was a child. A young boy who clung to a bit of debris that had probably come from the ship he'd been on. The boy was crying. Wendy never would have believed that the boy was Hook except for the intense blue of the child's eyes. As vividly blue as the forget-me-not pools.

WENDY'S EVER AFTER   227

Peter swooped in and hovered in the air above Hook-the-child. "Why are you crying?" Peter asked. The past voices had a watery echo to them.

"Because I'm about to drown. And there are probably sharks."

"Don't be silly. Just fly up. Getting above the storm's no trick."

"You don't be silly," the boy hiccupped. "People don't fly."

"Well, I'm people," Peter said, looking at his arms suspiciously as if maybe he wasn't sure about that.

"No," Present-Hook said. He tried backing away from the pool. "No. I don't want to see. I don't want to remember." But instead of stopping, the pool's reflection seemed to scramble to other memories. Child-Hook and Peter playing in the jungle and teasing the mermaids in the lagoon. Child-Hook and Peter cutting their palms and then clamping their hands together, declaring themselves brothers by blood, promising they would always be together. Other boys joined them eventually. And then a girl. "She's our mother. She'll tell stories, and make you take your medicine," Peter in the past said.

Wendy stared hard at the pools, expecting to see herself, but the girl wasn't her at all. A different girl from a different time.

The boys in the pool's memory all looked excited, but Hook looked mesmerized as he gazed at the girl Peter had brought to them. The memory in the pool scrambled again as Hook shook his head. Then the girl was leaving. "My sister needs me," the girl said.

"I'll come with you," young Hook had answered.

Peter begged young Hook to stay. "You promised you'd never leave!" his pitiful voice cried.

There was a mix of images. Flowers. A kiss, a wedding.

"No, not this. I can't bear to see her get sick again," Present-Hook said, but he kept staring at the pool, as transfixed by the reflections there as Wendy.

And then Wendy saw the girl, now grown to be a woman, lying in a bed. Her eyes sunken in a pale face. Hook was kneeling beside her, sobbing that he didn't know what he would do without her.

Wendy recognized the woman's face as the same one from the portrait in Hook's quarters.

"Go back to Peter," she said. "He will keep you busy and help you forget your sorrow when I am gone. And check in on my sister from time to time. Make sure she's cared for."

"I promise," Hook said.

The pool rippled, and Hook was back in Neverland. Only he and Peter were fighting. "You left me!" Peter shouted. "You promised you'd be my friend forever—my *brother*, and you left."

"But I'm back," Hook pleaded.

"You can't come back. You're old. Old. Old. Old!" Peter flew away, leaving Hook standing alone on the shore of the beach that Wendy recognized as Pirate Cove.

"What have you done?"

It took a moment for Wendy to realize that it was Hook in the present asking Liam this question. There was fury in his voice and fire in his eyes.

Just in time, Liam dodged the slash of his uncle's hook.

"Why would you bring me here to show me these things? You're in league with that devil!" Hook slashed again. Wendy covered the scream from erupting out of her mouth as Liam moved out of the way.

"No!" Liam insisted. "I only wanted to see what brought you here. I had no idea . . ." He clearly didn't know how to finish that statement. Though he had to have had an idea that *something* would happen, he obviously hadn't expected it to be so painfully raw.

Peter had saved Hook. Like all the others. Peter found boys who were lost, boys who would die without Peter's aid in whisking them away. Wendy felt profoundly sorry for them both.

Peter and Hook. Hook and Peter.

Neither one had a genuine reason to be at odds with the other. They were both stuck in their eternal war because, at the heart of it, they were both lonely little boys.

They gathered their little armies, Hook with his pirate crew and Peter with his lost boys, and they fought over and over and over.

"You betray me," Hook snarled at Liam before swiping his hook in Liam's direction. He missed, but he'd already started stalking away at that point, not even bothering to check behind him to see if he had damaged his nephew.

Liam stood by the pools and held a hand to his cheek where a trickle of blood seeped through his fingers. Hook must have grazed him after all. Wendy stepped out from behind the shrub. She wasn't sure what she expected from Liam in that moment.

"Wendy," he breathed.

"I'm sorry," they both said at the same time.

"Really?" she said, sure she'd misheard.

"What?" he asked, clearly thinking he'd misheard.

"I was wrong," he said at the same time she said, "You were right."

Then they both quietly laughed, and he whispered, "You first."

"You were right when you said Peter doesn't let the boys go when they want to go. You're right to want to put an end to it. I need your help to get Theo home safely. I can't have him involved in the coming battle. I can't have any of them involved."

He took her hands in his. "And my uncle is not the man he once was. He's angrier. Fury radiates off his every breath. He's lost all sense and reason. Did you see his memory?"

Wendy admitted that she had been spying for long enough to have seen the whole thing.

"That softer man is the man I have known. But he's darker somehow. He's venom and loathing. He's changed like that shadow fairy. I watched him closely when I returned to him. It's like something's controlling him. And whatever that something is, it wants your little imp friend."

Her fingers tightened on his. "So he is trying to turn Peter to shadow?"

As if encouraged by her grip on him, Liam adjusted the way he held her hands so that their fingers tangled together. "I think so. But it's not him, Wendy. You have to believe me."

"I do believe you." It surprised her that she really did. "Whatever's going on, something's wrong in Neverland. It's not just things turning to shadow. I think that's a symptom of something more. Neverland is sick." She explained all the things she tried to tell Peter about the tremors and the dead foliage. Relief flooded her heart when she saw in his eyes that he believed her, too.

Liam rested his forehead against hers. "So what do we do about it? I can't go against my uncle. When I returned, he made me swear a pirate's oath to protect him. By the salt in my blood and the wind in my sails, I'm sworn to give up my own life in the protection of his." Liam pulled away, the look in his eyes earnest and pleading. "Besides, whatever's going on isn't his fault. Something *is* controlling him."

Wendy chewed on her lip, feeling like she might get a headache from the fierce way she was frowning and thinking. "Go back to Hook," she said, and it seemed to echo when Hook's wife had told him in the memory to go back to Peter. "Find out what's controlling him. I'll go back to Peter and see if I can keep him from attacking, but you must be ready. Peter isn't easy to persuade. If the battle has to happen, we need to do whatever we can to mitigate damage. No child hurt."

"No crew hurt either."

"Fine. No pirates hurt, either. I have an idea that can keep lost boys from inflicting damage. But you have to find out what's controlling your uncle. I can't let Peter be turned to shadow. If Peter turns to shadow, Neverland will sink into total ruin."

The two of them shared a long look and then Liam leaned down and swept a brief, yet fervent, kiss across her lips. She almost toppled over since she'd started to lean into it, and Liam broke it off much more quickly than she'd anticipated. But he was right. There would be time for such things later, wouldn't there?

WENDY'S EVER AFTER

Liam left to catch up to his uncle. Wendy flew up to return to Peter—to try to talk him out of his foolishness once and for all.

When Wendy landed in the middle of the lost boys' encampment, it was to the sound of the finalization on battle plans. She hurried to Peter, working to prevail on him any sort of wisdom that would allow him to see reason.

No luck.

The lost boys were easier to be entreated—especially since Theo shadowed Wendy as she spoke softly to each boy. "Do no harm," she told them. "Defend yourselves if you're forced, but right now, the game is Capture the Pirate."

Nods and giggles followed her instructions. This sort of game was the kind they understood—the kind they liked.

Before she could truly feel prepared, they were marching to Pirate Cove. Well . . . she flew alongside Peter and Tinker Bell, but they stayed with the lost boys.

The boys unlashed two of the jolly boats from their sand anchors. With them engaged in that particular task and the brief arguments over who would sit at the front or the back or next to one boy or the other, Wendy snatched hold of Theo's hand and tugged him behind a large boulder. "You stay here," she whispered, tossing back a glance to the others to make certain none of them saw her remove Theo from their midst. She had no intention of letting the small boy join the battle in any capacity.

"Stay with me?" he asked.

Wendy shook her head. "I have to protect the others. And by you staying here, I'm protecting you too. Don't come out for anyone but me."

He nodded as he huddled against the stone.

By the time she'd turned around, the jolly boats full of boys were already on their way across the water.

She faced the looming shadow of the *Jolly Roger* anchored in the cove. A tremor vibrated the ground under her feet as if compelling her to move with greater urgency. Waves frothed on the water in response to the shaking ground. "I am Wendy Moira Angela Darling," she said to herself. "I'm the closest thing this island has to a mother, and I will protect it all." The tremor stopped—a breath held, as if waiting to see what would happen next.

Wendy squared her shoulders and raised her chin, determined to preserve her promise to Theo by keeping the other boys safe. Then, she flew to the *Jolly Roger*.

Onboard the ship, the lost boys made quick work of incapacitating the few pirates who'd been left by Hook while he was away on land. They tied up their captives even though Peter frowned and said they should be killing the pirates. They hid the pirates down in the galley and in between the crates and settled in to wait for the rest to return. They wouldn't attack the rest of the pirates immediately when they showed up. Peter wanted to make a grand entrance. And they needed to guarantee that Hook was aboard. Hook was Peter's ultimate goal.

Twilight had settled over the cove when the first sounds of returning pirates thumped on the deck. Wendy heard Hook rally his crew to get ready for battle. "Pan comes against us. By nightfall, it will be over. And we will be the victors. Leave Pan to me. And may our days be filled with fortune and our enemies tremble at our name!"

Wendy peeked out from where she hid behind a wooden barrel.

"May our days be filled with fortune and our enemies tremble at our name!" The pirates all repeated the last sentence and then laughed and raised their weapons in a salute, reminding Wendy of an older, taller version of the frenzied lost boys as they had prepared for battle.

It didn't take long for the pirates to lose their frenzy and settle in to wait for the attack, completely unaware that the attack had already begun. "Where are you, Peter?" Wendy murmured. The boys couldn't continue the battle until Peter had arrived. A low fog rolled in over the cove, which set the men on edge. Wendy didn't blame them. With the strangeness that the island exhibited every day, a fog like this would alarm her too if she hadn't known that the boys had created it.

"It's just fog, Mullens," Wendy heard Liam say. Wendy was glad to hear Liam's voice. She hadn't known if Hook would accept Liam back.

Mullens seemed extraordinarily spooked, though the acrid smell coming off the fog had to reveal the fact that it wasn't natural.

A slight scuffle sounded where one of the pirates was keeping watch over the port side of the ship. "Wibbles?" Mullens asked.

No one responded.

"Wibbles?" Mullens walked away. Wendy knew that when he went to check on the man, no one would be there.

"What devilry is this?" Mullens whispered when he returned. "I bet the fog-men got him."

"There are no fog-men," Liam said in response to his friend. The cynical response made Wendy raise her eyebrows. She'd seen dozens of impossible things since coming to Neverland. Maybe there were fog-men. How were any of them to know?

Another scuffle of shoes on the deck and another pirate joined the others who were bound and gagged between the crates.

"Mullens," Liam said since Mullens looked half-crazy with fear of the fog-men. "The captain wants you to take a jolly boat back to shore and wait there."

"By meself?"

Wendy held in her laugh.

"No. Of course not. He wants you to take Skylights and Jasper."

"Right. Of course. Not alone then." Mullens went to gather the two men and get off the ship as fast as possible. Liam had eliminated three from the fight.

Liam stealthily moved to the starboard side closer to where Wendy crouched behind several crates. Seeing he was alone, Wendy stepped out of the shadows.

"Curses, Wendy!" he hissed, brandishing his sword and only putting it away when he saw her. "What's the plan?"

The man was a sight for sore eyes. "Right now, the game is Capture the Pirate." She indicated the space between the crates to reveal two of his uncle's crew tied up and gagged. The pirates looked fairly surly over the fact that they'd been bested by children.

Liam grimaced at the pirates. "Sorry, Bronson. Sorry, Keb."

The pirates glowered at their captain's nephew.

"We've got more tucked away in the galley and on the other side," Wendy told Liam.

That news earned her a grin. "I could kiss you here and now," he said. "Though maybe it's better if we stay on task. I've sent eight of the men back to shore. Told them it was Captain's orders. I'll get a few more gone that same way. Since no one has sounded the battle alarm yet, everyone is still just waiting. It gives us time to manage the potential for disaster."

"Thank you," they both said at the same time and then they chuckled softly. The man Liam had called Bronson rolled his eyes. Keb, who sat next to him, gave a repulsed shake of his head at the show of silly sentimentality.

"Did you discover what's controlling your uncle?"

Liam shook his head. "But I talked to some of the men. And from what we can all gather, the changes happened when Uncle James killed the crocodile." He glanced over to where Keb and Bronson sat. Both men shrugged and nodded their agreement.

"Any ideas what that could mean?" She'd seen the new crocodile-skin coat Hook wore. But what could a coat and the shadows have to do with each other?

They agreed to keep an eye out as they continued thwarting the battle as much as possible.

Liam managed to get five more members of the crew to row a jolly boat to shore to await orders, while Wendy and her little band managed to disarm several more and get them gagged and tied up. She was suddenly glad that Peter was waiting for a grand announcement before he revealed himself. It allowed them to get several pirates out of harm's way. Unfortunately, their luck didn't last. The clang of the alarm bell sounded while Smee shouted, "Intruders! Intruders! We're under attack!"

Peter treated the bell clang like a personal herald. He crowed from the rigging before he flew down, insisting Hook come out and face him.

That put an end to stealth and caution. Wendy and Liam's efforts were foiled as pirates and lost boys alike came together in a clash of fighting. Wendy rushed to join in to make sure the boys weren't injured. As she moved, she spied Hook and Peter circling each other like wild dogs. There would be no saving the lost boys if Hook managed to turn Peter like he'd turned the fairy, like he'd tried to turn Mira.

Peter's level of childish selfishness would be magnified a million-fold if he turned to shadow. The dark fairy would be a ray of rainbow light in comparison.

A shadow skulked across the deck near the ship's helm toward Peter. Panic rose up in Wendy's throat, strangling off the cry of alarm she wanted to sound. *No.* This would not happen. Not while she stood watching. Wendy flew to where the shadow prowled closer. Upon closer inspection, it wasn't a shadow. It was Smee. Hook's bosun held a shroud of something like a vaporous net in front of him. He meant to throw it over Peter. He lifted his hands higher. Wendy had seconds. Less than that, really.

Without another thought, Wendy pulled at a knot in the ship's rigging, dropping a sail between Smee and Peter. The dark net hit the sail and tumbled harmlessly to the ground in a puddle that looked oily and frightening in ways Wendy could scarcely understand. Peter took the distraction to lunge at Hook. Their swords clanged on impact.

Wendy faced Smee.

"You foolish girl!" Spittle exploded from the gap in his large front teeth when Smee spoke.

"You wantwit!" Wendy retorted. "I know what that is." She

indicated the oily puddle of shadow netting on the deck. "You want to turn Peter. But I won't allow it." She held her sword at the ready.

She lunged first, striking out and nicking Smee across his bicep. She had told the lost boys to do no harm and yet here she was, drawing first blood.

Was it the nearness of the shadow net?

Or was it the shadows that had been within her all along and that she fought back continuously each day?

How could she know?

Wendy only knew that she was tired of this strange Neverland. It needed her to defend it. At that moment, its attackers were Smee and Hook. Wendy would defend her island.

Smee scrambled against her attack. Wendy had the upper hand, keeping him from moving his own blade close enough to inflict any kind of damage.

She heard Peter and Hook on the other side of the helm, locked in their own battle. She tried not to pay attention to them because she had her own fight to worry about, but she couldn't ignore that Peter's safety was a priority.

"It's over, Pan!" Hook said with a sneer. "Your childish games end here."

Wendy glanced over and saw the look in Hook's eyes. This was no game for him.

"My games are just starting," Pan said before thrusting out his dagger and nicking Hook's hand, much like she had done to Smee's arm.

Hook let out a strangled roar and slashed his blade out with more fury.

"You're getting slow, old man!" Peter said. "You should trade that hook for a walking stick!"

But the truth was that it was Peter who looked like he was growing tired. Hook fought with the ferocity of a man determined to win at any cost. Just when Wendy worried the battle was going Hook's way, the boat began to tip. Wendy grabbed the bulwark to keep from sliding and looked down at the vigorous splashing of large fish tails and tiny, delicate hands. Mermaids. They were shoving the boat, making it rock.

"You've got company," Peter said with a triumphant laugh. "I think they want to talk to you about their daughter that you had locked up."

Unfortunately, for as much as the rocking had been in Peter's favor, it unbalanced Wendy's footing. Smee swung his blade and sliced her hand. With a cry of pain, she released her sword and fell. She landed with a whump on the deck. Smee steadily approached her, his own sword high and ready to strike.

"Wendy!" It was Liam calling her. Liam rushed to the helm but also fell with the new force of rocking. Their eyes locked, and Liam slid his sword in Wendy's direction. She growled when the sword went just out of her reach because of another tumultuous rock to the side. But Smee also fell back with the new motion. Wendy found her feet and rushed Smee. She snatched up the sword and pinned him to the bulwark. "Not today, pirate!" she yelled. "Now drop your sword, or I will gut you like the carp you are."

Smee dropped his weapon. With shaking hands, Wendy began the work of tying him to the bulwark.

Emboldened by her victory, Peter began taunting Liam's uncle once again. "That fancy coat makes it look like all of you got swallowed up by that crocodile," the boy said. "Not just your hand." Peter threw his dagger in the air so that he could wave his hands and then shot up into the sky to retrieve it.

Hook's eyes flared to the red of hot coals. Couldn't Peter see? Something in the pirate captain had shifted, even before the forget-me-not pools. Hook was not playing a game. He was fighting to win.

"And that necklace!" Peter hooted. "When did you start wearing jewelry?"

Necklace?

That was when Wendy saw it.

The leather corded necklace swung as Hook struck out again and again.

At the end of that necklace was a tooth—large and menacing. The slightly curved, yellowed surface had fine cracks and splinters along the sharp ridges. It was a crocodile tooth. Not just any crocodile, either.

The crocodile.

Wendy knew Hook had killed the beast that was as eternal as Neverland itself. The jacket he wore was proof of that, but the tooth . . . something about the tooth was wrong. The fine cracks were like the oily netting Smee had tried to use to capture Peter. Shadow vapor leaked from those cracks and swirled all around Hook.

How had she not seen it before?

She was too far away. She couldn't do anything about it. "Liam!" she cried out. He was closer. "Liam, the tooth! Hook's necklace! The tooth is controlling him."

Liam looked over and saw what she meant. He moved to snatch the tooth from around Hook's neck.

Hook didn't even see his nephew as he blindly raged, slashing with his sword and hook over and over, enraged by Peter's taunting.

The leaking tendrils of shadow vapor swirled around both pirate and boy.

"Oh, did I hurt your feelings?" Peter asked. "Or are those just crocodile tears?" Peter then laughed hard enough he rolled back in the air while holding his belly.

Peter was distracted with being impressed with his own humor when the captain lifted his hook to strike.

Wendy felt as though she'd touched one of the time-twister vines. Time slowed, and she could see everything clearly, perhaps for the first time in her life. Peter was once Hook's best friend. Peter was all Hook had left. If Hook followed through with this moment, he would unravel and become unrecoverable.

Liam was moving toward his uncle, his hand outstretched, reaching for the tooth. His fingers wrapped around it.

Someone shouted, "No!" at the moment Liam slid between Hook and Peter. Had that shout come from her?

The sharp metal tip of the hook slashed through Liam's chest, looking as though it had cut away the flesh from his ribs and flayed him open. What had Wendy said to Smee? "Gut you like the carp you are." That was what Liam looked like—a carp with red hot blood spilling from him as he flopped back against the deck. He had the tooth still in his grip.

Hook staggered back in surprise and horror. Shaking himself as if shaking off a dream. "What? What have you done, lad? What have *I* done?"

But Liam didn't answer. His eyes rolled toward Wendy, who had reached him and now cradled his head in her arms.

He was dying.

Stars are beautiful, but they may
not take an active part in anything,
they must just look on for ever.

CHAPTER TWENTY

"No." Wendy repeated that word as if by saying it, she could make it true. No, he wasn't hurt. No, he wasn't dying. Wendy's heart broke. No, not broke. It shattered, splintering and bouncing off the walls of her soul. If a baby's skipping laugh could create fairies, the shattering, cracking sound of Wendy's heart could create demons. No. No. No. She couldn't let this happen. "You'll be all right. I've got you. Someone!" She began to shout. "Someone, help me!"

Little faces appeared from the stairs. The lost boys had crept up to see her wailing and begging with the stars to save Liam.

Peter had been able to subdue Hook only because Hook had been so stunned to have harmed Liam. From where he was lashed to the helm, Hook watched, his face twisted in confusion by what he saw.

"Save him," Wendy hissed at Peter. "Save him with your pixie dust. Save him with your mermaid's breath. Save him like you saved all those boys." Her begging was a pathetic keening.

She couldn't stop the noise. She just didn't know how to reconcile her heart to being without Liam. "Please, Peter."

"I can't. I don't know how." Peter's face was shrouded in something she'd never seen on him before. Regret.

Wendy had to gather her wits. She couldn't sit here crying and pleading for someone to help. She had to act. Gently settling Liam's head to the wood of the deck, she knelt over Liam and inspected the wound. "He's losing so much blood. We have to bind the wound, close it off to try to keep some of that blood in his body."

"What good will that do?" Peter asked.

"It will buy us time!" she snapped. "Now get me Hook's belt."

Peter did as he was told and retrieved the belt from Hook, who was whimpering about the crocodile and shadow. Wendy was glad Peter hadn't asked why it had to be Hook's belt or what she was doing. The truth was that she wasn't sure. Looking at the gaping wound, all she could think was that she wished she had a needle and thread to sew him back together again, which might have worked if there was time and tools. But there wasn't time. Hook's belt was long enough to do the job and made of sturdy leather with a buckle that would allow it to be pulled tight. It was all she had.

Wendy wrapped the belt around Liam's abdomen and cinched it tightly enough to staunch the flow of blood but not so tight as to hurt anything.

"I'm not a doctor," she muttered over and over as she worked.

The continued mournful wails from Hook rent the air. "Cursed crocodile! I promised I would take care of her family. I swore to keep them all safe. And now look what I've done! I failed her, failed her, failed her. The crocodile forced my hand. No choice. No choice. Failed!"

Wendy refused to be distracted by his lamentations. She might have put her blade through him for the impertinence of daring to be upset when it was she who deserved to lament. Rage filled her. A fury that bubbled and boiled and was close to eruption. That was when she remembered the tooth. This rage was not hers. If it was affecting her like this, what was it doing to Liam? Could it hurt his chances to heal? She eased open Liam's hand and pulled the tooth free from his grasp. Then with a guttural cry of rage, she flung it into the ocean.

WENDY'S EVER AFTER   243

As the tooth touched the water, the ocean rippled out in glowing circles, washing up against the *Jolly Roger* and onto the shore of Pirate Cove. The ripples reached the sand but did not stop. The water ripples turned to air and whispered across the grains of sand as they spread over the beach and through the leaves of the jungle. It was as if the entire island took a breath of relief from a pain that had been bothering it for a long time. With that breath came the faint *tick tick tick* of a clock in the distance.

The island had reset itself. But Wendy couldn't make herself rejoice even knowing that she had won a battle. She looked down at Liam.

What did a battle matter when she had lost the war? Perhaps such thinking was backward. Shouldn't the island matter more than a single man? It didn't, though. Not to her.

She had to think. This couldn't be the end. She had healed an island. Surely she could heal a man?

The idea came to her so suddenly she gasped out loud and jumped to her feet. "Healing! We need a neverflower. Immediately!"

"But Wendy," Peter said. "We used the last of the neverflowers for Theo. There aren't any left."

He was wrong. He had to be. "I don't believe you've looked everywhere. I refuse to believe that." She turned to the boys on the stairs. "Lost boys, think. Where could another flower be growing?" It was night; surely a flower that glowed like a star would be easier to find in the dark.

"The forget-me-not pools," Peter said.

Wendy wanted to shout that she knew of that location already and that flower had been used, but she maintained her calm. She had to if she wanted to think clearly enough to save Liam. There were so many things they hadn't done yet. She'd never been able to beat him at fencing. She'd never been able to invite him to dinner. They hadn't been able to go to Mrs. Connolly and tell her that she'd been right about them and that they got along famously. They'd never been out for ices, or to Hyde Park to row around the lake. They'd never gone to the museum. She'd never convinced him to come to her way of thinking when it came to pies and cakes.

Stop! she told herself. *You will stay calm. Right now, you will save him so you can do those things later.*

"Where else?" she asked them again.

"Lunar Meadows, where the six elder brothers live, had some a while back," Jinx said. "But they're all gone now."

"You're sure?"

"I took the last one myself." He hung his head over having to admit such a thing.

"Where else?" She would not lose Liam. They would have time. Time to spend together, to learn more about each other. Time to become best friends.

"The cliff edges where the gnome tailors live had a bunch at one point, but it's been a long time since I've seen any there," Ollie said, also hanging his head.

"I've seen them near Pixie Hollow," Flint said. "Maybe Tink knows if there are any left."

Everyone looked to Tinker Bell, who chimed low, mournful tones. There weren't any.

"What about Theo?" Bookworm asked.

"He's on the shore in the cove. He's safe," Wendy absently tried to assure Bookworm as her mind raced for what to do.

Bookworm shook his head and tugged on the end of Wendy's tunic. "That's not what I meant. I meant Theo has a neverflower in him."

"We can't take it out of him to use again, Bookworm." She was losing hope. Liam had stopped moving, and his eyes had been closed for several minutes. He was still breathing, but for how much longer?

"I know that." Bookworm was growing impatient. "But I read that just like we use the stars for figuring out where we are, the stars all know where other stars are shining. They use each other as maps too. Theo has a star in him. Maybe he knows if there's another one nearby."

Wendy's head shot up in the direction she'd left Theo on the shore. She had to get to him immediately. Hope surged through her and then she was in the sky, flying toward Theo. Flying on her own, on the happy thought of her own hopeful determination. Starna flew next to her, chiming that she didn't want Wendy to be alone in case she needed help. Wendy had never soared faster, barely registering that Starna was there. She landed on the sand much harder than Peter ever did and immediately was running to the rock where she'd left the boy. She called his name several times until he appeared, wide-eyed. She dropped to her knees. "I need a favor before we can go home. I need you to look inside yourself and see if you feel other stars shining close by. Maybe they'll look like stars to you, but maybe they'll look like neverflowers. Can you see any?"

Theo squeezed his dark brown eyes shut and scrunched up his face as if he was concentrating very hard. "I see one."

"You do?" Wendy almost broke down sobbing in relief. "Where?"

"It's under the big willow. It likes it there because the willow whispers in the wind."

"Do you know where the willow is? Can you show me?"

"I can show you," Theo assured her.

Wendy thought about carrying the boy but worried she wasn't strong enough. She looked at Starna, who seemed to be reading her thoughts. Starna nodded and chimed that she could do it easily. She grabbed a vine and looped it under Theo's armpits then tied it to herself.

"Let's go get it."

They raced through the velvet sky. The stars that hadn't fallen twinkled their approval of Wendy's mission. Their light seemed to fill her with an energy she hadn't had on her own before. She flew faster with Starna and Theo right next to her.

"There!" Theo shouted. "There's the willow."

The willow was illuminated from within the umbrella of its branches. Wendy landed on the ground and entered the confines of the sweeping limbs and saw what she needed so desperately. A neverflower was snuggled in among the willow tree's roots. It glowed impossibly bright.

Theo rubbed his nose. "She said it's okay to use her. It's why she's here."

Wendy nodded. "Thank you, little star, for your gift," she said before plucking the flower with the teardrop-shaped pearlescent petals and the golden glowing center from the ground. Wendy leaped back into the Neverland night.

She arrived at the *Jolly Roger* only moments later, but it felt like she'd been gone too long. When she landed on the deck of the *Jolly Roger* with the flower, it was as if she'd landed with an entire lighthouse. Its glow brightened everything, including Wendy's determination. She held the flower over Liam, then frowned.

"How do I use it?" she asked Theo.

"Pour the light over the wound." He pantomimed the pouring motion.

Wendy poured the golden liquid over the gash across Liam's chest. She poured until there was no light left in the cone of the flower. She pressed the spent petals together in her hands like she was praying. Then she waited and wished on stars. All of them, but specifically the little one who had bravely given up her place under the whispering willow.

Faith, trust, pixie dust.

You need not be sorry for her. She was one of the kind that likes to grow up. In the end she grew up of her own free will a day quicker than the other girls.

CHAPTER TWENTY-ONE

Wendy had to believe Liam would open his eyes.

Hook watched from where he knelt bound to the helm. "I'm sorry, little bluebird. She asked me to protect her family. She asked me to make them my family. To keep them safe. What have I done? I killed the island's timekeeper and kept bits of it as a souvenir of my triumph. How was I to know what it would do? How was I to know the cost of slaying that eternal creature?"

Wendy didn't answer. She couldn't let herself care about Hook. He didn't deserve her attention. She watched to see what the neverflower would do while she murmured, "Stay with me. I promise we'll have adventures. Please stay with me. I promise to let you win at fencing when we're back in London. Granted, I'll probably only let you win once, but that's more than I do for anyone. You can ask my brothers. I promise you the very best friendship. I'll let you fill up my dance card even if we aren't wearing masks. I promise we'll be happy if you stay. We'll be so happy." The starlight shone on them from above, but now it seemed like it shone from within Liam's chest, too. The glow spread and then the wound began to knit together. Through the tear in Liam's shirt, Liam's skin smoothed until it was entirely undamaged.

Wendy held her breath until Liam gasped and coughed. He

sucked in air hard and released it with another hacking cough. Then his eyes popped open.

"You're alive!" Wendy sobbed as she pressed kiss after kiss on his eyelids, his cheeks, his mouth.

She hardly noticed that Hook also sobbed or that Peter looked away or that the lost boys made noises of disgust. Her Liam was breathing.

Wendy looked down at Liam. "You're safe now. I've got you," she murmured into his ear while she stroked his hair. She felt Peter's eyes on her. She glanced up and smiled at him. "It's as you said, Peter. The stars are not content to just look on. They want to be involved."

"So they do," he said, looking up to the sky while Wendy looked down at Liam.

So they do.

Wendy wondered how completely Liam had been healed. Could he walk yet? Would it take a while, or was it all done?

Her question was answered when he moved out of her arms and stood on his own two legs. Liam standing in front of her was her undoing. She began sobbing all over again.

Peter, not one to let a good win of a battle go to waste, immediately began claiming victory of their game. "The ship is ours, lads! We've won the *Jolly Roger*!"

The boys began cheering and crowing along with Peter.

"No. Stop," Liam said.

Wendy wasn't sure if it was because of the commanding tone he'd used or because they were feeling humbled by the fact that he'd been saved from certain death, but everyone—even Peter—fell silent. "No more wars. No more games of little boys against pirates. No more."

He turned to Hook. "And I am not your heir apparent. I will return to London with Wendy, and I will resume my life there." Then Liam rounded on Peter. "And Wendy and I will take any of the boys who want to go with us. They will go home. We will find their mothers and fathers. Do you understand me? And you will not ever keep a child who chooses to leave again, or I will pick up the mantle of Captain Hook and hunt you down." Liam looked fairly dangerous as he raged out his list of demands.

The playful spark in Peter's eyes flickered like a distant shining star, and Wendy wondered if Peter had ever been healed by a never-flower. His response to Liam was to tilt his head to the side and say, "If the boys want to leave. *Truly* want to leave. Then they can leave. I would never force them to stay. What's the use of a bunch of surly whiners crying at me all the time?" Peter smirked at Liam and twirled the dagger in his hand. "As for you? You think you can pick up the mantle of Captain Hook?" He made a scoffing sound. "You could never be Captain Hook. You don't have any sense of the relentless adventure needed. You don't have it in you to be my dark and sinister rival. There is only one Captain Hook!" With that, Peter flew to the helm and cut Hook's bonds, freeing the villain of Wendy's youth.

She gasped and waited for Hook to strike.

He didn't.

Hook straightened his crocodile-skin coat, removed it, and laid it over the balustrade before saying, "We have a truce for tonight. It's good form. I will give you this win, and we can start over in the morning."

"No," Liam said. "Did you not hear me just now? No. We don't start over. You involve your crew in this madness, and you!" He pointed at Peter. "You involve these children. If you two want to fight then you do it, just you. Not the rest of them. You leave the crew and boys out of your squabble. And you should stop this feud anyway. The feud is your enemy, not Pan."

Hook shook his head. "You're wrong about that. Boredom and contentment are my enemy. I will not involve my crew if they don't want to join in, but I do not promise to not try to kill Pan tomorrow."

"That's a relief," Pan said. "Because I do not promise to not try to kill you."

"Excellent," Hook said.

"Good," Peter said with a firm nod. Though Wendy really didn't feel like there was anything excellent or good about it.

"We're agreed." Hook grabbed the burgundy velvet coat that had been stowed in a box by the helm and slid his arms into it, and Peter put his hands on his hips and nodded some more. They both looked pleased with themselves for being so reasonable.

Wendy and Liam shared a look over Peter's head. Reasonable was exactly what the boy and the pirate were not. Wendy sidled up to Liam and slipped her hand in his. "Well, you tried," she whispered.

Liam might have tried to respond, but Hook boomed out in his big pirate voice. "Until then, I am a man of my word." Hook swept his hand to indicate the ship. "You've won for tonight and tonight only. Enjoy it while you can."

"You heard him, boys!" Peter crowed. "The ship is ours!" The boys cheered with the announcement. "So where to, everyone? We have a whole pirate ship! What do you say, Wendy? Are you ready to be the pirate queen?"

Wendy didn't answer. She was too busy kissing the man who was alive and breathing and who had been looking down at her with the same relief and tenderness she felt.

• • •

The mermaids were glad to have had their revenge, but they didn't bother to stick around while the boys enjoyed the spoils of their battle. The boys wanted to sail around the cove in their newly acquired ship. But they had to release their captives to help them run it. The ones who had been on shore were signaled to return to their posts. Wendy was surprised by how much cordiality existed between the two groups. Was it because the shadow was gone, that eternal power returned to the island?

Wendy didn't know.

WENDY'S EVER AFTER

Once the revelry was done, the boys went off exploring, and she felt it necessary to trail after them to keep track of their doings.

Bookworm had found a small library in Smee's quarters and claimed several of the books inside, much to Smee's dismay. Jinx did the handshake buzzer on Mullens and laughed himself silly when the pirate yelped and yanked his hand away. They explored, ate, and danced around the deck and then grew bored and decided to drop anchor.

"Is it time to go now?" Theo asked Liam.

His eyes found Wendy's, and she smiled. "Yes, Theo," she said. "It's time."

Peter sat up on the crow's nest and looked down on the whole of them. If he'd made Wendy pirate queen, then he had definitely claimed the title of pirate king even if he hadn't said so out loud.

"Is he all right?" Liam murmured in her ear.

"I don't know," Wendy answered. She had more pressing matters on her mind. "How do we get home? The cave entrance to the cemetery is blocked, and you can't fly."

"We sail," Hook said, interrupting her thoughts.

"The *Jolly Roger*?" Wendy asked.

Hook nodded.

"You sail a pirate ship home?" Wendy felt incredulous. "A whole ship?"

"Naturally, we change our colors when we cross borders." Hook pointed to the skull and crossbones flag. "Only fly that when we need to restock provisions."

Wendy pretended to not know that he meant he was plundering other ships for provisions.

"I miss the open sea," Skylights said from where Rock had been showing him how to maintain better balance in a sword fight. "Sometimes we spend so much time looking for lost boys that we get to feeling lost ourselves, you know?"

Wendy wasn't certain if Skylights was trying to be poetic or not but decided it was safest not to comment.

Being around pirates made for awkward conversation.

"So you'll take me to London immediately," Liam said, looking at his uncle. "No strings. No tricks."

"No tricks," Hook said.

Liam raised his voice so all the lost boys could hear. "Anyone who wants to go back with us will find a home with us until we can locate your families. Your mothers and fathers." He looked down into Wendy's face. "Is that all right?"

She nodded. "It's how it's done."

Last time, all the boys went home with her, leaving Peter alone with Tinker Bell and his feud with Hook. This time, Wendy felt surprised when several boys expressed an interest in staying. Ollie, Rock, and Flint stood behind Peter and declared they would stay with him in Neverland. Nathan and Bridger vacillated back and forth, but when it came to load those who were staying onto the jolly boats, they lined up with Peter.

The others stayed behind Wendy and Liam, and they held their heads down, already mourning the loss of this magical place but determined to go just the same.

Wendy released Liam's hand and tightly hugged each lost boy who was staying. "Look after each other," she admonished. She said farewell to Starna and Tinker Bell and finally went to Peter, who wore Hook's captain hat and was giving orders to the lost boys who were staying.

Wendy stood next to him until he was still and silent and watching as the first light of a Neverland dawn filtered through the distant trees along the shore. She reached out and took his hand. "I'm leaving now, Peter."

"You could stay," he said softly.

"It would be no good for either of us."

"Your adventures will come to an end if you leave. They'll just be over."

Wendy looked back at Liam and smiled. "No. I think they'll be just beginning." Wendy took a deep breath, steadying her emotions.

"You be good and take your medicine and watch after the lost boys. And remember, you know the way to my window. Come listen for a story every now and again."

"Just always be waiting for me."

Wendy felt her lip tremble. "Yes. Always. Goodbye, Peter." She kissed him on the cheek and stepped away.

"Goodbye, Wendy." Peter then straightened, shrugging off whatever unhappiness he may have felt. "Goodbye, Wendy," Peter said again, only this time, the words had not so much as a hint of "sorry-to-lose-you." He gave her a smirk, a small salute, and turned away from her to the boys who were staying.

The sounds of the ship getting ready to return to London grew louder than the Neverland birds singing good morning to one another. The jolly boat full of boys who were staying was lowered, and Peter lifted up into the sky as the *Jolly Roger*'s sails filled with wind and the ship moved out to open water.

Wendy continued to look back at him until he was nothing more than a dark silhouette against the rising sun.

"Goodbye, Peter," she whispered to the wind, trusting it to carry the message to him.

Wendy watched the flag shift from the black and crossbones to the British flag.

Sailing away from Neverland felt like twisting the handle of a music box backward. It felt all wrong and loose and broken, like time was shattering around her. Wendy's only consolation was that she knew it was not broken. Whatever had been wrong with the island had been healed.

"I have something for you," Liam said.

She had to force herself to turn away from the railing and focus on him.

Liam was holding her father's coat.

"How?" she gasped, taking hold of it and hugging it to her.

He smiled, clearly pleased to have given her something of such value. "I asked Mira to fetch it for you if she could. She gave it to me while you were saying goodbye to everyone."

"Thank you. You cannot know what this means to me." Hadn't she cried enough? Where were all these tears coming from?

"Are you all right?" Liam asked, taking her hand in his and pressing a kiss to her fingers.

She looked down to where their hands joined together. "Yes. I know these leaky eyes of mine don't look like it, but I am. You're alive, and I'm alive. And it was a great adventure, wasn't it?" She smiled at him. "And won't Mrs. Connolly be so pleased that we actually do get along as she predicted? She loves being right, you know."

Liam laughed at that, then sobered. "Will you be happy? Living an ordinary life?"

Wendy squinted into the horizon, trying to imagine her future. She could almost see a home with a family who sang together at the piano and practiced with swords in the backyard, where her children gathered around her legs as she told them stories of a boy who can hear when children are sad and crying. A boy who has trouble making his shadow stick until a clever girl sews it to him.

It was all hazy and clear at the same time. But it was the future. Far enough away to be called distant because she had decided she would tell her mother that she would not be taking any more callers out of obligation. She would not accept a marriage proposal just because it was expected of her. She would marry some day when it was her choice and when she was ready to do so. But not today. Not any time soon.

"I'm not saying I won't miss this." She released his hand to gesture at the sky, where time twisted and warped around them, creating a symphony of colors in the air. "But I will also be relieved to not be in a place where it is tempting to not change. I don't want to stagnate like a puddle filled with mosquitos. My life will be full, Liam Blackwell. There's nothing ordinary about that."

"But won't you be sad that you'll never see any of it again?" Liam asked as he frowned into the horizon of twisting time. He was clearly uncertain about his choice to leave.

Wendy smiled and wrapped her arms around his waist. "I wouldn't say that." She pushed up on her tiptoes and pressed her lips to his, layering kiss after kiss on his lips, each one a promise of years they would get to grow old and become whoever they were meant to become. "Never is an awfully long time."

Then Wendy Moira Angela Darling sailed headlong into her future.

ACKNOWLEDGMENTS

I do not consider myself a great scholar of *Peter Pan*, and I'm sure no one else would think of me as such either. However, I am a great fan.

I always wondered how Wendy found love in her life after Neverland. After all, who can compare to that first love when he's a boy who can fly? I honestly worried about Wendy because I didn't want her to be alone, or worse, with one person while pining for another. Giving her story a different type of ending with the possibility of a future of her choosing was my privilege.

For me, writing *Wendy's Ever After* has been a journey filled with imagination, wonder, and fun. I didn't even mind writing the kissing scenes, which, if you know me, you know that is its own special miracle, and it wouldn't have been possible without the support and inspiration of many.

First and foremost, I would like to express my deepest gratitude to J. M. Barrie, whose timeless tale of Peter Pan sparked the imagination of generations and provided the foundation for this reimagining. The personal losses he suffered in life are reflected in his work, and I hope I reimagined his world with respect to him and the story he created.

I can never (which we know is an awfully long time) be grateful enough to Heidi Gordon at Shadow Mountain. She is a champion of my stories and was excited about this one from its very first pitch. I appreciate her vision, her tenacity, and her friendship. Thank you, Heidi, for putting up with my neurosis and for being such an exemplary friend. I love that I have Lisa Mangum as my editor. She is magic at seeing where I fall short and works tirelessly to shine light on my stories. I appreciate everything she does and is and value her friendship. Callie Hansen is another editor who challenged me to do it better and provided edits that stretched the story in all the right ways. And Kristen Evans put a wonderful polish on the whole thing as she fixed mistakes and fact-checked everything. Thank you to all of you.

And to the rest of the team at Shadow Mountain: the designers, marketing team, and production team, THANK YOU for everything. My cover is stunning and gives me joy every time I look at it. I am grateful to be able to make a living doing what I love, and you guys make that possible.

So, this was a tight deadline for this book. Like intense kind of tight. It didn't help that I lost access to all of my technology for over three weeks because of breakages and tech lockouts. It was awesome (or not). And so my family had to put up with a lot of me ignoring them. A lot of me having full-blown panic attacks and a lot of lamentations and handwringing. The thing is that they *did* put up with it. They're great that way. Thanks, McKenna, Dwight, Theo, Lily, Merrik, Charisma, Chandler, Julianna, and my parents and siblings for loving me when I make it hard to do. Thank you, Gary, for calling me every day to make sure my mental health was intact. And to my Mr. Wright, I love you forever and am so glad to have been young with you and to get to grow old with you. You are my happy thought. You are my happily ever after.

A heartfelt thank you to my friends and first readers, who provided endless encouragement, listened to my ideas, and offered invaluable feedback along the way. Heather Moore, who is always there for me and by her example shows me how I can be a better human in

ACKNOWLEDGMENTS

every way, Janette Rallison and Melinda Carroll, who brainstormed all the motivations for my characters and who make me smile every time I see them. Thank you for everything. Your enthusiasm and brilliant plot fixes kept me motivated to keep flying.

I would also like to thank you readers, whose love for adventure and belief in the power of imagination keep stories like this alive. I appreciate your support. Even when I hop genres as often as I do, you stay with me for the ride. May *you* always find a happy thought.

Lastly, to the dreamers, the believers, and those who refuse to grow up, this story is for you.

Thank you for keeping the spirit of Peter Pan alive in your hearts.

With faith and trust,

Julie

DISCUSSION QUESTIONS

1. As a child, J. M. Barrie experienced a terrible loss when his older brother died. There is a theme of loss in the original J. M. Barrie story of Peter Pan. That theme of loss is continued here in *Wendy's Ever After*. Wendy has lost her father. Liam has lost his mother. Mrs. Connolly has lost her son and her husband. Peter Pan lost his best friend. And Hook lost his wife and then his best friend as well. In what ways does that theme of loss find hope as the story progresses?

2. How well do you know the original story of Peter Pan? The play, which the author soon published as a novel, has been adapted many times. Some of these adaptations and sequels are very similar to the original book, while others bring in new settings, themes, and characters. What do you think makes a good adaptation? Should it stay close to the original, or is it more important to bring something new to the story? Why do you think Peter Pan's story has been adapted so many times? What themes or characters make it timeless?

3. When Wendy sees the time-twister vines, she wonders if Peter has traveled through them to see his face as an old man. She wonders if that image is what made Peter decide he didn't want

to grow old after all. What do you think? What made Peter Pan decide to be Peter Pan?

4. So much of this story is about the difference between childhood and adulthood. Wendy decides by the end of the book that she is glad to grow up; Peter insists that it's better not to change. Who do you think is right? Are there things children do better or more intuitively than adults? What benefits come with aging?

5. Wendy vacillates between her affection for Peter and her affection for Liam. Discuss the complexities of Wendy's feelings for both Peter and Liam. How do love and loyalty influence her decision to stay or to leave Neverland?

6. What does Neverland symbolize for Wendy, Liam, Hook, and Peter? How does this magical place impact their views on reality and imagination? How does it help some (Wendy and Liam) cope with their loss while at the same time enabling others (Peter and Hook) to deny that loss is a part of their life?

7. How is the struggle between good and evil portrayed through the characters of Peter Pan and Captain Hook? How does Liam's relationship with his uncle complicate this dynamic? How does Wendy's relationship with Peter affect the dynamic? Is someone always all good or all evil? What are the complexities and layers that form our opinions on who is evil and good?

8. How do Peter Pan's and Captain Hook's perspectives on life differ from Wendy's and Liam's? What lessons do Pan and Hook learn, if any, by the end of the story? What about Liam and Wendy?

9. In the original *Peter Pan*, Wendy is the pretend mother figure for Peter, the lost boys, and her brothers. In what ways do you see Wendy stepping into the role of mother now that she has returned to Neverland?

10. Finally, here are a few fun facts: The Joy hand buzzer wasn't actually invented until 1928 by Danish inventor Soren Sorensen Adams. I would love to take credit for this fun fact, but the truth

DISCUSSION QUESTIONS

is that my editor, Kristen Evans, was the one who let me know. We decided that since Neverland is a place where time runs amok, it was okay for one of the lost boys to own the gag toy. In the original J. M. Barrie telling of Peter Pan (both the play and the book), Tinker Bell was a fairy, and her dust was fairy dust. The term "pixie" came into use in reference to Tinker Bell in Disney's adaptation. In a nod to both iterations, I used both interchangeably. I hope that doesn't cause too much twitching for those who prefer one term or the other. Some people have given J. M. Barrie credit for inventing the name Wendy. However, the name was already in use. What J. M. Barrie did was popularize the name for baby girls all over the world, all because of the character Wendy Darling. So now you know the facts in case anyone asks.